DISCOVER

READ

EXPLORE

LEARN

irreversible

ALSO BY CHRIS LYNCH

irreversible

CHRIS LYNCH

SIMON & SCHUSTER BFYR

New York · London · Toronto · Sydney · New Delhi

SIMON & SCHUSTER BFYR

An imprint of Simon & Schuster Children's Publishing Division
1230 Avenue of the Americas, New York, New York 10020

For information about special discounts for bulk purchases, please contact Simon & Schuster
Special Sales at 1-866-506-1949 or business@simonandschuster.com.
The Simon & Schuster Speakers Bureau can bring authors to your live event. For more information
or to book an event, contact the Simon & Schuster Speakers Bureau at 1-866-248-3049 or visit our
website at www.simonspeakers.com.
Book design by Krista Vossen
The text for this book was set in Minion.
Manufactured in the United States of America
First Edition
2 4 6 8 10 9 7 5 3 1
Library of Congress Cataloging-in-Publication Data
Names: Lynch, Chris, 1962– author.
Title: Irreversible / Chris Lynch.
Description: First edition. | New York : Simon & Schuster Books for Young Readers, [2016] |
Sequel to: Inexcusable. | Summary: Keir Sarafian must finally confront his past when tragedy
strikes during his first year of what has been an eye-opening first year of college.
Identifiers: LCCN 2015037853| ISBN 9781481429856 (hardback) | ISBN 9781481429870 (ebook)
Subjects: | CYAC: Conduct of life—Fiction. | Fathers and sons—Fiction. | Colleges and
universities—Fiction. | Family life—Fiction. | Rape—Fiction. | BISAC: JUVENILE FICTION /
Social Issues / Sexual Abuse. | JUVENILE FICTION / Social Issues / Dating & Sex. | JUVENILE
FICTION / Law & Crime.
Classification: LCC PZ7.L979739 Irr 2016 | DDC [Fic]—dc23
LC record available at https://lccn.loc.gov/2015037853

Dedicated to my brother, Marty.
He deserves better.
He's always deserved better.
But this is the best I've got.

PART ONE

HOME

O wad some Power the giftie gie us
To see oursels as ithers see us!

—Robert Burns, "To a Louse"

didn't even know who I *wanted* to come for me.

Not Carl. I knew I didn't want the first person through the door to be Carl. Because a boyfriend was always going to think the worst about another guy who was with his girl. And I was only with her because he wasn't. He let her down, and if he hadn't, things would have been way, way different. He wouldn't want to hear that, but it was the truth.

I might have wanted my sisters to come, because they loved me, and that's a good thing to have when a guy is in trouble. Fran, though. Fran would have been better than Mary, because Fran would listen to my side.

My dad, Ray. Ray would take my side before even hearing what my side was. Maybe that wouldn't be the best thing. Maybe better if the campus police came, impartial, taking my statement and seeing there was nothing to this.

Nothing but craziness, mistakes, and misunderstandings.

I didn't know what I wanted. I just knew I was going to wait for it to come.

That was a lie. I knew what I wanted. I knew who I wanted.

I wanted Gigi Boudakian to walk back through that door. I wanted Gigi Boudakian to come back and say how crazy all that was, how the fresh piney air and the clarity of morning light breathed sense back into her and back into the whole universe. Because I could never rape anybody. *Rape.* Even saying the word, even saying it to myself, nowhere else but inside me, caused my head to crackle with lethal pain, caused my stomach to try to launch right up my throat and out of me.

And to think I could do that to Gigi Boudakian? Hurt Gigi Boudakian in any way at all?

How could she? How could she think that? How *dare* she? How fucking *dare* she? How fucking *dare* you, Gigi Boudakian?

No. No, no. This was a nightmare. Was this even a nightmare? Even nightmares needed to make some sort of sense, come from some real place somewhere. There was nothing real about this.

No. It was not her fault. Nothing was, nothing could be. I didn't know whose fault it was, but I knew it was not Gigi Boudakian's fault.

I also knew I was a good guy. Good guys didn't do bad

things. All we needed was for Gigi Boudakian to remember that, to know it like she always knew it, and come back. So we could all know it again.

"Get the fuck up."

It wasn't like I was unprepared for this. But I couldn't have gotten "the fuck up" if I tried. I didn't try. I stared at the cinder blocks in the wall, counting them like I had been doing ever since it got light enough, tracing the straight, right-angle lines of mortar holding them together.

"I'm not gonna say this a whole lot of times. And I'm not gonna just let you lie there, and I'm not gonna kick the shit outta you while you're already down. So, if I have to pick you up and put you on your feet first, that's what I'll do, so you might as well just get the fuck up, *now*."

The wall had 120 cinder blocks altogether. You would think they could slap a layer of something, anything, over the blocks so they didn't have to look so cold, penal, and punitive. How much could something like that cost anyway? Hardly anything, I would guess, and the difference would be transforming. Anything would be better than this soul-sucking business here.

He was good to his word, though. To all his words. He wasn't having any of this nonsense of mine.

I felt weightless as Carl lifted me up off the rotten little bed. It was like it was no effort for him at all, as if he was doing it almost tenderly. Like a dad taking a little kid out of bed to get ready for preschool. He must have remembered. Carl. He must have remembered when we were friends and who we were and how we were and that's why this was all wrong and why when he manhandled me it was with a gentleness almost. This was the reality, and soon enough everybody would be back to the right reality, the one where I was the guy I always was and the insanity would go away and Carl and me and naturally Gigi would come back to earth and realize how everything just went a little mental and forget about it. Because we knew better, didn't we? Carl thought I did something terrible to someone we both love. We all knew better than *that*. Right?

Carl's surprising and reassuring soft grip, lifting me and then lowering me, said as much. You can tell more from touch, and from every other human connection, for that matter, than you can from words. That's what I have learned. And Carl's manner told me what I needed to know, that everything was going back to okay.

Until it told me otherwise.

At the best of times, Carl was a man of the minimum of words. Now was not the best of times, and he minimized even the minimum.

He held on to me with his right hand, pulled the collar of my shirt up over my left ear, and the intensity of his expression almost, *almost*, pulled my attention from his big gnarly fist thundering down and crashing into my eye socket. I heard the snap-crack of bone-at-bone and remembered how deadly

Carl always was. Left-handed, smooth, great balance. He had unfeasible hands, huge, hard, and almost as big as his head when he held fists up either side. He had a small head anyway, but still I marveled, and admired and cheered him on and never once considered those fists would be a problem for me.

But right then, that expression on his face was almost as alarming. Famously stone-faced, Carl allowed his features to crack like pond ice, and I was sure I saw him start something like crying as he dropped the hammer on me.

I didn't see much else after that. *Felt* quite a lot of sensations, though. Anyone who says they felt nothing throughout a violent trauma because they were in shock is talking crap just so they don't have to keep feeling it forever. Because I was deep into shock already and still felt a whole lot of sensations that Carl handed out to me. Felt every one at the time, and will feel every one for as long as I can feel.

After the massive left overhand exploded the right side of my face, Carl met my nose with a right uppercut that shocked me back upright before I could dive to the floor and be done. I couldn't even get my bearings before he hit me with the exact same right uppercut, catching my chin this time, clattering my teeth and hopping me briefly in the direction of the ceiling.

It was only when I landed, when I felt my feet galumph back to earth, that I realized I had left it. It was only then that I realized I could seriously be leaving it for real if something didn't change here quickly.

"Just talk to me," I said, reaching out semi-blindly to try to wrap Carl up in a boxer hug to get him to stop punching me. "It's not the way it looks—"

I got nowhere near tying him up, as he got nowhere nearer to talking to me. He had already decided. As if to return my words to sender, the next thing I got was the full force of Carl driving his whole self behind a straight left hand that hit me flush and drove my jaw back so ferociously I could hear it bang, both sides, into the base of my skull behind my ears.

I went almost entirely deaf with the impact. Now my eyes were bleary with blood and mucus and panic and probably all that additional blood I was picking up off Carl's knuckles, and the front of his powder-blue button-down shirt, so I was as close to deaf-blind as possible when I threw my first serious angry punch with malice aforethought toward my old friend's head.

I had to. You have to, at some point, unless you have already given up the will to survive. I didn't want to hit Carl, because I didn't want to make this horrible nightmare of a lie any more real. Fighting him made it real, but not fighting him could kill me.

He surely wasn't expecting it at that stage, because I felt the pop from my knuckles right through to my heels as it landed bang-on his silent, fuzzy orb of a face. He backed up two, three awkward paces, and thunked into the yellow closet door.

"Okay now," I said, surprised and I suppose also a little

bit jacked at what it seemed I could do. "Let's cut the shit, Carl, okay, and sort out what's really going on here." I held my hands up as I approached, still only able to make out a slushy, sloppy outline of the guy I once knew, from that fading world I once knew. I thought it was going to be all right now. Or some version, some approximation, of all right.

My hands-up approach to him was like surrendering, or like greeting an old pal after a long time away.

He came launching off the yellow closet door to meet me before I could get to him. I saw his mouth motoring and thought this was just perfect, Carl finally deciding to talk back to me just when I couldn't understand a word he was saying. Someday we'd laugh about this, probably. Probably. When all was put back right. Maybe not laugh, though, okay. But get there, and be better, and be sane about everything.

But not today.

I could not even count the number of sharp, scorching punches Carl threw at me then. He banged and battered my face, my skin, my skull, with left and right and left and right-hand shots that had me reeling rapidly backward. My blood was shooting in every direction, the globlets clearly visible to me as they sprayed off, like pulpy tiny rats abandoning the sinking ship of me.

I landed eventually—half landed—back on the bed where he'd found me. Perfectly halved, with my spine backbent between the mattress and the floor. Carl let himself fall dead on top of me.

"It's not like you think, Carl," I said, freaking myself out with the underwater sound of my own voice.

I was thinking my only chance was to read his lips and hope to read just the right things on them. But even that small chance was dumped when he roared, or howled, or made whatever lipless big noise that was before slamming his head into my chest with enough force to snap me like a jackknife. My chin cracked into the back of his head, and one or both of us opened up a whole new flow of blood that finally turned us into one great disgusting indistinguishable soupy mess.

How? I thought, as I lay there flattened, back-bent, blood-swamped, with Carl's head embedded in my chest and not going anywhere anytime soon. How did we get here? I thought, as the two of us, or one or the other of us, made the whole room shake with the sobbing that nobody could hear but anybody anywhere surely could feel.

I would not have budged if I could.

Anyway, I couldn't.

When I finally woke up, I was not on my back, not on the mattress. I was on the cold, whitish, blood-awash floor. I was on my face, and I was alone.

off the floor

K eir?"

It was an awful sound, hearing it said that way. A bruised, regrettable ache of a sound. Too close to the last howl of a dying great beast. My eyes were closed and so I had only the sound.

"Dad. Dad? Ray, I'm all right. I'm fine," I said as I found myself helping my father, to help me, up out of my own vast blood puddle. I looked at the hunched hulk of him through swollen slitted eyes, and I just wanted to shut them tight again. I hated to see him like this. I'd have rather endured the same beating all over than to have him see the results just once. "Really, it's nothing. You know how it always looks worse than—"

"Jesus Christ, Keir," Ray said, depositing my ass decisively onto the bed, just like old times.

"Jesus Christ, Ray," I said, attempting a smile that didn't get very far.

• • •

It was, to say the least, a little blurry, the hobbling shuffle that eventually got me and Ray to his car together. It was the beginning of the proper time of the morning, when the joggers and couples striding toward breakfast someplace nice had taken over from the night crawlers and made a place like Norfolk shine just like in the brochures. I saw, fleetingly, these sights, these good people trying to ignore my old man and the mess he was transporting. Or trying to appear not to have any morbid curiosity about the scene. Hard to imagine anybody really disinterested, though. I'd have been staring good and hard if I were them; I know I would because I would not be able to help myself. Maybe these people were all just better than me.

Or maybe I hadn't seen them. They looked awfully close to the scenes I had pored over so hard, for so long. I had projected myself into every page, picture, and paragraph of the Norfolk University prospectus for two solid years, planning my exquisite existence here. The images that flashed through my mind were spooky close to those images I had lived with for so long.

"Where are the girls?" I asked when Ray was leaning over me to buckle my seat belt. He forgot to do it when he lowered me into my seat and only remembered after buckling himself in. He growled his frustration as he thrashed around, getting himself free to take care of me.

"I don't know," he said.

"Who called you?" I asked as he impatiently roared out

14

of the dormitory parking lot without bothering to do up his own belt again.

"I don't know, Keir. I don't remember."

"You don't *remember*?"

"Keir," he hollered, scaring me. I jerked forward, raised my hands up and spread them wide at the windshield the way you would instinctively prepare for an upcoming head-on. Or for warding off a pummeling. He had my attention. Counting just now, I could still tally up on one hand all the times Ray had shouted at me in my whole life.

"Yeah, Dad," I said.

"I don't know, I don't remember, I don't care. Look at you. Who called me is not the goddamn point, all right? I don't care about anything else right now except this right here beside me. Do you get that now? Do you have any concept of how . . ." He turned to look hard at me, sort of punishing us both for the state I was in. I heard him swallow hard just before I reached over and pushed his big crazy loving-me face back toward the road.

"Watch what you're doing, Ray, or you could wind up making a whole bunch of people on the road look like me before it's over."

"Don't joke," he said.

"Wasn't joking," I said.

"You wouldn't joke if you could see what's left of your . . . my boy's face. My lovely little boy's face . . ."

"Stop it, Dad," I said, because he was killing me. "I wasn't

15

joking." I almost wished it wasn't him who came to get me. I almost wished anybody else, anybody other than Carl, that is, came to find me and bundle me off.

Except it wasn't even almost. There was nobody I wanted bundling me off at a time like this other than Ray. If only he could have done it without having to suffer seeing me at the same time.

"What about the rest of you?" he said as he got to open road and pounded the accelerator.

"There's nobody else. I'm on my own."

"No, Keir, I meant the rest of you, your body, your injuries. Ribs, guts, what else do you have going on there that I need to know about?"

"Nothing," I insisted. Nothing that you need to know about.

"Nothing at all?"

"Nothing at all."

"Well, that's lucky, considering how it looks. Good, good. Now, I could take you to a hospital here, but I was thinking of trying to get you in closer to home, as long as you are not in too much—"

"Nope," I said firmly.

"Nope what? Which do you prefer? How's your head feeling? You think maybe you got a concussion? Yeah, maybe we shouldn't take the chance, get you checked sooner rather than—"

"No, Ray, no. I feel not so critical. Definitely no concussion, and definitely no hospital."

He inhaled so deep and long I wondered if when he let it go the windshield was going to blast right off the car into oncoming traffic.

"Keep breathing, Ray," I said, and he blew it all out as if he had been waiting for the order.

"All the blood, though, Keir. We can't even tell how much you lost. There might be other things you can't even—"

"Orange juice."

"What?"

"You'll get me home and fill me up with orange juice, and the blood will be back to normal levels in no time."

"I don't think that is the—"

"Ray? Dad? All I want to do is go home. And the only person I want taking care of me is you. This whole situation is already bad enough, and to be honest, the only clear idea I have right now is to retreat. I don't want anything for now other than to burrow in back home, to know that you are there and that the whole rest of the world isn't. 'Cause, I don't, at all, understand it, what's happened and what's happening. There was some alcohol and stuff, and that doesn't help, I know. But I still don't understand. I do not understand this. It's all wrong." There was a long pause then. This was the point where the crying came in, and I couldn't say with any certainty which one of us got it started. "Ray . . . ?" I said with the intention of saying a lot more, but I wouldn't even know what it was going to be until it came out of me.

"Okay," he said, big sniffles bracketing each syllable. "I'm gonna take my boy home, and take care of him. You need to run for the cover of home, well, that is what home is for after all. Whatever you need, Son. What*ever*."

"That's it, that's all. Get me back where I belong and do what you do. Then I'll be showroom new again before we know it."

He nodded vigorously, leaning a little harder on the gas until I had to point out to him how much worse the day would get if the state troopers pulled us over. He decelerated promptly.

A period of welcome quiet passed as I looked out the window, through my letter-box lids, just watching the trees and the granite outcroppings whiz by. Then I felt heavy and nodded off, but that didn't last long. Then I watched the blur of roadside again, then nodded off again. It went like that.

"You are a good boy," Ray said. I could tell from the pitch of his voice he didn't know whether I was asleep or awake. He would have to say what he had to say regardless, I knew. As long as he could say it at the lump of me, something in him would be satisfied. I wasn't interjecting anyway. "I'm sorry, Son. I never should have let this happen. I should have been able, somehow—"

Okay, I was interjecting. "Don't be mental, Ray. This was not in any way your responsibility."

"Oh. I thought you were asleep. Did I wake you up? I'm sorry. Don't mind me, go back to sleep."

"You have nothing, nothing to be sorry about. I can't listen to that. I mean it, if you don't stop that kind of talk—and that includes that kind of *thinking*, and I will know—then I swear I will pull up this door handle and toss myself right out onto the road."

"Jesus, Keir," he said, sweating a little from the strain of it, of everything. He mopped his brow, then put a hand on his chest. "You know, there is a limit to how much load my system can take in one day."

"Right," I said. "So it's good we are done for now."

"It is," he agreed.

He went back to concentrating on the highway and getting us home. I went back to gazing and dozing.

Ten minutes later he was at it again. "I was thinking," he said.

"I thought we agreed you wouldn't do that."

"No, it's funny."

"Oh, well, funny is welcome. Desperately welcome right now."

"I know. So, I was thinking, even if you did fling yourself out there into the rocks at sixty-five miles an hour, when I doubled back to come and get you, you'd probably look exactly the same as you do right now."

"Oh, is that right?" I said.

"Yeah," he said, nodding and smiling. He was pleased with himself and his contribution to my healing process through therapeutic hilarity. I was happy I could do that for him.

"And you woke me up for that?"

"Ah, you weren't sleeping."

"Nah, I wasn't. But I think I will now, okay? So . . ."

"Sure, of course," he said, waving me toward my window.

It took less than a minute.

"Keir," he said, his voice all the way back to solid.

I gave him a huffy dramatic sigh for his troubles. "Yes, Father?"

"You are a good boy. A good man. Come what may, you know I know that."

I looked at his big, sad, proud head. I had no impulse to look out the window anymore, or to sleep. I twisted my body toward the inside of the car, toward my father, and settled in with an eye on him for the rest of the way.

"I do know that, and it means everything to me."

At that, he whale-inhaled again, this time so deeply and for so long that by the time he breathed out again he could have delivered air from one state into another.

"I remember now," he said. "Nobody called me. Rollo came to the house."

I got a blast of hot blood filling my head.

"Rollo?"

"He didn't say much. Chauffeur's code or some stupidity. But under ordinary circumstances, Rollo don't worry. It's practically his motto, 'Rollo don't worry.' He came to my door, Keir, so that I could *see* him worry."

"Don't worry, Dad."

"Is there anything for us to talk about right now, Son?"

20

"Nothing, Dad."

"Where is Gigi?"

"I thought you trusted me completely."

"I do. Nothing changes that. I just need to know what I need to know to help you as best I can. A gentleman would see her home safe. Or, from where I sit, a gentleman asks about the lady. So, I'm asking."

"The lady is at home, Dad, same as the gentleman would like to be. That's all he wants at this point, to be home. Please. Just home, and quiet."

What I got, on command, was quiet at least. A lot of dense, thick quiet.

It was still a marvel, still a surprise and a responsibility I needed to be more aware of. How simple and effortless it was for me to make the man smile like he was a few minutes ago. And conversely, how easily and lethally I could make him suffer over me.

ties binding

One of the old man's greatest accomplishments was shielding me from whatever nastiness lurked outside our doors and windows, waiting for a shot at me. I heard phones ringing and knocks at the door, muffled and not-so-muffled voices. And even if some percentage of all that was a product of my scared imaginings, or my increasingly torturous nightmares, that still left plenty of scope for unfortunate reality. I burrowed farther and farther into the darkened spider hole of my bedroom and hid from whatever I could.

If you talked to some people, they might say Ray shielded me from too much nastiness. My sisters might be among those people; certainly Mary would. She'd say it didn't do father or son much good, for him to be taking my lumps when I should have been learning to take them for myself.

But she would be wrong. He always did his job when it came to me, and he was always brilliant at his job. And even if it felt a little uncomfortably familiar to be in the defensive posture we were in now, it didn't make Ray wrong and it didn't make Mary right.

The familiar part of this was probably because I was innocent. I was innocent of ever doing anything wrong to Gigi Boudakian. And I was innocent of doing anything wrong when I made a hard tackle and somebody got hurt. He wasn't crippled, like people said, and he obviously wasn't killed. But he never played football again.

When you hit a guy with all your being, hit him the way a car hits a moose, you would expect it to hurt both of you. But it doesn't hurt the hitter, if the hitter has hit perfectly. It is a strange sensation, almost a magical sensation. The car takes a crumpling, and the moose takes a mangling.

My timing was perfect. The defensive back hit the receiver at the instant the ball arrived. A beautiful pop and explosion, like fireworks.

And that was that.

I never received so many hard slaps on the back.

"Way to bang him, Keir," somebody said, and banged me on the back.

"Way to stick."

"Mowed him, Keir. Absolutely killed him."

• • •

There. See there? Right there? That was a moment. Only I didn't know it was a moment because I guess I had not had many moments of that type in my life, so I didn't recognize it. I recognize it now. That there are precise moments in your life where you can grab hold of a thing and get it under control or you can miss that chance and let the thing get away from your control altogether and forever.

I was no kind of killer. You could have asked anybody who really knew me, and they'd have told you there was nothing like that in me anywhere. I was just not that kind of guy. All I did was, I did my job and I did it very well, and as a consequence somebody got seriously hurt and I somehow got a reputation out of it.

I made my name as a two-way player. I was a consistently good kicker, but I was a sporadically good defensive back. I made a lot more field goals than I did tackles, but when I made a tackle, I made it *hard*. I made it loud and I made it count and I made it hurt the receiver so that he would have to be thinking about it all day.

In the big picture, my field goals mattered more, and that was what I loved. As for my reputation and what people wanted out of me, well, I was the only back in the state who could hit hard enough to be worth a damn. Except when I didn't hit hard enough.

Although everybody—teammates, coaches, parents— seemed to agree. I was gonna someday hit hard enough. And whoo-boy, when that day came, everybody hoped to be there to see it. Might even kill somebody, I heard once. Then I heard it again.

I should have said right there on the spot, I did not *kill* him. I tackled him. Nobody's going to bother nicknaming a guy "the Tackler," and if they did, who would notice, or care or carry it on?

But "the Killer"? That sticks to a guy. And no matter how wrong it might be, it follows him.

It was news. There were inquiries and investigations and editorials. I was home from school for a week, for my own good, for my peace of mind, because I couldn't possibly concentrate, couldn't hear a word with the constant roar in my ears coming from inside my own head and from all points around it. The phone rang all the time, and my dad answered it. He never put me on the phone, never shied away from a question, never lost his patience with school officials or local radio or whoever. He took off work and stayed there with me and played Risk, the game burning on all week as we took great chunks of continents from each other and then lost them again in between phone calls and lots of silence and lots of talks where he said not much more than that everything was going to work out all right and that it didn't much matter anyway what any investigation said because he already knew, knew me, and knew that his internal, in-his-own-heart investigation had cleared me.

"You're a good boy," he reminded me every time I needed reminding.

· · ·

By Friday of the week I stayed home, everybody had looked into the accident. It was an accident. And also, it was no accident, anything but an accident. Everybody concluded—though not happily—that I had not done anything wrong. I had not done anything out of line. I had not done anything blameworthy.

"An unfortunately magnificent hit, in the universe of football," was what the writer called it, in the article about my being cleared.

I was cleared of having violated either the letter or the spirit of the laws of football. A whole lot of people would have said that I had *honored* the spirit of football. I was cleared because I never did anything wrong. Because good guys don't do bad things. And it seemed like my father was the only person in the world who didn't need an official report to tell him I was a good guy.

But by the time I returned to school, I was the Killer. Even if I wasn't.

There was only one breach of Ray's steel curtain defensive operation, a week or so after he'd brought me home.

I didn't even know for sure where I was when I first saw them. It was like one of those hokey movies when a dead person sees all the loved ones ringed around his hospital bed and saying wonderful things about him. But this wasn't going to be one of those.

Ray was standing at the foot of my bed. Fran was sitting to my left, on a plain oak chair brought in from the kitchen table. Her hands were folded, but opening and closing repeatedly in a worried exercise of distraction. From the way she studied my face, I'd say that would have been the source of the worry. Mary was standing, to my right, arms folded, her face all pinched up and dubious. She would have been worried too, but determined not to show it until I was judged worthy. That was pretty much them. I had been dying to see them, and dreaded seeing them.

"Wow, hi," I said, propping myself up with some effort to a sitting position. "This is a surprise. I didn't expect to see you guys here. I didn't expect to see them, did I, Ray? Or did I forget?"

"You forgot," Ray said. "But it's understandable. Everybody understands."

"Yeah, that's the thing, though," Mary said, sitting abruptly down on the side of the bed, right against my hip. I was wishing she had also brought over a chair, as her gesture of sibling solidarity might have looked like a comfort, but it felt like a challenge. "There is a problem with that, which I'm sure is not a surprise to you. There is a lot of not-understanding going around just now."

"*Mis*understanding," I said as directly as I dared.

"That is an important distinction," Mary said, nodding.

This was exactly the fierce, lawyerly, social champion quality Mary always had and I always idolized. I remembered thinking that if you had Mary on your side, you were always

27

going to be all right, and how lucky I was knowing that I had her. I never considered what it would feel like to be on the opposing side to Mary's side. She was making me consider it at this moment, though, and it took no time to conclude that I much preferred the way it used to be.

"Oh, stop with that already, May," Fran said. There was something I loved about the way she would call Mary "May" sometimes, and that nobody else ever did. Dad and Mary both used to correct her and she never heeded them. Then Mary switched to saying that Fran was just reducing her to one syllable out of jealousy. "Look at him. There's no need to intimidate him further, is there?"

Mary made no move to speak, just held my eyes locked to hers while Ray echoed softly, "No, no need for that."

"What *happened*?" Fran asked, finally.

I had not been asked that, which after all was something I knew should have happened already. Ray the gatekeeper was the answer there. Nobody short of law-enforcement types would get anywhere near me with that question as long as I was recuperating. And the only person who did get close to me before now was Ray himself. And he would have considered it maximum treachery to even think the question silently to himself. Ah, my Ray.

"Nothing," I insisted in a pitch of urgency that would have embarrassed my twelve-year-old self. That self would have also well recognized the absence of any detail or substance in my response.

"Nothing," Mary said. "That, Young Brother, is the kind of statement that isn't likely to inspire anybody to rally behind you. And in case you haven't been keeping up with things outside this one house, rallying behind you looks like a tough enough proposition already without you lending that kind of hand."

"May-*ree*," Fran said, throwing her hands up in protest and scold. This caused her sister to sigh with frustration and her brother to nearly weep with gratitude. On the inside, there was no nearly about it, and I struggled to hold it together. Ray, now slumped over my footboard, may have been losing that same struggle.

"Oh, May-ree what?" Mary snapped. "Please, Fran. If it was any one of our friends at school, we'd be among the first ones to rush in and support her."

I turned quickly to the left, anxious to hear Fran's defense of me. There wasn't one. Her eyes turned down.

"Exactly," Mary said. She appeared extra emboldened as she turned fire back on me. "Now, Keir," she said, with force but also now with a small, really small, note of old recognizable warm feeling for me. "You must realize that 'Nothing happened' is not going to satisfy anybody who doesn't happen to be your dad." Fran growled low at her; Ray showed no sign of noticing the remark. "You have more to say than that, I know you do. I'm trying to be fair. I want to give you a chance, to have a voice, and I really want to believe only the best things about you because you're my brother and I love you."

"No matter what," Fran ventured cautiously.

When I then quickly looked toward Fran with a nod and a weak smile of thanks for that much, this seemed to provoke Mary, who grabbed my forearm and my attention but good.

"But like I said, if it was a friend of Fran's or mine from school, we would be right there stuck into it. No matter who turned out to be her attacker."

"I never *attacked* anybody!" I yelled in my sister's accusing face. I found myself surprised when that did not seem to back her off even a little. When I realized she still held a grip on my arm, I yanked it roughly away from her. When she still remained planted defiantly, on the side of *my* bed, right up against *my* hip despite my obvious desire to get up, I had had enough. I took my forearm and applied it to Mary the way coaches taught me to apply it to tight ends, and receivers who wanted to block me off the play. I swatted her with all the force I had stored up lying in that bed all those days, batted her off the bed, out of my way, and into the wall with a thud.

"Keir!" Fran gasped, smacking the side of my head furiously as she ran to Mary's aid. I had been head-slapped by brutes three times Fran's weight, but none of them ever rocked me more. I held my skull tight with both hands in case any fragments tried to shoot across the room.

"She can't just hold me like that, like her prisoner," I yelled. "She can't *do that.*"

When I passed Ray, he declined to rise from his personal huddle position. He remained instead folded and faceless, over the glossy blue footboard of the bed he'd bought for me eleven better years earlier.

It took Fran ten minutes to come and find me. More like, it took nine minutes to see to Mary and one minute to walk to where she knew I would be.

"Oh yeah, this should fix everything. Good plan, Keir."

We were in the timeless basement, where I had learned to love the scents of damp, dust, and decomposing fabrics, and to associate that with solitude and peace. She was standing over me, fists on hips, as I sat in the tiny wooden toddler chair wedged between the big ancient furnace and an exposed and decaying stone wall. But it had always been decaying, and would always be, so it was all right.

"You found me," I said, something like joking.

"Yeah," she said, "I'm clever like that."

It had taken me years to work out that nobody went looking for me when I ran away because they knew where I was and that I was safe. It wouldn't have killed them to fake a little worry, but I suppose waiting me out was better for making me grow more self-sufficient. Maybe. Who knows?

"You can't be shoving people like that, Keir."

"Some people need a shove," I said, sounding every bit my six-year-old self.

"And some people really, really need not to be shoving."

"Hnn," I said. "How's Ray doing?"

"Ray? Ray, Keir?"

"Ray, yeah, Ray. Our father. The guy who's been doing

all the taking care of me. I'm not going to worry about Mary, because Mary's just fine. Mary's always just fine, so I won't be losing any sleep over her, that's—"

"Shut *up*, you petulant little brat, and get over yourself. Mary's methods might need a little work, but at least she is here trying to help you somehow. In spite of yourself, and yes, in spite of Father Ray. You are in potentially serious trouble now, Keir, and you will do yourself no favors by posing as the tough guy you most definitely are not. That is the very type of swaggering macho *bullshit* you've been pulling for the past year or more. It doesn't suit you and it doesn't get you anywhere you really want to be and it does not ultimately shield your true softy marshmallow self from all the same stuff that scares everybody."

It might have been some form of dignity I was trying to achieve then, stiffening my back to straighten me up in my child's chair, in my child's hidey-hole in our dirty safe basement. I kind of already knew the absurdity of it, but that didn't mean I wasn't still bullheaded enough to hold the pose until my sister relieved me of duty.

"Oh, please, Keir," she said with a sigh.

I slumped forward at her word, clipped, a stringless marionette.

I looked hard at the floor between my feet, with my head between my knees. So much cellar dirt I couldn't tell, and I couldn't remember, if this was unpaved earth under me or just accumulated filth.

"Is there anything you want to tell me, Keir?"

It took me a very long time to say the word "No" and a very short time to stuff "Thereisnothingtotell" right up behind it.

"Right," she said. "Okay, then. This is what you should know. When Gigi left you . . ."

The sound of her name, here, now, in this air, sliced like a ceremonial sword bisecting my heart, pouring my blood out everywhere.

"Are you even listening to me?"

"I am absolutely listening."

"Well, she ran into Grace going out for her run. She was crying, and confused, and didn't know which way to go, and when Grace tried to bring her inside the apartment, she refused to come in. She said someone was coming for her, and she would be fine and she just walked, fast, then abruptly stopped where our road forked, and just stood there, weeping. Like you're doing now. Do you want to say something to me now, Keir?"

I shook my head definitively no, and stared at the floor becoming mud beneath me.

"Grace took care of her. Brought her over for coffee and to pull herself together in the bathroom and to kill some of the waiting time. And they talked, of course, quite a bit. And Grace stayed with her, walked with her down to the bus shelter after a while to wait with her there, and to listen. Mr. Boudakian finally pulled up in a big Lexus, stopped and sat without even looking at her. Never even got out. Carl did, though. Just couldn't wait, apparently. He didn't look at her either, just bolted in the direction of . . . well, you know where he went."

Did I *ever* know where he went.

That was where Fran left off telling me any more specifics.

"Now," she said, the softness in her tone starting to sound like effort, "are you sure there is nothing you want to talk about?"

Big silence filled the cramped basement space while I struggled to build sentences and sense, for her as well as myself. Then, "Remember that thing you said about me?"

"Which one? I'm sure I said a lot, way more than I meant. It was not my intention to hurt you. I know how easily wounded you are, and I don't want to contribute any more of that to what you have to cope with already. But sometimes somebody has to say something."

"You said that I make things up to be the way I want them to be. I don't remember a lot of other stuff if you did say it. I remember that one really clearly. That doesn't sound like a heat-of-battle, blurting sort of thing to say."

"No. It doesn't. It wasn't."

"Do you really think I do that?"

"Oh. Oh, now. Aw, Keir, look at you. You've gotten into a state already just by asking the question, never mind my answer."

Fran was always my middle way. She was the baby bear

34

measure in my life, not too hot, not too cold when it came to telling me things that needed telling. There were maybe people too eager to lay on the sugarcoating, and maybe one or two who were overly vinegar-happy. Fran was always trying to balance all that for me whenever she could.

"'Never mind my answer' sounds like the real answer to me, Fran. Coming from you. Thanks."

The silence came back, filled up all the empty places between and around us, and we came to something like an understanding. A partial, temporary, insufficient understanding but one that would have to stand for now.

"You're welcome," she said, and left me there.

to minimize risk

I t was when I made the inevitable trip down the hallway that changes were obviously in motion. Ray had finally used up all his available sick time, though his only real sickness was ever me, and he was reluctantly back at work. In a somewhat parallel move, I forced myself to confront the weight bench and free weights that I had set up in the girls' room as soon as they had both vacated the premises.

It was the shock of the lonesomeness that spurred me into motion to begin with. I had no idea it was going to hit me like it did, but that first day with Ray gone and me left only with myself for company blindsided me. I wasn't up for more than a half hour before I found the silence and the relentless presence of all that nothingness unbearable. I started pacing the house from one room to the next and back again, just to find something, just to escape something else. I started talking gibberish to fill the joint up with nonsense that might help displace the dread that was filling the atmosphere rapidly, like some poisonous gas leakage out of nowhere.

A closed door was just an invitation to even more harrowing places, so I passed the girls' bedroom door on three or four circuits of the house before the thought of the weights and the physicality and the old life and football normalcy came to me and I burst through the door as if the whole of the Baltimore Ravens defense was waiting in there to brutalize me.

They weren't. And it was with a kind of joy and relief that I slung myself down onto the weight bench and got right to work building myself back up to the man I was going to need to be to face the bigger, angrier, most unforgiving world that was waiting for me to come and play.

God, was I unready for it. That was clear enough when the bar carrying the weights came crashing down to my chest with only the feeblest resistance from my arms. The sound of life escaping from my lungs was as scary as the silence it had disturbed. But that was one of the simple beauties of brutal physical necessity. It doesn't matter what was frightening you just seconds before, because you have to throw all body and soul into getting out from under the thing that would crush you otherwise.

I grunted and growled, straining completely against the force of the weights. I lifted them off my chest, then noisily up the next couple of inches before stalling out and watching my arms shake with the effort of shifting the load farther up to the hooks that would rescue me. I nearly screamed with the extra surge of strength I needed to find to get the weights moving again, and it seemed to take twenty more sweaty, trembling minutes for the load to travel the final half a foot to the point where I could just barely urge them, shout them, will them over the edge of the hooks, where they clanked to rest directly above my skull.

I was occupied now, for sure. The sight of my chest rising and falling dramatically was a morbid fascination that I watched as if somebody or something else was attached to it. I had trouble believing that this was the result of one measly rep of a weight I had surely bench-pressed before at some time in a distant other lifetime, or else why would they be sitting there waiting for my return?

I was weak. I was soft and breathless well beyond what I ever would have figured.

I tried to keep it in perspective despite the alarming deterioration I had suffered since the last time I laid my body down on that bench. How long had it been? Too long, sure, but no layoff, no setback, no breakdown had ever caused me this much regression before. Maybe I was hurt more than I realized.

"It was just the time," I assured myself as I went through the indignity of loosening the cuffs on each end of the bar to reduce the weight to something I could manage. "Time away from the workout got me to this state, and time back at it will put me right again. And then some."

I was talking a good game, at any rate. And that was critical, always the first step to rising to any challenge. Psych yourself up properly and all things are possible. Talk a good game, and your good game will follow.

By the time I realized I was no longer alone, I'd become a barking, grunting, smack-talking madman. I was brought all the way back, to better days, high school days, workout days and game days. When the team was winning more than losing, when I was as fit as a Doberman and when I became so aware of being liked. And so aware that I liked being liked.

When Ray stepped into the doorway of the girls' room/weight room, he brought me back from the two places I was visiting, two better places. Through the sweat and the strain I had managed to reach back, to my pinnacle self of senior year. And for the brief moment before the interruption, I had just about hit the sweet spot of exertion exhaustion, the zone where I could briefly escape being any version of myself at all.

"Didn't Mary tell you not to mess with her weights?" he joked as I swung up and sat on the bench to look at him. I got a bit of the dizzies as I did it, and looked down at my feet to let it pass. A few seconds later I could turn to him and see properly.

Aw, hell. Despite his attempt at light humor, he wore the sad sideways mixed emotional smile I was never happy to see.

"What's wrong?" I said.

"Nothing's wrong," he said, plainly trying to reconfigure his face into something more acceptable.

"Was going back to work really *that* bad, Ray?"

Sad sideways smile popped back into place. "It sort of was, but only because I'd got kind of used to hanging around here with you."

"Oh, you missed me?" I chirped.

"Shut up," he said, showing me a large, completely unmenacing fist.

"Don't try it, big man," I said, holding up two of my own. "I've been working out. The big comeback is under way, and it just might include kicking your ass."

"Hah," he said, which was refreshing, since the thought was indeed so laughable. "But you do look good there, boy. You surely are on your way, huh?"

There was a relentless sadness haunting this small conversation, and I couldn't stand it but I couldn't talk it away, either.

It was the *on your way* thing. This was my first healthy step forward. Forward, to reentering life, getting strong and independent. And to getting back on schedule to move out and leave my old man finally alone in the house. This was going to be one long *See ya later, alligator,* before I left him to this house's wicked deep silence.

"I am still a long way from on my way, I can tell you," I said as I stood and nudged him along out the door. "If you saw me a little while ago, you would have been worried that I would never get out of here, I was so weak and pathetic. So don't even think your job is done, old man." I gave him one final great shove, which made him rumble out a genuine, thrilled roll of laughter. "Now go make my dinner. That's just weird, you hanging around watching me lift. Go on."

He was still chuckling away when I closed the door between us. I poured myself into one last painful session, to try to regain some of what I had lost since last season. And to try to put some distance between myself and the man with the sad sideways smile.

I was drenched in a whole new coating of sweat when Ray came back through the door some time later. I could see him behind me as I did dumbbell curls in front of the three-panel mirror on top of the vanity. I kept curling to reach the end of my set.

"What?" I groaned.

He aimed a cell phone at me. "Mary says why don't you answer your phone," Ray said.

I finished my last set of biceps curls, let the weights fall with a thump to the floor.

"Well, if I ever dreamed Mary would call me, I'd carry the thing with me every place I went."

I took the phone from Ray, who pulled it back to grab my attention. "Try to be nice to your sister. We're all on the same team here, remember."

"I'll try to remember, Ray."

"Good, and knock off the workout now, and get a shower. Dinner's in fifteen."

"Okay," I said, shoving him again, to hear him laughing again. "Hey, Mary, what's up?" I said flatly.

She matched my flatness and added a chill that came like a frozen mist through the phone.

"Well, Keir, it seems you have gotten out of it, out of the mess you made. Got out of it like you always do."

"What are you talking about, Mary? And stop with that voice, it's creeping me out."

"She's not pursuing it," she said in exactly that voice. "Gigi. She wanted to. Still wants to. And she has her evidence. But it's her family. The shame of it all, of her being with *you* and then taking that situation into account, and all that went on up there, into public? It was too much. She's not even home now, because they sent her traveling around South America or something to get her away from the whole thing. So well done, you. You managed to humiliate a whole family into backing down from doing the right thing."

I dropped almost involuntarily back to a sitting position on the weight bench. I squeezed my throbbing and dehydrated forehead with my free hand.

"How do you know all this?"

"Grace. Gigi and Grace talk now. And so Grace came to us with this. I don't know if it's supposed to be shared with you or not, but there it is."

Grace. Right, Grace. Grace was Fran and Mary's roommate, the only one home when Gigi and I came all that way to see the girls and share our graduation night with them. They had lied and said they couldn't make it to the ceremony, and I was still good enough to bring the ceremony all the way out to them over three hours away. But they were out, which they were not supposed to be, leaving us with only Grace.

It was Grace who tolerated us for several uncomfortable, uncelebratory minutes in the doorway of the sisterless on-campus apartment. It was Grace who told us Fran would be back in an hour. We went for a walk, and came back to an even more awkward meeting with Fran. So we left, Gigi and I, and spent the night together in an unoccupied campus apartment nearby.

And it was Grace who was heading out for an early run just when Gigi Boudakian was running away from me the next morning.

Gigi Boudakian should never have been running away from me.

Fran and Mary should have been there when we showed up. Goddamn it, they *should* have been at my graduation. None of us should have been at Norfolk University and that apartment and then that other apartment, and none of us *would* have been there if Fran and Mary had done the right thing and just *come home for my graduation*.

How different would things be then?

Grace was there the whole time, though. Grace the Graceless, guarding the door. Grace the witness. Grace almighty, who rushes to judgment.

"It was a misunderstanding," I said quietly.

"Yes, well, just so you know, Grace thinks she understands pretty well, and she is no fan of yours whatsoever. I wouldn't recommend you coming here, to be honest. You are free now to go wherever you like otherwise."

"To tell you the truth, Mary, I had no intention of coming to your place again anytime soon, so don't worry about it."

She held her chilly silence for a few uncomfortable seconds before finally getting to it.

"I didn't mean my place, Keir. I meant you probably shouldn't come *here*."

Oh. Oh no. At least now it made some sense, Mary calling me. This was her mission all along.

But, no. Jesus, this was my dream, my place, my life game plan just about to come together the way I had envisioned it for so long. Norfolk was the only place I ever seriously considered going.

"I didn't do *anything wrong*!" I bellowed into the phone, holding it out in front of me so I could face her somehow as I did it.

"Hey, hey, hey," Ray called, rushing into the bedroom. "What are you doing, yelling like a wild man? And what are you doing, not even in the shower? Dinner's ready. I told you . . ."

I was still staring at the phone. I didn't bother bringing it up to my ear because I knew she would be long gone. I continued to stare at the thing and to hold it at arm's length.

She did not have the right, or the power, to tell me where I could not go. Especially since I had not done anything wrong. Especially not my place, that I worked and planned so long for, so hard. Especially not there, nobody had the right.

She ruined my sleep, that was one thing Mary accomplished with her hateful phone call. I might have been lying on an outcropping of a stony hillside for all the peace I got. The mattress felt hard and jaggedy, causing me to turn and shift over and over again, and each time I did, I was jolted with the feeling that I was rolling over the side of that ledge and headed for a crash hundreds of feet below me.

"She is not right," I said to myself as I got up at the first sign of light. I wanted to run. I had begun the strength training and had the aching muscles to prove it, and now it was time to work in the cardiovascular stuff. Legs and lungs, upper body and core, I was going to be ready when the time came to show my stuff to the new team, at the new school, in my new life at Norfolk.

I would be the complete package. Hard and fast and lean and untouchable.

This was the Plan, goddamn it. The Plan was right and I had done nothing wrong.

I stretched extra carefully before even leaving the bedroom. But there was no avoiding the strain and almost audible squeal of my rusty hamstrings, calves, Achilles tendons. Fair enough. This came with the territory, and it was territory I was ready to reclaim.

I squinted at the surprising brightness of the morning as I stepped out onto the porch for the first time since the day my father brought me home to heal. I should have been out before this and felt a little ashamed of myself for hiding. There was no reason for it. I was careful to pull the door shut quietly behind me so Ray could enjoy his last twenty minutes of sleep before getting up for work.

The sun was uncommonly strong for this early, and I was holding my face up to it, absorbing it with half-closed eyes as I started down the front stairs.

"Jee-zuzz," I yelped as I bumped my chest right into Ray's big chin. He was coming up the stairs just as blindly as I was going down them.

"Jee-zuzz, yourself," he said, looking up, sighing heavily, slapping my chest. "What're you doin' here, at this hour?"

"Goin' for a run," I said. "What're *you* doin' here is a better question."

"I'm going to work," he said, snappish.

"This early?" I snapped back.

"Yes, Keir. Sometimes I go to work early. You wouldn't necessarily know that, because why would you need to know that? This is still sleep time for you. Go back to sleep."

He brushed past then, in a gruff way that felt completely strange and foreign to me. I almost asked, *Who are you all of a sudden?* Then I saw that he was scurrying toward the side of the house, where the trash barrels are. He had a lump of something bunched under each arm.

"Hey," I called, then ran to catch him when he didn't immediately respond.

"Hey, *what?*" he called back without looking. He started jamming the lumps into one of the barrels.

"Hey, *this*," I said, lunging into the trash before he could even fully pull himself out.

I retrieved the junk from all the other stinking junk, then stood in front of my old man with one of the things in each hand. I examined them intensely as Ray looked everywhere else.

In one hand I held an array of flowers, carnations, pink roses, one white lily, done in the shape of a heart and held together with a spine of something like a coat hanger. It was very much like a miniature version of a funeral arrangement. And at the center of the heart was a postcard sort of thing that read, NEVER TO BE FORGOTTEN.

In the other hand I held up a teddy bear, wrapped in cellophane and holding a single red rose along with another card. This one read,

DEAREST KILLER,
DO NOT
EVER
R.I.P.

Ray lunged and slapped both "tributes" out of my hands and straight back into the trash barrel.

"Don't even waste a minute on that," he said forcefully. "There are jackasses everywhere. They got nothing better to do

47

with their sad selves, and the only thing to do is ignore them."

I was still staring at my hands as if the things were still in my grip. Then I looked into the bin, at *them*, and to see what else was beneath them.

"This is why you were up so early," I said.

"Don't be stupid," he said. "*That* is a pathetic reason to get up early. I get up early because I get up early."

"No, you don't."

"Well, I do now. That's what I'm like now, one of them early risers. And it feels great. That shows how much you know about me. The new me. So." That was always his last word when he wanted to conclude, when he wanted to have the last word even if he hadn't earned it. So.

I had gotten all the logic I could get out of staring at my hands, then staring into the trash barrel, then staring at my hands again. And it was a sad tiny teardrop of logic, at best.

So I turned to my father instead.

"So," I echoed his so inconclusive *so*. "How long have you been doing this?"

"Three, four minutes at the most," he said. "No trouble. Hardly worth talking about."

I smiled, nodded, pointed at him the way a quarterback does to his wide receiver when they've just connected on a long bomb touchdown pass.

"I mean," I said, "how *long*? How many days? How many mornings, when I was in there all comfy, curled up and cowering from the nasty, scary world, were you out here cleaning up the nasty, scary world in case I might see it?"

He couldn't avoid my gaze now so, cornered, he checked his watch. Corniest delaying tactic of them all, so of course the watch check was Ray's move.

"I really am going to be late, Keir," he said. He was probably correct, and he sincerely meant it, but it meant nothing all the same. We both knew he had to answer, even if it meant he didn't punch in till lunchtime.

"They're just punks, Keir, little nobodies. Just jealous of you. They've always been jealous of you. It don't mean nothin'. At all."

This did not put me at any kind of ease, no matter what his intention was.

"How long, Ray? How many days have you had to do this?"

"This fence. You know this fence, stupid iron bars. There's always crap winding up caught in this fence, every day. I been cleaning the crap out of this fence every damn morning since you could even remember. Remember?"

I didn't want to remember. "I don't want to remember. *Ray.* How many days, since I've been home, have you had to clean up after this shit?"

He had by now gotten as tired as I had, of fighting dogged, relentless, inevitable fact.

"All of them, Son. Since the morning after you came here from . . . you know, the dorm. Every day brings more."

We locked stares on each other for as long as we could

hold it, maybe forty seconds. I remained frozen, so he broke the spell because he was the man here, with the job and the responsibility and the sense of time that comes with it. He lurched across the couple feet of space between us and grabbed me up tight in his awkward, primitive beastly hug. He hung on just a bit longer than usual and leaned his head flat against mine while stroking my hair flat. Just the way a trainer does when he's telling a beaten fighter, *It just ain't your night, kid*.

Then he let go, unclamped himself from me, and walked toward his car and his work and away from me and the trash barrels and all that stuff inside them.

I went for my run. And when I returned, approaching the front steps, everything suddenly looked filthy and disheveled. Like an abandoned house. I dropped right there and started picking up leaves and candy wrappers with my bare hands, and about a dozen of those cellophane rectangles that fall away when someone opens a pack of cigarettes. I thought nobody smoked anymore. Why do people have to be thoughtless pigs?

I got a broom and went over all the steps, twice, before picking every bit of litter up out of the modest patch of a front yard we had behind that sturdy iron fence. When I thought I had it under control, I stood on the top step looking down over it, and feeling all whooshy with pride. Then I looked up, and beyond our place to all the places surrounding us, and all the places surrounding them.

It could have been just one punk. Or two. Maybe it was an organized thing, or something more spontaneous and copy-cat, leaving stupid shit at my door to scare me or threaten me or whatever it is that ignorant vigilante types think they're accomplishing with this hero bullshit.

I didn't even do anything. One or ten or five thousand of them, I didn't care, they got their facts wrong.

But it didn't matter. Didn't matter how many were at it. Didn't matter that I didn't even do anything. This house was marked, as long as I was in it. This *life* was marked.

I went inside and hit the weights hard for another hour. I paced, and paced around the old house I loved so much. I felt the emptiness of it right now and it gave me the twitches. I felt utterly alone, and at the same time, surrounded.

I burst out the front door again, down those clean stairs, and onto the streets for another run. A long, long run as far out as I dared with my lack of conditioning, and then back again, just about.

The stairs looked dirty again. Could have been I was a little sensitive to it, could have been I missed a spot or two, or it could have been just the filthy filth of people, gathering all over our property. There's always crap winding up here, like Ray said.

I cleaned and swept again, the way good people do with their places, like they should do, to show the world a decent face. Then I went in the house and lifted some more, but I couldn't last in there for very long this time. I scuttled back out the front door, breathed in a couple of anxious lungfuls like a guy coming to the surface after a dive too deep. Then I sat on my clean, proud steps to rest, and to just be there.

I couldn't have Ray blocking for me all the time. He shouldn't have had to. Cleaning up my messes, before I could see them? No, we couldn't have that.

"You been right here all this time?" he said, startling me. My head was hanging, my elbows on my knees, as I must have dozed right there on the steps.

"What?" I said, snapping slowly out of it.

"You're right where I left you this morning, knucklehead," he said with a laugh. "Were we playing a game of freeze tag I wasn't aware of there, Tin Man?"

"Don't be stupid," I said, taking a weak swing at the air in front of his big-target face. "I've been everywhere today. This is just where I happened to wind up. Sitting, waiting for you to come home from work."

I knew it as soon as I said it, but I had not thought about it one second before that. His big gooey features told me all I needed to know anyway. Looked like he was going to burst out in both giggles and tears at the same time. "Remember?" he said.

"Yeah," I said, trying not to fall all the way into this one or I might not be able to climb back out. "Every day, practically, when I was little."

"Every day," he said.

"Waiting right here," I said.

"Right exactly there," he said. "Same *step*, even. Third from the top."

I looked down at the step under me, then back to him. "Even I didn't realize that," I said.

"Ha," he said, tromping up and past with a small smack to the back of my head for good measure. "Why wouldja need to? That's what you got me for."

This was starting to hurt. I had to shift it.

"No, what I got you for is to feed me. You going to make my dinner, old man?"

"Maybe. If I feel appreciated, ya rotten punk."

"You want me healthy, don'tcha, Coach?"

"Of course I do," he said, continuing on through the door and toward the stove beyond so that I might be cared for properly. As I ever was.

"Good," I said, "then get to it. I can't be waiting for my dinner, because that's not part of the program."

He stopped, and I could feel him reverse enough to hover in the doorway looking down at me. I continued to stare out into the world and not at him.

"Ah, that program of yours," he said with a mix of pride and reluctant farewell. "It sure seems to be picking up steam very quickly."

"I guess it is," I said, holding back anything more. There was more, and I was only just now beginning to grasp it all myself. In his Ray way, he seemed to be working on it right along with me. Then he shut the door and left me to it.

Mary was right, and damn her for it. I was a big fat wrong-magnet here in this house. And I'd be a big fat wrong-magnet at Norfolk. The Plan wasn't going to work. The Plan, after all the planning, was dying right in front of me.

I couldn't burden anybody with any more of this shit of mine.

And I couldn't allow anybody to handle any more of this shit of mine for me.

I had to go away, and not just three hours away, where my sisters, many classmates, teammates, and much, much else would be there with me. Like it or not. And where weekend trips home would be so easy, so expected, so necessary.

commitment

can't say it wasn't my fault, because it mostly was.

Backing it up, it went more or less like this. I committed to Norfolk, where my sisters, Fran and Mary, were. We were so great, such a team. They were the kind of sisters a guy would choose a college for even if it sucked, which Norfolk spectacularly did not. The fact was, I had been missing them monstrously since they left home. Especially Fran, who kind of mothered me when I needed a mother but was never uncool about it. I missed Mary, too, though Mary was always the tougher nut, the one who gave it to me bare-knuckles if she thought I was out of line. Wouldn't have thought you could miss the knuckles, but that's what I did.

And a full-ride scholarship, essentially because of my abilities as both a placekicker—I was a lock inside of forty yards—and a defensive back—I crippled a receiver one time, but mostly I was decent reliable coverage in a zone setup. But as a kicker—especially of field goals and point-afters—I was lights-out, automatic on point-afters. They assured me I was valued as a kicker, and that my ability to fill in at DB in a crisis was just a massive bonus. Which would provide me just enough excitement—and, once in a while, glory—to live the football life while avoiding most of the life-threatening business that the game is kind of renowned for. Sweet. It was my dream arrangement, Norfolk.

But then things went wrong. Life didn't do things the way it was supposed to. As an above-average graduating senior football player and all-around contributor to team and school and home and community and world, I had a right to expect a smooth ride on my way out of high school. Things went all wrong, and in the span of a little more than a couple of harrowing, upheavaling weeks, I did a turnaround. I turned completely away from everything I had known I wanted out of the next stage of the life thing—familiar friends, family, football, far but not too far from father, impossible good fortune for a guy like me. That was my idea of having it all, and I was this close to having it.

Then, all wrong. A situation got out of control and there was poison in my life that just would not flush out no matter what. And I started thinking how everything needed to be 180 degrees from what I'd wanted before, because now I wanted out, and away from anything familiar. Because everything that was familiar to me before was turning, rapidly, elsewise. The town that was so mine, so recently, was now a foreign place, a place I feared showing myself, to such a degree I knew my original choice was no choice at all. Coach, at Norfolk, said he understood. Said it was late for changes of heart. Said he understood the complications over which I had no control. It was almost as if he wasn't surprised. It was almost as if he wasn't terribly upset. Best for everybody, he said, and so he released me from my signed letter of intent to him and his fine program and the fine community that supported it unreservedly.

Shame. I could have used such a community.

But the silver lining appeared much farther west, with big skies, smaller expectations, and not one familiar face between me and home two thousand miles behind me. Carnegie, a very successful NAIA school, sent me a hopeful long-shot offer back when the NCAAs—mostly Division II and III schools with the odd limping Division I sniffing around—were paying me all the attention. I vaguely remembered the offer, but we had no contact after that.

As I sifted through all the paperwork from all the interested programs, Carnegie's location and size and campus and moderate approach to athletics leaped up at me out of the pile of more feisty competitors. Much the same way and for the same reasons, I'm sure, it must have shrunk away and buried itself the first time around. Back when I was a spotless and bloodless kicking machine, splitting the uprights cleanly nearly every time. When the choices were still all mine to make.

It was a step down in prestige, going to Carnegie. And they weren't even offering the full ride that Norfolk was.

But they were taking my call, which lately didn't feel like a guarantee, putting them immediately at the front of the line. If there even was a line now. So when they got over the surprise of my sudden dramatic rethink and offered me a half scholarship and a full new existence, we had a phone call handshake deal.

Bliss. Troubles could trouble somebody else now.

But it wasn't as easy as that, of course. Even a desperate broken simpleton like me knew better than that.

When I got off my sneaky whispering phone call to my new coach, I got instant butterflies at the thought of telling Ray. He had just spent every minute of a whole lot of his days nursing me, to the point where I was probably physically better than I was before the beating.

Physically better.

It was a hard time, diabolically hard, nasty weeks of me and Ray against the world, only I wasn't any good for shit. So it was Ray and Ray against the world, in defense of me, and he was magnificent. We were never closer, he was never truer blue and steadfast, and I had the conviction that if I decided to hibernate in that house under his Papa bear eye, I would be safe and without care for the rest of my days. I hadn't thought I could find any more love for my old man, but lying there like a pulpy lump day after day, I'd be damned if it didn't find me.

And when I finally gathered myself enough to make the first cautious foray out of hiding, out of my room, it was to locate him. Just to tell him . . . whatever. The stuff somebody should say to somebody once in a while. I found him, utterly wiped and recharging in his Barcalounger. His mouth was wide open and his left arm dangled over the arm of the chair toward the floor. The pins and needles would not be long in coming to that hand, prickling him awake and back on duty.

I was very happy to back away now and give him what peace he could get. There would be time to say the stuff.

When I had dinner on the table for my father as soon as he walked in, he looked at me sideways.

"Are you having a relapse, Keir? Post-traumatic brain disorder or something?"

I suppose the balance of caretaking and caregiving between us had never been anything close to equal, but this level of shock was not necessary.

"It was my turn, that's all. You gonna eat my food or do stand-up comedy while I dine alone?"

He scrambled down into his chair as if he was terrified it all might vanish before he had a chance. A few moments later, we were sizing each other up across a sloppy mash-up of scrambled eggs with cheese, corned beef hash, and french toast. We both adored breakfast food for supper, and it occurred to me that it had been a sad long age since we'd had it.

"Nice," Ray said after we ate in near silence through most

of the meal. It wasn't that kind of tense horrible silence, and not all that unusual for us, since we always agreed on respecting good food while it was still hot. There was always going to be time for the words once the food was honored and devoured, and anyway, we exchanged grunts of companionship that filled the gap.

"I'm really glad you like it," I said, gathering up every possible granule of taste, scraping my plate clean with my knife and fork together.

Without the food as the sort of third party at the table, the reality started rising, and obviously we both knew something was up.

"So, you gonna tell me what god-awful thing you need to stoop this low for?" he said, and it was sweet that he was making the effort. He wanted to put me at ease, when clearly he wasn't finding anything funny in what he had to guess at. His discomfort pulled him, down and toward me, his shoulders hunching, his spine giving out to a big sunflower wilt over the table.

"Ray . . . Dad," I said, reaching across to force him back into his best big-man posture. "Don't do that. That's so awful, I can't stand to see that. No matter what, nothing's ever so bad you have to fold up like that. It's like you're stabbed, destroyed, filleted, and gutted when you do that move, and it kills me. It's hard enough without you killing me."

He got less animated then, less responsive. "What move?" he said without a trace of a joke. His mind was occupied now, guessing probably every kind of crazy wrong thing that I might be going to say to him. Though the crazy right thing wasn't going to be any great improvement.

"Okay," I said, standing up and gathering plates and utensils and condiments, very much the elements my father and I had constructed a pretty nice life over, through it all. "I have to wash up now."

"No," he said.

"No?" I said in return, keeping my back to him as I deposited things noisily into the sink. "Since when is *no* to cleaning properly, immediately after meals, acceptable in Ray Sarafian's house?"

"Since Ray Sarafian is being kept on edge in a suspicious way by the only roommate and dinner companion currently residing in Ray Sarafian's house. It's pretty damn noticeable and distracting, so the freakin' dishes could wait for once while you talk to me, Keir."

Why was this so hard? I hung over the sink, still refusing to address him directly because, why was this so hard? People did this *all the time*. It was normal, it was correct, in a lot of ways, a positive step in a person's life. It was a natural move, an adjustment—okay, a big adjustment—but completely natural to millions of people just like us, just like me and just like Ray, who do what I was going to do. Millions, just like us, every year.

Why was this so *hard*?

"Are you all right, Son?" he said from back there, a voice

just about bursting its seams with suppressed anguish.

I was so weak. I couldn't even force it up just a little bit quicker and save him from the dread of anticipation. I couldn't even give him the word that I had made a big decision, because I was frozen stuck in knowing that telling him would be the moment of impact that would certify it as actually happening.

I wasn't yet man enough to live with that moment.

"I tell you what, Ray," I said, turning on the taps and squeezing a ridiculous stream of green liquid into the mix. "I'll just put a few things away and leave the greasy stuff to soak. Then I'll meet you in the living room. I went and dug out Risk from the games closet. I set it up for us, in the living room. What do you think about that, Dad? Up for a game of Risk?"

I got no response. He had escaped while I was waffling on like a sad, sorry fool.

But of course he was up for a game of Risk. We had played Risk, me and him, practically in an unbroken campaign of conquest that lasted all of my senior year. We played it, invested in it, dedicated ourselves to the great epic game as if it really was countries and continents and the whole of the world at stake.

And when we faced each other across that board for all those months, I suppose it pretty much was.

"You leave me enough time on my own and even I can work a thing out," he said, posing like a bored teenager, arms folded, legs splayed out from his chair. He was seated beside the awaiting Risk. "You're leaving. You're getting itchy feet and you don't want to spend any more of your exciting new lifetime oafing around with your old-fart father. I can't blame you. Hell, it's the right thing to do. It's gonna be sad, but I'm gonna have to face it anyway, whether it's now or a few weeks from now. Right?" he said with his droopy tired eyes watering up over his performance.

And this was when he still thought it was relatively just up the road. Denial maybe wasn't the worst thing, for a time. It could be a stage, on the way to something better, lots of things better, if we took it by degrees. Could we even pull this off? We were both drifting toward some sort of chicken-heart treaty, where we would agree to fool ourselves for just a little bit longer.

Could work. It was already working for me. I would delay beyond reason if I had half a chance, because I knew why this was so hard. It was willfully ignorant of me to compare us to the millions who pull this off, because they were not us and we would never be anybody else, even if sometimes that would be a very good thing.

When my ma died, the Ray Bear turned inward, in to us—me, Mary, and Fran. He wrapped us in Ray, and that was all the life he was ever looking for from then on. And then it was time and Mary left, and then it was time and Fran left, and Ray just kept bear-hugging tighter to what he was still holding, because what else would you expect a bear to do?

And I hugged him right back. I was his cub no matter

how much I grew, and I always felt special about it. It just got more muscular over time, the bears holding on, and I only hardly noticed when the girls didn't come back the way they said they would. And I never even hardly allowed myself to think about what would be left in that house once I left the old bear on his own inside it.

Now I couldn't not think about it, even as I made my plan to do it big and bold and more emphatically than anything I had ever done in my life.

But we could kid ourselves, kindly, thoughtfully, for a little bit longer, couldn't we?

I went to sit across from my longtime adversary, the esteemed old commander who had taught me everything I knew and was going to have to pay for it. I prepared myself for at least one more battle and possibly a couple of hunks of coffee cake and some trash-talking to rattle the old man's thinking.

And in one musket flash of a moment, all that burned away into the air when I saw Ray's face that he didn't seem to see I could see. He was staring at the board, bearing down like it could and would tell him something that he couldn't work out on his own. He flashed a stranger's frightened look, lost and suddenly, shockingly aged in his heavy, and heavily scored, face. Like a geographical map of his life. Like, Mongolia.

"My turn?" he asked politely.

I couldn't do this. Finally, this was the breaker that forced me to step up to the line.

"No, Ray," I said, "it's my turn. After all you've done . . . I have to be fair to you."

He raised his bulky head and showed me his softy eyes and tried one last stalling, diversionary maneuver.

"Who says you have to? I never did. I never expected you to be fair, just to be *there*. To be *here*. That's all I needed."

"Ah . . . Ray. Ray—"

"I know, Keir. I couldn't expect that indefinitely. It's no more reasonable to expect you to stay home than it is to expect you to be fair."

"Hey."

"Hey, yeah, hey yourself," he said, sitting up schoolboy straight and folding his hands. "We are going to have to have this conversation now."

I nodded a good number of times as a sort of flying start. "Yes," I said. "Well, Ray, it's probably a lot more drastic than you imagined. . . ."

"Well," Ray said, very deep into that hard night, "you sure know how to spoil holy hell out of a game of Risk, I'll give you that."

To be more accurate, I didn't spoil it so much as obliterate it. We poised ourselves for combat, angled ourselves toward it, sat on opposite sides of the waiting board, and even occasionally glared at it just to break the tension of staring at each other. But we played no Risk that night, not one skirmish.

Instead we talked each other into submission. I told him,

calmly, simply, and repeatedly, why I had to go away. I was a lot more patient about it than even I would have expected beyond, maybe, the second telling. That was because of the situation, sure, and because Ray needed and deserved the kid gloves on this. But I realized, listening to myself try to get him to understand a thing he would never truly understand, that I was making sense of events right along with him. I was explaining it to both of us.

But I was already altering the details, editing myself on the hoof because, *exactly* because, I wanted to spare him the pain, the worry, the drama, the trauma that was going to come to a certain kind of guy, with a certain kind of profile, in a certain kind of situation, even if he didn't do *anything* wrong. And that pain, that worry, that drama, that trauma would inevitably be inflicted on the guy's innocent beloveds. The conversation was a sort of mini play preview of the bigger picture: I was cutting out the unbearable facts in order to leave something much finer behind after I was done.

And I was done, with home, and with Norfolk, too. Ray didn't need to know every thought in my head. He didn't need to know that the boy he found waiting for him on the third step down thirteen years ago and the one he found there just recently had very, very different feelings about home. It was enough that he knew his son was in fact alive but maybe he got beat up and worn down enough by people and place that there was really only one thing for it. And Ray didn't need to know how tough things were between me and the girls, especially Mary. It would slaughter him to learn that his oldest daughter told his only son to basically fuck off and don't show your face on our campus, so he wouldn't ever be learning that. If what he learned instead was that my concerned sister phoned because she was looking out for me, and she wanted to give me the best advice, which of course you won't get anywhere like you would from your big sister, that would be a finer thing for him to hear. There were groups on the Norfolk campus who were planning to make trouble for me. Because they tended to make certain specific types of transgressions—which I didn't even do, but that didn't matter—into their own crusades and generate all kinds of noise and conflict and agitation wherever they went. And if I was going to be an angry mob's cause, to launch my very first semester, well, my sisters were going to worry that I would never make my way after that. Mary never even mentioned the obvious point of how difficult things could get for *them* at the same time, any spillover from my troubles. And they were up there and already established, Ray, you know, and that would be all wrong, to let something like this poison all the great stuff they have going on for themselves up at that beautiful campus. So, you see? Ray? This just has to be, my moving now. To clear up the atmosphere, to give everybody, all of us, a chance to live whatever lives we're meant to live and not have to be fighting people and getting into hate wars and having to defend yourself from a past that isn't even there when you look behind you. It's only there when other people *make* you see it and make you live with it forever. And who can live like that? Right, Ray? You see. We all need me to go, to let things get back to right again. Okay?

"Bullshit," he barked, again. Only a wearier bark now. "How come we never discussed this so I could talk you out of this nonsense?"

Even I never knew, during almost the whole of my lock-in stay at Club Ray, that I would be changing course and tacking west and breaking out of my cell inside his huge, hairy heart. It came to me in a flash of clarity that beat the pants off any kind of certainty I had ever experienced all at once before. It was the nearest I would ever get to calling something a *vision*, and I wouldn't be calling it that now. Ray was having enough trouble wrapping his big head around things without bringing mumbo jumbo into the game.

"It all makes sense now, Ray. I know you know it, so just say that for me and we'll call it a night."

For a few seconds I thought I might be losing him, as he let his chin drop to his chest and then didn't move. We were worn out, the two of us. It had been three hours since my father consumed an entire coffee cake out of spite, and we had gone over a lot of rough terrain in the time since. We got through all the cake and crying, all the pleading and scolding, all the remembering and laughing, though that didn't eat up a lot of clock. All the remembering, and all the crying again. We got through all that and had now eaten well into the available eight hours for Ray's sleeping before work. He was a wreck when he didn't get eight hours or close to it, and this day emotional wreckage was all but guaranteed. Fortunately, he would be gone before I woke up. And if he wasn't, I was just going to have to fake it. I'd spread enough sunshine and sugar cubes around the joint to get him out the door before he could start bawling all over again.

I began packing up the game, getting it all back tidily in the box while the old man snoozed alongside it.

We used to not even bother with putting it away. We would leave it right there in place and come back to the same epic battle between us across the globe and across days and weeks and more weeks. Because we could. Because it was just us, and just the way we liked it.

"You're going . . . Keir? Keir, where *is* that? I never even heard of the place. What's this all about? Is it happening, really? How is it happening? Surely it's too late now to switch—"

"Done," I said, pulling him up from the chair with a mighty tug of his burly bear arm. "I had to move fast, Ray, as I have already told you, and as you can certainly appreciate. I was fortunate enough . . ."

And blah, and blah, and balls to it all anyway. Blah. I sounded like a recorded message. Like a machine, a robotic nonperson selling a new kitchen to an old man who didn't need a new kitchen but did need his well and truly adored son to stay.

I knew all that. I knew exactly, how profoundly I was loved. And still.

How did we get here? How far, how fast, how wrong, totally wrong every which way?

We were not the type of people this was supposed to happen to. We were a great family, a really special, lucky family, and I said it many times to many people. I knew it then, when we were in it, and I knew it now, when we were apparently not.

Fran could say as much as she wanted that I made things be the way I wanted them to be, but that didn't mean anything. Because I was not wrong about this.

didn't have to worry about my father coming into my room and getting all soppy the morning after I told him I was leaving. I didn't have to worry about it any other mornings either. Because he turned out to be as determined and hard-hearted as I was, and that was pretty good for a couple of sappy saps like us. It was a crash course now, the accelerated program for getting used to the new world order in our tight little world.

Life without Ray.

Ray without me.

Those thoughts were always unimaginable, and I had decided that they would remain unimaginable forever. I started concentrating, thinking hard about not thinking about it at all. Ray was going to have to look out for himself, and himself only, from here on, and he would be fine once he got the hang of it. He would be in his old familiar home, and he would simply get familiar with it all over again, but with more elbow room, more freedom, less grief. He had earned it.

I was going on to all things unfamiliar, and that was what I focused my entire consciousness on. We were pulling off a screecher of a turn here, and it was taking all of Ray's efforts on this end—talking to the bank, redoing the loan paperwork while I filled out the Carnegie application to make it official. Coach Muswell was either a warlock or just a very can-do persona at that school, because somehow a lot of wheels got greased in setting up my football arrangements, housing, food plan, and he even looked into all the various travel options to get my body delivered onto that campus, the cherry on this very swirly cake.

Ray and I were reading the printout when he intoned, "Well, it's not a choice at all. You'll fly. There, that flight is the one. You don't want to be dealing with those connecting flight nightmares. I'll take care of this."

He went to get up quickly, to avoid my eyes the way I had been likewise avoiding his. I grabbed his arm and guided him back to the seat across from me at the kitchen table.

It was a perfect summary of how haywire all the old familiars had gotten for us, that this was the first time I could remember us ever sitting across this table together without having one scrap of food. It felt perverse. It felt like shame.

He knew it too, I could tell. But he couldn't do anything about it now, because that would be to recognize it. To acknowledge that small but damning oversight that he had never committed before.

Anyway, this was the better way. If you don't want to recognize a thing, then don't. If you just don't acknowledge a thing, who is to say that it is there at all? Or that it ever was?

"You are not to buy me a plane ticket, Ray, and that is an order. And before you say anything, even if you do buy it, I won't use it. This information from Coach Muswell is great, but I already pretty much knew how I wanted to go. And *there* is the trip." I flattened the page out for him on the table and tapped it several times. "That is how I want to go. And that is how I'm going."

He read my choice, did a small dramatic recoil from it, and made a sound like *yuck*, but as if a bear made it.

That didn't bother me one bit. This life was mine now, and I had been snap-crackling with nervous energy to get it out and on the road since practically the moment I finally said it out loud.

I slapped Ray's arm and stood up over him because for once, there was no discussion necessary. I kissed his overheated head on my way to my room to change. I came back out a few minutes later, kissed that same spot as he sat in that same spot, and crashed out the front door for my final distance run from this house.

It was just starting to rain lightly, and I never at all minded having the rain accompany me on my runs. So this was right, for my final lap of the old town. Victory lap? Farewell circuit?

Didn't matter. I wasn't feeling it. Wasn't feeling anything, not even the rain doing its best to weigh me down.

PART TWO

LEAVING HOME

bloodletting

Something inside me popped. There was already a weepy leak that opened up inside me around the time I made the decision to go far away from home and everything I knew. But then, the night before I was leaving, Ray got himself worked up well beyond any state of melancholy, any abject dam-broken-open suffering I ever saw before. He paced around the house endlessly, noisily. He kept talking to people who were not there: Mom, Mary and Fran, even me. I was there, all right, in the *house*, but not in the rooms where he was having conversations with me. And even if I was there, in the same building with the man, I wasn't *there*, in the same *space* as him.

"Go to bed!" I finally yelled from my bed, when I couldn't sleep and couldn't take it any longer.

"Go to Norfolk!" he yelled back, just in case there was any

confusion about what was standing between him and sanity.

I could not feel guilty about this decision. I had been over it every which way, and it was the right move, every which way. If I dared roll it around in my head any longer, I would wind up just as demented as he was acting. I imagined us like a couple of those robotic vacuum cleaners, blindly patrolling the rooms, sucking up every particle of family history off these floors and crashing into each other over and over and over and over.

Breaking point, camel's back, no return came at 4:47 a.m. I could tell the very instant that Ray lost consciousness after his mania of pacing and haunting his own house to the limit of his endurance. You could tell that, in a house like this, in a family like ours, when somebody finally went unconscious, even if they had stopped making noise an hour earlier. The breathing of the walls changed, and you just knew.

And when I knew it finally, I got up. I grabbed my full duffel bag, and I slipped through the house, between those walls, out through the front door quiet as a cat in slippers.

Like a coward. Like a reverse home invasion.

"What're you doing?" came the big embarrassing bellow at my back. It felt extra conspicuous tearing its way through the neighborhood through the stillness of the predawn.

I tried to shush him by waving my hands downward the way traffic cops would tell you to slow down.

"You were just gonna leave like that? Keir? Like that?" He hadn't adjusted his volume at all. Not that I had use for any of these neighbors anyway, but I was embarrassed all the same. Then I was embarrassed about being embarrassed, and then I was just fucking irritated.

"Just go back inside, Ray, please," I shouted at him because he was seeing me off, wishing me luck and bon voyage in his own style, which involved great gales of noisy crying and spectacle-izing himself with such determination I had to switch him off, turn my face toward fresher air, and just get on with it. "You're free," I called, hurrying away from him, doing a shit job of making my voice sound jovial. "Go and have fun now, empty nester. You earned it."

"I *did*!" he yelled back, doing a shit job of making either one of us feel better about this.

Every single particle of my existence, he took care of. It felt like murder now, what I was doing. Leaving him bloody in the street.

It felt necessary, though. I only wished I had the skills to do it without butchering the whole thing like I was doing.

But I lacked those skills, and who knew what others as well. I *had* to start figuring everything out. I had to start doing things right, which meant doing things differently.

"Keir," I heard my old man call out, and knowing him, he was going to tell me I forgot something and needed to go back for it.

And that was the first thing I would be doing differently. The old me would have answered that call, but this one would not be going back.

Removing yourself from your life sounded easier than it felt once it got started. I didn't doubt what I had to do, but I did doubt whether I was man enough to do it. From the moment Ray caught up to me fleeing the scene of the crime, I had the sensation like I'd been shot or something. I had a pain start stabbing me in the left side, around the kidney, and the faster I walked toward the bus station, the deeper it jabbed me. I kept touching back there, feeling and looking to see if anything was bleeding out of me, that's how real it felt. By the time I got to the station, I had downshifted from power walk to stroll to shuffle, trying to appease the stabbing, jabbing pain. And I was favoring my side, hunched forward and left, so plainly that a kid held the door for me like I was some kind of old duffer. He wasn't more than two or three years younger than me.

But he held that big heavy glass door, and I thanked him, and then I was through and officially on Greyhound's ground.

Greyhound's ground, and westward bound, was what I was thinking as I heaved my duffel into the belly of the bus. The pain had gotten bearable as I mounted the stairs, but not so bearable it would let me ignore it. I felt again at my side, certain that somehow I had gotten myself punctured. Nothing on my hand, nothing on my shirt. Nothing. I continued checking the spot as I went into the small, stale shop to get a couple of things for the ride. I did not appear to leave any trail entering or leaving the shop, and told myself how stupid this whole thing was and to grow the fuck up right now.

But in my seat waiting to depart, I scanned the terminal floor all over for any trace. Like a murderer leading the cops to his hideout by the trail of his own blood.

The puncture was going to have to seal itself rapidly, because this was the first leg of what would be three days, five different buses, forty stations, and two thousand miles of American experience that I sorely needed to experience. The very last thing I wanted was to leave a trail for any posse— real *or* otherwise—to follow all the way back to me. So if it wasn't going to heal, it might as well just go the other way and bleed me right out, because that would be a more tolerable outcome than being found.

I was done with that guy. I didn't want anybody to find him.

solitaire

Springfield, and a young woman gets on.

When the journey began, we set sail with maybe ten of the bus's fifty-plus seats occupied. Which was a surprise to me but probably should not have been at this prebreakfast time of day. Stopping at Worcester doubled our population, and Springfield is doing even better, filling us up with bodies at the expense of breathable air. Although nobody knows or cares, I'm still embarrassed that I thought Greyhound buses were all going to be cool and quiet, roomy and airy, based on the pathetic sample size that was my life.

Still, folks were largely groggy and muted until the young woman joins us, with her whole kitchen in a large plastic bag and two little girls clinging to the belt loops of her battleship-gray jeans. It's hard to tell whether the girls are trying to cling tight to their mom or to keep her pants up for her, but both ideas seem to be good ones. This is a sinewy, carnival-midway-slim woman.

She soldiers on, struggling, banging and crashing her stroller and that giant green trash bag full of clangy noise until she makes it to the driver's tiny ticket window, where she drops everything on the floor and simply leans forward with her forehead against the Plexiglas.

"Go find seats, girls," she says without removing herself from the ticket window.

The girls tentatively make their way down the aisle as the driver barks at the woman to get her skinny ass in gear and present her ticket.

Her ass stays right where it is, wherever it is, but she does straighten right up to address the driver. "I prefer 'narrow,'" she says, and I laugh out loud, but I am in a minority. Folks all around start barking at the driver to move, and the driver barks back that nobody is moving till narrow-ass finds her ticket and hands it over. It's all getting tense now as the woman gets down on her knees to start rummaging through that great big Dumpster of a bag, which does nothing but irritate everybody on the now sweaty and angry bus.

I jump up and head toward the front, passing the girls on the way.

"Here," I say, reaching and taking the stroller from her. Because a gentleman doesn't just sit there and watch. I must be the only gent on board then, because nobody else even offered. It's a stroller that's seen a lot of duty as a bumper car, and so it won't stay folded up. It's also no use to the five- or six-year-old kids she's got with her, so I wonder what it's even doing here, but I will just wonder that to myself.

She looks up at me for a couple of seconds, expressing nothing with her voice or her face, then dives back into the critical rummaging.

Just before I get back to my seat, after stowing the stroller in the cramped overhead space, a great cheer erupts from the majority of my fellow passengers. For an instant I actually believe they are doing it for me and my gallantry, my stowing ability, but it is obviously directed past me, to the front, where someone has located a bus ticket at the bottom of a big bag and against all expectations. The bus's brakes hiss, we jerk into motion, and I have to grab a seat back to keep from falling on my face and definitely getting my own round of applause.

"Hey," I say when I get right and catch on. "What are you doing?" I am addressing the girls, who have occupied my seat and the formerly vacant one next to it. They do not acknowledge me, but continue eating and looking out the window.

"What are *you* doing?" the mother asks, jabbing a finger into my painful side.

"That's my seat," I say, pointing at the window seat, where one girl is now willfully kicking at the seat in front.

"They're all the same, mister. Go find another one."

She throws herself down into the aisle seat in front of the girls. In the window seat next to her is a guy wearing a full Cleveland Cavaliers outfit, tank top, shorts, socks, headband, and he should have known better fifteen years and forty pounds ago. He got on in Worcester and started snoring before the bus even pulled away.

"There are no other window seats," I protest. She looks straight up at me, expressionless as ever. "What are you, four?"

She has really sizable hair. Her face is rigid, but I can see traces of who might be in there, and I think I may have known her. I think I may have gone to grade school with her. But the girl I knew didn't have a nose that took a severe left-hand turn halfway down the bridge. This nose has known knuckles.

"Actually, I'm the same age as you," I say.

"My age is none of your damn business," she snaps, and turns front again.

"Fine, what about my seat?" I demand.

The driver's voice crackles to something like life over the speaker. "Please take a seat, sir," he calls out.

"I had a seat," I say, pointing.

"If you do not take a seat, I am going to have to stop the bus."

My fellow travelers turn sharply on me. There are growls and worse, and I lean down close to the woman, as if anyone would think this is going to pass for sitting.

"I am going to sit in that seat," I say.

"Right," she says, loudly, theatrically, effectively. "I knew it. Another pervert."

"Don't *say* that," I plead, waving her down.

The Cleveland Cav bursts up out of his seat, and I think I'm about to get a beating. He snarls, climbs over the woman roughly, and then pushes right past me. He stomps toward the back of the bus and throws himself hard into a seat near the bathroom.

"He doesn't care that you're a perv," she says. "Nobody does. He just can't stand the noise and the kicking and what all. Happens all the time, so I'm used to having an extra seat, but I will let you have it if you sit down and shut up."

I am already leaning to climb past her into the window seat when she scoots over and snags it. "Y'snooze, y'lose," she says as I reluctantly sit in the aisle seat.

"I didn't snooze. I was up very early, as a matter of fact. And I got myself a window seat. That one right behind you, where a little lady is right now sitting on my jacket."

"You'll get your jacket back," she sighs, sounding bored with me.

"And my food?"

"What?"

"They're eating my sandwiches."

Her face makes its first attempt at expressing itself, and I think she's going to laugh, before she fights it off. "You complain a *lot*," she says, folding her arms, closing her eyes, shutting me out. "It's no wonder you got no friends."

That was rude. I am carefully thinking of how I am going to express how appalled I am without making her laugh. But before I can assemble it, my seat back starts thumping. And thump-thump-thumping. And giggling.

I turn to peer through the space between the seats. "Could you not do that, please?"

The thumping stops, the giggling doesn't. I turn frontward again just in time for the thump-thumping to resume and the stabbing side pain to rise sharply.

I growl and start turning.

"Mister," the woman says, low and serious, "if you do not leave my girls alone right now, I am going to start screaming and bring holy hell down on your head."

I work up a wild fury, feel my face flush and my muscles tighten all over, my breath quicken.

And I exhale, uncoil, and settle as low down into my thumping, thumping seat as I can get.

After stewing for several angry miles and realizing these children's legs were never going to tire, especially since they teamed impressively to trade places every few kicks, I gave up altogether.

"I'm just sorry I didn't bring you a sandwich too," I say, unaware whether the woman is asleep under those eyelids or not.

"Next time," she says.

Her eyes remain closed. Which is good, because I'm staring. She looks just like her. From school. Except for the nose, and the remarkable wiriness. Could be her.

I have no business even thinking this, since the last time I saw the girl, we were twelve. I loved her. She could be in there somewhere, though, behind the nose that I can't stop staring at. I hope not.

"Are you staring at my fucking nose?" the woman snaps from what looked like a dead sleep. I nearly topple into the aisle with the surprise of it. "Ha!" she says then, covering her mouth with one hand and pointing at me with the other. I have to say, she flips from enraged to amused impressively.

"No," I say, "I was not, I assure you."

"You're staring at it now, though."

I surely am. For the life of me, I'm glued to the thing now. "I am really sorry," I say. "I don't mean anything. I'm just . . ."

"A total rube who's never been anywhere or seen anything, and so you stare, like you're invisible and nobody'll notice."

"No," I say, almost happy to be the offended one now.

"No? Sorry, it's just that you seem like a total rube who's never been anywhere or seen anything and that's why you're socially awkward and friendless."

She's really getting under my skin now, making these assumptions and insulting me based on nothing at all.

"And I can understand now why somebody wanted to punch you in the nose."

I didn't want to say that. No matter what she had said, that was not something I meant to say, and not something that was okay to say. I'm about to grovel for all I'm worth when she cuts me off by giggling.

"You can understand because you want to punch me in the nose?" she says, leaning a little closer, closer, practically flattening my own stupid nose with hers.

"Absolutely not," I say in a confession-box whisper.

We stay sort of suspended in each other's ether for several seconds. I hope my ether doesn't smell as sour as hers, but it quite possibly might.

"Good," she says, smiling on. "Glad to hear it." She gracefully backs away into her space by the window, and I continue watching her, thinking about who she is, where she comes from, how she learned to smile like that when most people would not be smiling.

"You're amazing," I say, just as involuntarily as I said that other thing I said.

She laughs, of course. She digs around in an inside pocket of her jacket and pulls out a squat, flat bottle of vodka. As she unscrews the top, she says, "And you are an easily excitable boy." She tips her head back and takes a short drink off the bottle, then offers it to me.

"Oh, thank you so much," I say, "but I don't drink."

She wobbles her head comically side-to-side-to-side and says, "Why would anybody not take a small sip of kindness off a stranger?"

Fair enough, it is a funny place to start saying no, to a person I'm starting to feel I never want to say no to.

"I'm just not a drinker," I say, because that is the truth. This me, who slipped off one layer of skin as he left home and stepped onto this westbound bus, is not a drinker. Truth.

"What, you think I'm dirty or something?" she says, and I am halfway into matching her jokey smile when I realize her face is showing no such thing.

So much for new purified me. I tentatively reach over to take the bottle, if she will let me have it. She does, and as her tragic magic smile reappears, I take a swig from her little white spirit of kindness. I lower the bottle and drink in her sweet expression.

"You want me to drink more?" I ask. "Because I'll drink more if that'll make you happy."

"Nope," she says, snagging the vodka right away from me.

She takes a more sizable slug from the bottle before tucking it away again.

"I take it back," I say. "I can't imagine anybody wanting to punch you in the nose."

She is nestling down into her seat and turning away from me to look out the window or more likely to sleep. "Nobody punched me."

"Good," I say, like I have achieved something.

"I just got thrown down some stairs."

After several seconds of trying, "Oh," is all I can say.

Which is probably for the best, since even that much provokes a "Shut up now," in response.

I can do that, shut up. But I do go on thinking about her, and her kids, and what life must be like. And it's only fair, since she was happy enough to draw whatever conclusions she wanted to about me.

Eventually I slip away to sleep myself, thinking as I do that I'm glad they ate my food and I wished I had had more for them.

I'm wearing cargo pants because they make me feel autonomous. It gives me a kind of peace knowing that in the case of hijacking or firebombing or what have you, I can always jump out the window and hit the ground ready to carry on a mostly functional life. My wallet, phone, secret cash stash, Kleenex, gum, and throat lozenges are all safely secured on my person. This also lets me be less freaked than I otherwise would be about getting separated from my jacket. The only item in the jacket pocket is a new deck of cards for playing solitaire. I've never played solitaire, but figured if there was ever a time to learn, this would be it.

But it is my varsity team jacket, from senior year football. There is a lot of stuff attached to that thing.

As I come up out of my cat nap, I glance back and see the window-seat girl has fallen asleep, comforted by my jacket. Her partner is still—or again, since I lost track—bravely managing the occasional halfhearted kick but seems to be running out of gas.

I have a sudden, overpowering urge to play solitaire.

My right thigh pocket jolts me by silently vibrating. It takes me several seconds, and I do contemplate my window jump, before I work out that it's my phone. I have never used the thing much, and it still surprises me every time it demands attention.

I fish it out and see that it's Ray trying to call. I can't talk. I cannot contemplate talking. I have to ignore this. I have to ignore you, Ray, and I hope you can understand.

I try to nap a bit more as the bus leaves Massachusetts and crosses into New York State. I may or may not achieve sleep a few times, but the phone's relentlessness is beyond question. I know he will eventually give up, and as we approach the next stop in Albany, he does. Sort of.

There is a little pulsating beeping tone, because I didn't realize that you had to set both phone and text tones to silent vibrate if that was what you wanted. We are pulling into the Albany Greyhound station, with the low rustling activity of people preparing to exit, as I read the text.

DID I DO SOMETHING WRONG?

I breathe deeply and noisily through my nose, and I try to recapture my dissolving autonomy. I reach for a throat lozenge.

"Girlfriend not happy with you, I guess," the woman says as she climbs over me.

"Hey," I huff, indignant to find that a Greyhound bus in Albany is shockingly not a private space to be respected, and strangers wouldn't read your phone messages just because they can.

She laughs heartily. My indignation is the final proof that she was right about me being a clueless rube out here. We both hear it the instant the huff comes out of me, and I think we're both glad I finally settled the matter.

"Yeah," I say, looking down at the message again for no good reason at all. "Girlfriends, right?"

"Right," she says, pulling down the stroller and nearly conking me on the head with it. She gathers up the stroller, the noisy trash bag, and with a quick "Yep," the children.

I'm looking at the phone again, this time trying to work out the silencer on the messages, when the three of them edge toward the exit. I look up and see the two girls occupying my varsity jacket together, each with one hand clutching a sleeve and the other Mom's saggy jeans.

I am a good guy, but not that good. I badly want that jacket, but I badly don't need "child molester" on my resume, even for a minute.

I scoot up to them and, reaching right over the top, relieve Mom of the stroller.

"Thanks," she says. "These aisles are stupid narrow."

"Stupid," I agree, still carrying the stroller over my head and trailing closely behind my varsity jacket.

It is a smelly, bustling scene we find in the bus depot, and I feel like things are getting away from me quickly. Things like the woman, who has grabbed the stroller firmly out of my grasp and turned away from me with a barely audible, "Thanks again."

Things like my jacket, which I see hot-stepping away from me on four little legs. Nobody but me seems to notice what's wrong here, unless that's the whole point and now it is going to be an even messier scene if I try to prevent this frail little family from stealing my jacket like they're doing.

Against my better judgment, I stay close on their heels, saying, "Hey, hey, hey," increasingly loudly at their backs and looking every last ounce the dirtbag I hoped not to be. But since I am being ignored comprehensively, I am just going to have to make the scene and risk the whole vigilante routine right here in this filthy bus station that has probably seen it loads of times before.

"Hey," I say one last time.

But I am topped by a triple-loud and angry "Hey," coming back the other way.

But it's not the girls and not the woman.

"What the fuck is this?" the man bellows, snatching my jacket off the girls forcefully enough to send the two of them teetering sideways like candlepins.

"Hey, hey, hey," I shout, rushing forward.

"Jesus Christ," the woman says. She moves like a martial arts ballerina, in one motion grabbing the jacket from the man and spinning around perfectly timed to hand it off to me. "I'm sorry, mister," she says, looking up at my eyes and carrying on a whole separate conversation there. "I didn't realize the girls had your jacket."

"Are you okay?" I say low, looking over her shoulder at the small stocky guy breathing steam at me while two little girls tangle up in his legs.

"Yes, I'm fine."

"You want me to—"

"Go? Yes."

"Ah, I don't know about this."

"You like me?" she says, seizing all my attention just like that.

"Yes, I do," I say.

"Good, because if you do, you will turn and go right this second."

I glance up again toward the bad guy.

"That's not a good guy," I say. "I think—"

"Right . . . this . . . second," she hisses. "*Now.*"

She gives me a shove firm enough to move me, subtle enough to go unseen. And warm enough to make me ache as we spin off in our opposite directions toward our opposite situations.

Several steps farther I turn back, which I know is probably a mistake. They are all walking off together, but the man is gripping her arm and sort of tugging her this way and that just enough to imbalance her and make her look helpless and messed up.

Which I know she is not. I'm less simple about things than when I first got on that bus—even if she'd surely laugh at me for saying so. I know he is not a good guy, and she is a fine woman, and neither one of them is getting what they deserve.

And I know that if I do what I badly want to do, which is run after them, I will wind up making the bad a whole lot worse.

I stop looking. I turn and head for the bus to my next destination.

rude awakenings

'd like to say this is the first time I ever woke up in Erie, but that would sound like a lie. Dropping that second *e* makes a whole lot of difference. It is, though, the first time I've woken up in Pennsylvania.

Erie the town may be a perfectly fine place, but the sensation I get, from the minute the bus bumps roughly to a stop and rudely awakens me, is eerie.

I've been on the road for twelve hours. I fell asleep shortly after we left Buffalo about two hours ago and was into some deep dreaming that I cannot now remember anything about. What I do know is that when I woke up, I remembered her name. Tracey. The girl I loved in grade school. She was unfailingly sweet to me all the time I knew her, and I am certain she only agreed to be my girlfriend because she was too kind a person to mangle me the way a rejection would have doubtless done. I asked her at the most awkward moment when I semi-accidentally crashed my bike into hers. I timed it perfectly and crashed her up over the sidewalk and into Paul Burnam's front yard on Sunnyside. I was only even in that neighborhood because Paul told me she hung around there with some friends, so I jumped on my bike that very day after school and motored down there like a guided missile, and then *bam*. You'd probably be right to call it a targeted hit, even though that wasn't exactly the plan. I just had an overload of emotion but a deficiency when it came to control.

We were an incident within two minutes of my arrival on Sunnyside, and an item within three minutes of that. The kicker was that how it started was all my reckless doing, but I came off the worse of the two of us, flying right over the handlebars, almost clearing Tracey and her bike completely as they lay there. But my shin cracked the handlebars and my face planted deep enough into Paul's lawn that I could come back out with a report that his tulip bulbs were sprouting roots already. I was a mess, dirty and disoriented and grappling to even get up to my feet and remain steady on them. I could have been an especially ugly baby bird just thrown down out of a nest. But I got the words out quick in case they were my last, and Tracey smiled shyly from her seat still on the ground and she giggled me a yes.

What we wound up really was to be exceptionally great friends. She was my girl, but that was a technicality. A technicality I had no intention of ever clearing up, mind you. But for two years we went off privately and secretly the way steadies do, walking the Muddy River, hiking up Peters Hill for the view and the sensation, and making use of all that opportunity to just talk, about stuff that was real stuff, stuff that was less real, and it was the easiest talking I have ever known with a girl. Still. I talked mostly about my family, who I thought were just magically perfect. And she talked, eventually about her dad punching her in the stomach.

She didn't finish grade school with us because her family had to move. She told most people that any bruises had come from her brother, who was certainly jerk enough in his own right. But brothers bashing their sisters sometimes are one kind of jerk. Fathers who punch their daughters are a whole different class of jerk. She protected her dad, and her brother could protect himself.

Until they were gone. Beamed up by aliens, I guess.

I can't stop thinking about Tracey since Albany. Tracey, and Tracey, because why not? Could be. The world can surely be that random if it's in a mood to be.

I hope Tracey is all right. I hope she gets away. She'd be all right if she was with me. I think now I dreamed of her. But she was not quite *with* me there, either.

I look all around, trying to get my bearings, and notice a total of about a half dozen other passengers as we depart the station for the next stop, Ashtabula, Ohio. It probably has more to do with whatever I was dreaming than with reality, but I feel like I've landed in a particularly gnarly neighborhood on wheels. There's a smell. Nobody else is within ten feet of me, and I'm still getting a powerful whiff of bad body business that's making me queasy.

It's dark outside, and as I make my way to the bathroom at the rear of the bus, it is dark inside as well. No reading lights or anything; the few bodies I notice are shadows.

As I reach the bathroom, it certainly smells, as it has right along, but it's not the same smell as the other one. It is, in fact, almost a relief to think of getting in there and breathing better-quality air.

The little window that's supposed to rotate and show us whether the bathroom is vacant or occupied ain't showin' me nothin' right now. Where one word or the other is supposed to be visible, there is nothing but a heavy green-brown smudge that I don't care to contemplate.

I knock lightly, saying, "Anybody in there?"

"Vacant," comes a quick, high nasal reply.

"Yeah, I don't think you're truly vacant there, bathroom. So I can just wait till you're out."

"Vacant," he says again. "Come on in."

Right. The toilet room is so small that if you were squatting and straining and wound up suffering a catastrophic Elvis Presley event, the only falling-down option would be forward, and when you did so, you would block the door so comprehensively that by the time they got you out, your rot would match the reek of every tortured ass that ever fouled a Greyhound convenience.

"I think that's a little impractical," I say. "Don't worry about it. I'm not desperate, so I can wait."

"What, are you saying that I *am* desperate?"

Jesus Hell.

"No. I'm sure you have no reason to be desperate. I just meant I was in no rush. No rush to be rushing you. Right?"

This, after all that, seems to have rushed him. I hear a little agitated bumping and thrashing inside as the man finally muscles his way out, passing with a snarling, "*Fine, then*," directed at me. Was I supposed to apologize for being patient? Maybe there is a whole upside-down etiquette to shadowy Greyhound Society, and I'd better get the guide-book before I commit something unspeakably heinous.

Finally in the bathroom, I do my best to catch up on the long-neglected clean-and-shine. I give it a good bit of soap and toilet paper wipe-down to the point where I can contemplate using the facilities of toilet and sink. The mirror is actually shiny sheet metal that distorts, clouds, and somehow even delivers one's reflection into a deep-looking-glass space about six feet away from the owner of that reflection. I stare at it, mesmerized by the distance between this me and that one. I don't like it. It gives me a zinging spine, and I have to shake it out. Then, just before sitting down, I glance back at it, and the zinging strikes again and I cannot decide if I need that other me to come closer like a regular reflection would do, or to just buzz off completely because this mid-range creep show is too hard to bear.

I'm sitting down finally, a little less anxious but not quite relaxed. A secure and relatively pestilence-free spot to do unavoidable business is one of the real basics of a civilization. Greyhound has been doing this for long enough to know that and to have the systems in place to make this work.

I dropped my vigilance too soon, and as the thought hit me—that lock doesn't work—it hit somebody on the other side of the door at much the same moment.

"It's occupied," I say in a screamy small dog/large bird cry of horror. My hands shot straight up too, like I was blitzing the quarterback. This guy is quick, though, and his upper torso is through the opening before I can shove the door on him.

"Ow," the guy says in a firm, but even, accusing tone. I have him pinched right at the waist and pinched mightily. If he were an ant, he'd be in two separate rooms now. "Will you release me?"

"Will you get out?"

"Release me."

"Get out."

"What's wrong, Cecil?" asks a new voice outside the door.

"There's a crazy guy on the toilet trying to guillotine me door-style. He's one of them totally hairless ones, so we already know he spends too much time down there to begin with."

"Well, that's not right. Hey, man, let the guy go, will ya?"

"Is he gonna get out?"

"Where else is he gonna go?"

"Shouldn't have come in here in the first place like that, just bursting in."

"Oh," Cecil says, sounding noticeably weaker, "I'm getting the death penalty for failure to knock? How did we wind up in Texas?"

Next thing I see is that either Cecil has sprouted a second head, or else . . .

"Hey, man, I'm Dirk. Listen, I'll vouch for my friend. He will back out directly if you let him. But otherwise he's gonna pass out, and who knows what kind of trouble you'll be getting into."

"All right," I say, more spooked than a real man should be by the mere mention of getting in some vague trouble. I pull the door hard toward me, surprising Cecil and dropping him to the bathroom floor. Or that's where his head and one arm lands, with the rest outside.

Dirk, the levelheaded negotiator, has not dropped immediately to the floor to tend his fallen comrade. I look to see him scanning *me*.

"God, look at that," he says. "You were right, Cecil, bald as a blind pinky rat. Whatever is *with* these boys today? Can I ask you something? What exactly is it all about, like what you get out of it?"

This has gotten strange in a way that couldn't possibly fit into any TV anthology of strange, strange things.

"Could you go now?" I say, trying as coolly as possible to

hook my underwear with one finger and drag them up to me with as little fanfare as possible. It is harder because Dirk won't stop watching every move to see if there is any more show coming. I once pushed a dead car home for a mile and a half up a gradual incline, and it felt quicker and easier than this.

Cecil is on his feet now, the rose of frisky good health back in his cheeks. They are both observing. I finally give up on any remaining discretion just to get it over with. I hop up and try frantically to get my underwear in place with speed, but the nervousness makes me fumble the whole thing, and the underwear gets tangled, then twisted on one side and . . . I have to pull them partly back *down* to get them right again.

The humiliation is something I could not have even contemplated before. I'm sweating, my hands still doing more flapping and tangling than just pulling my friggin' clothes up over my body the way I had been doing successfully for over a decade and a half now.

The two of them, remarkably, suggest no physical threat. But they also are not moving out of that doorway until I have underwear up, pants up, shirt tucked. I feel both relief and the greatest humiliation yet as I hitch up my pants and secure the pewter buckle of my belt with a snap-clank at the point directly above my fly.

The eeriness gets to its peak and conclusion as the two of them simply look at me when I make it obvious I am getting out. They nod, something like approval, or thanks, or yes to something I would never ever want to know.

Then, just as I am about to bump past them, there is another knock at the door.

"Vacant?" The guy says the same word, in the same high tone he used when he was in here—and lying about the vacancy. We all say yes, vacant, and as I exit last, the little man says to me, "See, shoulda came in with me when I invited you. And I got caramel corn, too. I bet them guys never gave you no caramel corn."

We are practically to Ashtabula by the time I make my way up the dark aisle feeling weak and sickly and unsure about pretty much everything around me. My hands are trembling slightly, so I jam them into my pockets. The bus looks exactly the way it did when I walked to the bathroom all that time ago. The shadows are all still shadows lying low in their seats.

Is this what everybody out here is like? Is this the way things are?

The trip to the safety of my own seat seems about five miles long, but I get there. When I burrow in, I go through all the pockets and spaces of my cargo pants. I was more preoccupied with *other things* in that bathroom than a guy would normally figure to be worrying about. Stuff could have fallen out of every pocket, I could have been left with most of my valuables taken from me and I wouldn't have known it at the time.

I check and I check, and everything I had when I went into the bathroom I still have now. I think.

They never even touched me. I didn't have to fight anybody. Nothing was taken. It was almost like some perverse form of admiration or something. Something thrilling for them. No harm, no foul for me.

It was a compliment. Just a bit of fun. Take the compliment, loosen up, and have fun, Sarafian. Who wouldn't like all that? You know you wanted it. You know you liked it.

I don't close my eyes, and I don't so much as shift in my seat until we have to transfer at the station in Cleveland. When all the passengers have disembarked, I stand far back from the luggage compartment in the bus's belly. I wait until every other bag has been collected before slowly making my way toward my bag, lying alone on its side where the driver dumped it on the pavement. I don't even glance up as I make my way through the people headed away. Suddenly I'm jolted by a hard shoulder banging into me and sending me two feet sideways before I continue my route, head down, to collect my bag and scuttle off, breathing heavily and squeezing my fists hard enough that I can almost make out my fingertips coming through to the back of my hand.

I didn't do anything. What am I holding my head down for? Could guys like that make me feel like this, just like that, so easy, by looking at me and saying things? Is that even possible to do to a person? Why am I supposed to be ashamed? And why am I going along with it?

Well, I'm not going along with it anymore.

I decide. I decide from here on, what comes with me to my new life and what doesn't. Layers of skin are coming off at every station now, left behind for good. I don't carry skin I don't want, skin that doesn't fit me now. And that goes for memories, too. If they don't fit, they don't come, because I'm the guy doing the packing.

Maybe skins and memories are the same thing. To be shed as needed so they can't weigh you down or get you overheated.

And anyway, that putrid shit can of a bus is gone from my life. I came out of it, and it isn't even a memory now.

We have to change buses again in Detroit, and the journey is feeling already far longer than it seemed when I mapped it all out. I've been traveling almost twenty hours when we pull into a little nothing of a station that seizes my attention anyway when I realize where we are.

Ann Arbor, Michigan. Home of the University of Michigan Wolverines football team. A recruiter actually came to our school to talk to a couple of linemen who had potential, and while he was at it, he talked to me. I was on a hot streak, and they were looking hard at any kicking talent they could dig up.

Michigan. They talked to *me*. I never even thought about going to a big monster program like that, but just a few words from their guy, and my head was swimming. There are, like, forty thousand students at the school, and over a *hundred* thousand seats in their stadium.

I couldn't imagine walking out and lining up for a field goal in front of one hundred thousand people. But for the next two or three weeks, I tried to imagine exactly that.

But my hot streak cooled off along with any interest from big-time schools at the same time that my senior-year life started heating up. The Wolverines went in a different direction, and so did I.

We pull out of Ann Arbor just as quickly and uneventfully as we pulled in. But I find myself staring out the window and looking for that big stadium like a little kid, staring and staring and getting all sad and stupid like I lost something there in a place I never even set foot.

An hour and a half later we are in Kalamazoo, and though there is a twenty-minute layover, I do not want to get out of my seat. I haven't eaten anything since Syracuse about fifteen hours ago, but that wouldn't be enough to get me up if I wasn't bursting to use the bathroom. There is no way I am using any bus bathroom again if I can avoid it, so I hop up and go.

After the bathroom I hit a vending machine for something resembling nourishment. It doesn't help that I am rushing through the decision, but Lord, I am sure if my new coach saw me put any of this stuff into my body, he would personally put that body right back on the bus and give it a good shove back east. But I'm just hungry, so I select the ten-inch all-day-breakfast sandwich, a raisin bran muffin because how wrong could they go with that, and lemonade.

I go all running back, tuck the loot under my arm, and run.
I may have improved on my hundred-yard-dash time as I
return to the bus.

Back in my seat, I am munching on the sandwich's tough
outer defenses, sipping my drink, and watching the arrangement of about ten fellow travelers gathered together in the
smoking area. They look relatively happy as far as bus people
go. They don't even seem completely like strangers, though
most or all of them surely are. They talk easily, they nod
a lot, they laugh a couple of times at some guy's remarks,
and they laugh all together and loudly at something right
after the driver passes by them to resume his duties. Then
they all have to scurry to get back on, because these drivers
are known to leave people who are even a minute late, just
because they can.

Even this activity seems to bring out something like a
team spirit as these men and women together stub cigarettes
and run desperately in a line toward the bus stairs and the
road to Chicago.

It's like dinner and a show for me, until everyone has
scrambled into a seat and my all-day sandwich defeats me
in much less time than that. I make the mistake of looking
inside to see which of the contents might be bothering me,
and I quickly slam the thing shut again. The breakfast they
were referring to was apparently prepared on one of those
Siberian islands where they eat things that are blubbery,
killed and dried but never cooked. I'm hoping the how-

wrong-could-they-go muffin will help me out, but when I bite it, I don't think it's even real, because it crumbles to dust like it was just a clay prop from when the snack machine was a demo model in the 1950s. The lemonade, though it contains the juice of only zero lemons, is refreshing. This stuff, I realize, is how they kill off the bus people of our country.

Once we're moving, life takes on its new familiarity. The rumble of the engine settles me into my seat. The swerve and sway as the bus negotiates the first streets of whatever city it is before flattening out on the long easy highway, stretches that just get longer and easier as we progress west and get more of the eastern United States behind us.

Get thee behind me, old home. Get thee behind me, past, and old skins and things that didn't look the way they really were. Get thee behind me, and stay there.

We transfer again in Chicago. Then, somewhere on the route to Milwaukee, I fall into my first deep sleep for quite a while.

All of it is wrong, and all of it can be straightened out.

"We just need to talk," I say. "Please, can't we talk?"

"No, we cannot."

"It's practically not even light out yet."

"It's light enough. Let me go. You have to let me go."

"Okay, Gigi. What if, even if I didn't, I said all right, you're right, whatever. What if I did that and then I said it so you can feel all right, and we can just leave it there, leave it right here

in this room behind us when we leave, and nobody, not Carl and not my father and not your father or anybody, has to be involved or upset about it? What about that, and then, like I said, we can leave it behind us, close the door on it, and you can feel all right and we can get on with stuff. What if I did that for you?

"Because I am sorry, Gigi. Whether I did something or I didn't, I am sorry because of how you feel about it. How you feel and how you feel about me."

She tries the doorknob again, and I grab her wrist with both hands.

I have both hands tight on Gigi Boudakian's lovely soft long wrist. She looks up at me, almost as if she is afraid of me. Things are so wrong.

"Please, Keir," she says, and her voice is a shaky whisper. She looks down at my hands holding her wrist, and Gigi Boudakian's tears drop, right onto the back of my hand, and this is a nightmare now. I should be the one crying.

Things are so, so, so wrong.

My dreaming has a lurid, beyond-reality vividness that wakes me up with a jolt, a headache, and a queasy stomach. I'm sweating and breathing heavily, unsure once more where I am.

"You all right?" asks a heavy, worried-looking woman seated across the aisle. She's wearing some kind of security guard uniform, which I almost find comforting.

"Yes," I say. "Fine, thanks."

"Well, whoever Gigi is, she must be awful scary," she adds.

I fold myself up and turn away toward the window.

There are twenty-minute rest stops at both Milwaukee and Tomah, Wisconsin, and at each one I go outside to stand with the smokers. The smell of the smoke is wonderful for some reason, and the jokes about the driver and about tobacco love are among the funniest things I have ever heard.

At Alexandria, Minnesota, a girl with a bruise on her forehead and a missing left ring finger offers me a cigarette. I have never smoked in my life, but at this moment I'm seized with a panicked certainty that this is some kind of test because the smoking community has caught on and they're going to force me out of the group for weirdness if I keep hovering among them without partaking. I take the cigarette from the girl and fight the urge to stare at the finger-space as I do it. She offers me a light, I accept it, and I smoke, right along with the smokers. I'm one of them now.

Until a different seizure takes hold and I cough loudly and violently for so long that three different people from the group take turns slapping me on the back, and by the time I am just about over it, the whole gang is laughing, and I don't care whether it's with me or at me because it's such a welcome thing to listen to from so close in. Even my side pain, which came back during the choking and back pounding, doesn't hurt nearly as bad now. And I can't find any leaks out of me anywhere.

As we board the bus again, I am thinking seriously of giving this some practice and becoming a real smoker.

It's not long after dawn when I open my eyes to find the hugeness of North Dakota and the Wild West opening up in front of me. I have been getting only the choppiest bits of sleep, and most of that consists of riding the rapids of nightmares I have already forgotten once I awake but that terrify me just the same. The landscape out here is something I have never seen before, and the effect it's having on me is like a combination of peaceful sleep, a good hot bath, and hearty food, all of which I am dangerously lacking right now.

I keep my face window-pressed for mile after mile of this, and as we pass into Montana, I'm like a charging battery, fresher every minute, stronger, and newer.

Then my phone starts silently vibrating, and it might as well be a direct current electrical charge right into my thigh.

I take the phone out and don't even think about it before shutting it off. I could have done that at any time, but at the same time, I couldn't. I just couldn't do it. That was a different time, different place, different Keir. That phone and its connections belong in that different place right now, and not here. Not till I'm ready, if I'm ready.

• • •

We transfer for the final time at Butte, Montana. I cannot believe how the flavor of the air here is like a different thing entirely from what I have breathed my entire life. I pull it in deeply enough and rapidly enough that I'm either going to use it all up or pass out before I can board that last bus.

But I make it aboard, then on through stops in Basin and Boulder, Montana, and finally into Helena. Home.

I feel myself grinning like a loon as I gape at the mountains in the near distance. But that is about the only thing I can feel for sure. The pain in my side is long gone. So is every other pain I ever had.

PART THREE

YOU CAN'T GO HOME AGAIN.
BUT YOU CAN'T NOT.

There to meet me when I take the last leaden steps up to the entrance of my residence hall are not one, but two people who greet me by name. It is, I believe, mid-afternoon.

Just one would have been remarkable enough. I expected it to be at least a week before anybody called me by name, at least not without checking a roster sheet first. And I didn't think that was any bad thing. This, in fact, kind of spooks me.

"Mr. Sarafian?" says the tall gent with the white handle-bar mustache framing a broad, welcoming smile.

"Yes, sir," I say, stepping right into his handshake as he steps around the big reception desk.

"I'm Mr. Rivera, residence halls manager. Pleased to meet you."

"And hey, Keir," says the anxious young guy beside him. "I'm Fabian. I'm going to be your roommate. And you are right on time, which is an excellent way for a new roommate to announce himself, I have to say."

"Is it?" I say, shaking hands with Fabian while I try to catch up with the speed of progress here. "Can I ask how you know whether I'm on time or not?"

"Your father forwarded your itinerary," Mr. Rivera says. "Just in case you got waylaid somewhere on the road between leaving his jurisdiction and entering mine. That was quite a journey."

"Yes," Fabian says, nodding and shaking his head at the same time. "I was tracking you the whole way, door-to-door, and I was wiped out just keeping up by computer."

What am I supposed to make of this? Do I feel welcomed, embraced, cared for? Do I feel spooked, stalked, monitored? Is this the kindest surprise in a long time, or the creepiest? This kind of scrutiny is not what I came all this way looking for, that's for sure.

So what do I do now? Turn right around and go back?

"Well, I'm pretty tired myself," I say.

"Good thing I'm here," Fabian says, picking up the long, stuffed duffel bag I dropped at my feet. "Let me show you to your accommodations."

"Go on, get some rest," Mr. Rivera says when I look to him for the okay. "Come see me later. I'm easy to find."

"Sure," I say. "Thanks."

I pivot and shuffle after Fabian, my rucksack pushing down on my shoulders in a final effort to stop me before I reach my destination. Bed.

I have no clothes, and very little fat, because I have been good about my health lately. She grabs, can't grab, scratches instead at my chest, then slaps me hard across the face, first right side then left, smack, smack.

"Say what you did, Keir."

"Why is Carl coming? Why do you have to call Carl, Gigi?"

"Say what you did, Keir. Admit what you did to me."

"I didn't do anything, Gigi."

"Yes you did! I said no!"

I say this very quietly, but firmly. "You did not."

"I said no," she growls. "Say it."

"I don't see why you need Carl. You can beat me up just fine on your own. Listen, Gigi, it was nobody's fault."

"Yes it was! It was your fault. This should not have happened."

"Fine, then it didn't."

"It did, it did, it did, bastard! For me it did, and it's making me sick."

"Don't. Don't be sick. I don't want you to be sick or anything. I just want everything to be all right. Everything is all right, Gigi. Please, can everything be all right?"

"It is not all right! It is not all right, and you are not all right, Keir Sarafian. Nothing is all right. Nothing will ever again be all right."

She is wrong. Gigi is wrong about everything, but especially about me. You could ask pretty much anybody and they will tell you. Rock solid, Keir. Kind of guy you want behind you. Keir Sarafian, straight shooter. Loyal, polite. Funny. Good manners. He was brought up right, that boy was, *is what you would hear. All the things you would want to hear said about you are the things I have always heard said about me. I am a good guy.*

Good guys don't do bad things. Good guys understand that no means no, and so I could not have done this, because I understand, and I love Gigi Boudakian.

"*I love you, Gigi.*"

As I say this, Gigi Boudakian lets out the most horrific scream I have ever heard, and I am terrified by it and reach out, lunge toward her and try to cover her mouth with my hands, and I fall over her and she screams louder and bites at my hands and I keep flailing, trying to stop that sound coming out of her and getting out into the world.

I am only trying to stop the sound. It looks terrible what I am doing, as I watch my hands doing it, as I watch hysterical Gigi Boudakian reacting to me, and it looks really, really terrible but I am only trying to stop the awful sound and the way it looks is not the way it is.

The way it looks is not the way it is.

When I wake up, it's dusky outside the window. It takes a good long stare for me to establish where I am and if it's true conscious reality. I figure I've slept five or six hours, and the world seems all the stranger for it.

"Hey," Fabian says.

"Hey," I say.

"That was quite some afternoon nap you had there."

I push myself upright so that I am in a sitting position propped up by my pillow and headboard. The window, with its view across rolling lawn to pine trees rising onto foothills in the distance, is to my right. My poky pine desk and chair are straight ahead, against the cinder-block wall beyond the foot of my bed. Fabian, seated at his own poky pine desk, is to my left.

"Yeah," I say, "I wasn't figuring on anything like that, but boy, I was dead to the world."

"Maybe, but you were pretty busy for a dead guy. There was a lot of rockin' and rollin' going on in that rack. And I'm not complaining or anything, because I wouldn't want us to get off to a bad start. But I hope you're going to tell me that this is just an adjustment period and you're not normally so loud when you sleep."

"Oh, cripes, Fabian," I say, swinging sideways to face him with my feet on the floor. "Are you serious? Was it really bad?"

"Well . . . it was sporadic. Like, in bursts. Then you'd go silent again. Then another burst."

I lean forward, putting my face in my hands. "As far as I am aware, this is not a regular problem. I guess I was having nightmares or something, which is rare for me, I think. But I don't have that much to go on, actually. I can tell you I've never woken myself up from stuff like that. And nobody else has ever made me aware of it. Though nobody else has ever been close enough to really monitor the situation."

I raise my eyes up over my fingertips to see how he's taking my answer, and he has already turned his back to me in order to get busy with something on his laptop.

"Okay, fingers crossed then, and hope for the best," he says.

"Yeah," I say, "we'll hope for the best."

He plinks around on his computer for several more seconds before he comes out with it. "As far as nightmares go, whoever Gigi is, she sounds like a real mind-bender."

I'm not sure what comes out of me into the room, but inside it sounds like a gasp. Whatever it is, it causes Fabian to swing around in his seat and lean in for a closer look at me.

"Are you all right, Keir?" he says, like he's some kind of paramedic.

"Yeah," I say, "I'm fine. I think the air here is probably a little thinner than what I'm used to, that's all. I'll just need to do some acclimatizing before I'm completely myself. It won't take long, I'm sure."

"Sure," he says. "I'm sure too. And I'm sorry if I was out of line mentioning this Gigi person. She's none of my business."

"No, no, no," I say, waving the whole thing away as I get up to go to the bathroom. "Not a problem at all. I don't even know where I got that. I don't know anyone named Gigi. So, no offense. No problem. But that's not what you heard, anybody's name. It was just a sound. That's a kind of sound anybody could make in a dream."

I walk the modest length of our room, patting my roommate's shoulder as I pass him, then pass his bed on my right, both closets on opposite walls, shared dresser on my right, sink on my left, and finally, the tiny bathroom.

"Too bad," Fabian calls before I shut the door between me and the words. "I was guessing she was pretty. That's a very pretty name."

I snap the door shut and latch it.

Fabian Delmonico turns out to be a very easy guy to get to know. He's happy to talk about himself, which is no knock on the guy, because he's just as happy to talk about most anything at all. That works out very much in our favor, because I arrived on the campus of Carnegie College feeling like I didn't have a great deal of talk in me, least of all talk *about* me.

As it happens, he's decided he can fill in a lot of the blanks on his own, and for now I'm willing to let him go for it.

Until he seems to be getting too close to any blanks that I am determined will remain blank.

"So you're a football player, obviously," he says as he lays my plate down in front of me. We are in the communal kitchen we share with eight other freshmen on our floor. It's very late for supper, but my monster nap, on top of the changes—of time zones, of air quality, of population and purpose—has left me in no state to settle into a normal schedule just yet. So I moved slowly through my paces and into new spaces in the hours after waking up. I unpacked and found places for the few clean things. Fabian brought me down to the laundry room and showed me how to deal with the rest and then left me to it. I stayed there, in silence and mostly in peace, through the washing and the drying and the folding. He was in the room when I got back up, when I finally slithered my way to an overdue shower, and when I emerged close to an hour later. He held off on his own meal because, he said, he had prepared something for my first night. Thinking I'd be in no shape after that grueling trip. Thinking we'd eat together. If I thought that was a good idea.

I thought it was a good idea. What kind of a shit would think otherwise? And what kind of an even worse shit would say so if he did? Not this kind, I'm happy to say.

"*Obviously?* Why is it so obvious that I'm a football player?" I say as I stare down at what he has made for dinner. I see strips of boneless chicken, several big pink shrimps, green and black olives, peas, tomatoes, chunks of garlic and spring onions. Spinach is snaking through it all, surfacing up out of the sticky rice here and then submerging again there. It's mesmerizing to me. The scent alone is putting me into a trance.

"Oh, no," he says, sitting across from me with his own plate, "I didn't mean it like that. Housing filled me in when they contacted me about you. In fact, I was going to pay you a compliment and say I know you're a football player but you don't seem like one at all."

I laugh at that and manage to pull up from my fascination with the food. "That's a compliment, is it? Well then, for sure I owe you one in return. Man, this is an incredible meal. I can't believe you went to this trouble for me, and you hadn't even met me. And I was a football player. I could have turned out to be, you know, a *football player*. And then, where would you be now?"

"Now? I'd be sleeping. Anyway, it's risotto. Easiest meal in the world."

"No, a banana is the easiest meal in the world."

"Nnn," he says, wagging his fork at me like a no-no finger while he swallows his food. Then, "Maybe you should eat before you start sounding like a football player."

I'd say we've reached an agreement there. I start happily in on my food, and it makes me feel so good, so quickly, I feel a rush of something stupid and unexpected, something I have to fight down because I am not showing this stupid something to anybody, not even the kind and thoughtful guy who is looking after me, feeding me, and forcing these feelings in the process.

I shovel food. Not in the way I know, not in the way I was taught, not in the way this fine classy cooking deserves. But I shovel, to occupy me, and to smother that spot that won't quit smoldering in the pit of me. I shovel to get me through the way only food can do.

"Glad you like it," Fabian says, a little leery of me now, eating like a pig, like a damn football player. But I will show better of myself, at every meal hereafter, just as long as I can be cool through this one.

I nod with great enthusiasm and appreciation, but I do not slow down. At least I don't try to talk at the same time, which would probably be all the information Fabian would need to put me into his do-not-feed category for good.

But I'm still not close to tapping out his goodwill yet. "I imagine I'd be ravenous for real food at the end of a journey like yours," he says. "I mean, myself, I wouldn't be putting another scoop into my mouth before the previous one was swallowed . . . but I would be very hungry, sure."

I have to say something, at least. I cover my savage mouth with my hairy hand, swallow almost completely, and say, "Sorry, man. I *am* starving. But I am better than this, I promise."

He nods, satisfied, and surprisingly relieved. He wants me to be better.

"I liked following your progress," he says. "Plotting your movement across the country, using your itinerary to guide me. I felt good about you coming—even though I almost had my own room until your late-decision scramble altered the equation."

I peer up over my last bite and give him my sincerest shrug apology.

"Oh, it's all right. Kind of a mixed blessing anyway, starting out at college not knowing anybody and then rooming alone. And then we got the itinerary. And I saw it, studied it with a kind of awe, and I felt for you having to travel all that way, through those places, on those buses. I felt really bad for you, actually. But I felt better about meeting you. Because, I hope you don't mind my saying so, but nobody comes all that way, *in* that way, if there is any other way."

I let it hang there, even though I had the offer of a plane ticket hot in my head. Even though I am not sure how I feel about where this is going. But I am not correcting anything, not going into any detail, about where I come from or why or how. I'm not doing that now, or ever.

And then when he finishes his point, I'm glad I don't contradict him.

"It sometimes seems like everybody I meet has got money. And I expect people I meet at Carnegie not to be worried about paying for things. I hope you're not insulted when I say I was looking forward to having a roommate who had to take three days of buses to get here."

I make sure he can see how closely I'm listening to him, that there are many kinds of manners that I actually do possess. I put down my cutlery, wipe my mouth with a precise and efficient left-right swipe of my napkin.

"I'm so not insulted that I'm practically flattered," I say, and quickly grab up both plates to go wash up before things get all sentimental.

walk on

When I finally come face-to-face with Coach Muswell, he looks just as befuddled as he'd sounded over the phone. He gives me a good hard handshake in greeting just the same.

"Well, I still can't believe you fell into our lap, but, son, I am pleased as Punch to have you here. I hope you are ready now, 'cause we may not be Division I, and you won't be playing in front of seventy thousand of your nearest and dearest on a weekly basis—or any other kinda basis, frankly—but this is a serious and high-quality program in its own right."

"I know that, sir. I did do my homework, and this is the kind of team any real football player would be proud to suit up for."

"Excellent. Exactly. That it is. So I hope you are prepared to get yourself in ungodly great shape for the task ahead, young man. And that you're looking forward to a season of kickin' and stickin' like the two-way legend you are surely cut out to be."

We'd talked for like a half hour on the phone. Forty minutes, actually, minimum. There was no way he didn't hear me on the subject of position. My d-back days were done, except for the odd desperation cameo appearance. My decision, at that, on what constituted a desperation scenario and what didn't.

"Coach? I'm a placekicker. I thought we were clear on that. I'm here to kick field goals, which I can and will do for you, very well. But at this point I'm all kickin', no stickin.'"

It is dawning on me already that Coach's expression does not have a wide variety of moves. When he's puzzled, happy, enthusiastic—all of which he has been over the past few minutes—or a little bit fierce like he is right now, he holds just that crack of a smile, eyebrows arched V-like the way little kids draw birds in flight. He also favors nodding yes all along while pretending to listen, as if to preempt everything with his rightness while waiting for the other guy to catch up.

"Keir, son, look around you."

Blue ridiculous sky everywhere, mountains, forest, compact campus, and a nice tidy football stadium no bigger than the one I played in the last four years.

"Gorgeous," I say. "One of the many reasons to be here."

"True, all true," Coach says. "And you are gonna love

129

Carnegie and never regret your decision. But top-level NCAA football this ain't. Them boys have eighty-five scholarships to dole out. We got less than half that. I ain't green or foolish enough to waste one of them precious notes on somebody who spends eighteen seconds of game-action time on the field per week, now am I?"

I know that it is a question because of the way his voice pops a wheelie at the end there. But by the time he got to telling me the color that he wasn't, my eyes headed up into the surrounding glistening hills and took me along with them.

"No, sir?" I say, half reconstituting his speech in my head, half guessing.

"No," he says. "No, that's right. Now, I am anxious to see you in action, 'cause I got a feeling you are gonna be a big help to this poor little team. You will need time to catch up, of course. I am aware you've taken some pretty hard knocks along the line, and that you couldn't be expected to be quite game ready yet. I have been fully briefed, and if I may say so, you've got some mighty serious backers behind you. Talked to both your high school coach and the head man at Norfolk, and both say I'm getting a stud for pennies on the dollar. That is the reason our program is rolling dice on you, and why you were allowed to arrive so long after everybody else. Coaches said you needed time to heal mentally and physically, and you needed just the change of scenery this place has in abundance, and if I cut you that slack, you would be paying me back big-time for the next four years."

I had no idea this went on. I have no idea now whether I would have allowed it.

"I feel like I owe you a refund already, Coach."

"Ha!" he hollers. "That's a good one. But of course you owe me no such thing." He could not be more enthusiastic if he had the haloed C of the Carnegie Fighting Saints tattooed on his forehead. Then he leans close. "But you do owe me something. I know, Mr. Sarafian, that you are smarter than ninety percent of the boys on this team, and *all* of the coaches. I also know you have the killer instinct that I have never once been able to teach to somebody who did not arrive here with it already. And as you stand here before me today, I'm not sure if I was sold a bill of goods or not, but I do know there isn't a damn thing wrong with you physically. You are a born free safety. Therefore, you need to get into *game* shape, and you need to learn the playbook. And then you need to be ahead of everybody on the depth chart by opening day, no matter how much earlier they reported. Are ya with me, son?"

If I thought there were any possible answers other than the obvious one, I would have to think about it.

"I am with you, Coach."

"Outstanding. Now, get to work. This poor little team has a big need, and you are the filler."

This poor little team has a coaching staff of ten. And the filler may have been wildly oversold to them.

"Where do I begin, Coach?"

131

"You just head down that way to the office and see Mr. Santos. He coaches up the backs for us, and he'll get you started off right." He shakes my hand even firmer as I try to leave. "I got a feeling this is gonna be remembered as a momentous occasion, Keir Sarafian. I truly do. Can't wait to look back on it someday and say, uh-huh, that was it."

"What about the kicking game, special teams coaching?"

"Well, we'll get to that. Don't be in such a hurry to be branching out. You need to concentrate, and right away. You're already behind most of the rest of the guys, who have no business being ahead of you. Some of them showed up over a week ago, and all of them have been on our scientifically developed off-season strength and conditioning program all summer. I trust you received your copy, though I'm not sure how much of it you were able to get through in that short a time."

"I got a start, Coach. I'm getting caught up quick." I read it over during the trip. The fitness equipment provided by Greyhound fell a little short of requirements, however.

"That's good. I'm sure you'll get yourself fighting fit in no time. Which is good because that's just about how much time you have. Anyway, we got a couple of walk-ons, came to us when we had no idea you were comin'. Not bad, either. Couple of them ol' soccer boys, but we can reform them if they prove to be worth the effort. But you won't sweat it, talent like you. My only worry would be if you *didn't* have any competition in camp to push you, give you a challenge, and force you to be your best."

"Yeah, Coach," I say, finally prying myself out of his grip and heading for the stadium offices and changing rooms, "Funny, that was my only worry too. My only one."

Is that what I achieved? By being so clever and boldly decisive with my eleventh-hour shiftings? I wasn't going to be asked to play much defense at Norfolk, if any at all. They didn't need me there with the recruits they were bringing in. That was one element that made my original plan such a brilliant plan. You didn't have to have much in the way of imaginative powers really, to picture the life I was going to have there. A very sweet life, indeed. With everything and everyone that mattered right there with me, or no more than three hours away, it was going to be too perfect. Too perfect. I did some good thinking, planning that life.

And then I did other things.

I'm not a crybaby. I have been many things but never a crybaby, and this is no place to start. No spilled milk puddling around me, because I got myself here. Me and nobody else had that responsibility. If anybody wanted proof, all they'd need was to take a look at that great big crying crybaby father of mine as I walked out of his house that day, headed for wherever in hell this is. If anybody ever saw that scene, that day, then they would know whose idea it was.

I wish I didn't have to have seen it.

Too close. Too close. You take it all with you, like it or not, when you only *sort* of move on. The great stuff trails along in your slipstream, but so does the rest. I needed to be substantially more than three hours away. I needed to not bring my bags and baggage to the same school as my sisters, which was already going to be a difficult place for them with my unhappily high profile throwing long dark shadows all over the place. I needed more distance from Ray, for his sake as well as mine. And I needed to have nothing to do with Norfolk. Nothing.

My hometown had become an ugly, filthy place, and I left it without knowing when I would come back, if I ever even did. The trade, for shrugging off the weight of eighteen years' accumulation of people and history and life, was that I am apparently going to have to return now to the real side of football, the brute side. I was sure I never wanted to *stick* anybody ever again. I was done with that. Gradually, as I make my way across the field toward the team facilities in the building ahead, I start feeling changes, again. More changes, sharp shiftings. I refuse to look up and out at the sky and the mountains that I've been finding so reassuring and distracting. I watch as one by one the white hash marks pass beneath my feet. I'm picking up yardage, quicker as I go on, and with every yard I gain, I sense myself regaining something else, something harder and maybe meaner, difficult and essential.

Why not? I could stick with the best of them when I had the desire to. Maybe this is the right time to let the desire back in.

I'm not so sure, after all, that I never want to *stick* anybody ever again. Maybe it was a brilliantly executed game plan by the coach. Trick me into thinking I need not play defensive backfield. Lure me all the way out here to the western end of nowhere. Then jerk me back into the position I no longer felt mean and motivated enough to play.

Thus making me mean and motivated enough to want to start banging into somebody again. Possibly. It would take a pretty awful genius to execute that play, that's for sure. Should I be petrified, or thrilled, to play for this guy?

I don't even know the answer myself. But either way I'm finding myself undeniably excited, about the possibilities, the newness, the unknowns.

real time

I was always supposed to be here. Every part of me was telling me as much from the second I arrived. I felt like what I imagine salmon feel like. Right, the spawning thing, where salmon make their way upstream through crashing white water and whatnot. And from the *ocean*, for Pete's sake, back up the river to the spot where they were born. Even though who can remember the spot where they were born, never mind somebody with a bitty fish brain? And why is a cold fish doing something that seems so emotional? But they do. And even though I visited several schools and none of them were Carnegie, I felt like a total salmon when I got here. I had made it, to the place I never even knew I always belonged.

And that was even before Joyce.

"Okay then," she said, clapping her hands crisply together

and snapping the next bunch of raw recruits into formation for the official campus tour.

This time, I did not lose focus at all. It's even possible I managed to remain *too* focused.

"Miss?" I asked as we crossed the footbridge over the tidy man-made duck pond. Joyce was at the head of our party of eight clueless frosh and herself as we headed for the campus's one big hill. A fancy spiky red-and-white brick building perched at the crest of that hill like a pointed helmet. A sign pointing up that way identified it as the main administration center, but to me it looked like a baron or somebody lived in there, with the pointed helmet and all to match his home.

She spoke without turning around to even see who was talking to her.

"Keir, I do wish you wouldn't call me 'miss.' Sounds like I'm your kindergarten teacher or your nanny or something."

She knows me already by voice. The thought just muscled everything else right out of my brain space, so I had nothing more to say while the rest of the group chuckled at the whole snappy exchange.

She finally glanced back my way. "Was that all you wanted to say?" she asked, amused. Everybody was amused. I smiled at her like a dope while I tried to recall my question and tried not to dwell on the fact that I had stalled after only one word, and even that was a word she didn't want to hear. It seems I performed a lot better conversationally when I wasn't paying attention so much.

So I bootlegged it. I shoulder-bumped my way from the back of the group to the front, being careful to excuse myself along the way, until I was right beside her. I couldn't do public speaking very well yet.

"Sorry about the 'miss' thing. Joyce."

"Ah, now. That's better. Friendlier."

"It just came out. I wasn't being a wise guy or anything."

She patted my arm as we swung into stride halfway up the hill. "We'll put the whole nasty business behind us now, will we?"

I sounded like an oaf, and she was letting me know. "Okay, now that was wise guy, right? Got it. Wasting time. The point."

"There. You do better with two-word sentences. Let's go with those for the time being."

"Ah, no," I said, making her laugh loud enough to get my peers crowding around to catch the next act. "Do you mind?" I said over my shoulder to a guy whose breath was actually warming my neck. He drifted back. "Right, Joyce, now I remember what I was going to ask you, but now that I do, I realize I'm just going to make things worse because it's a doink question."

She looked genuinely excited as she leaned closer toward me, like we were walking *together*.

For a second, just one second, this got to me. Feeling the warmth of lovely cool Joyce, her arm running parallel to the whole length of my arm, I caught a lump in my throat. It felt wonderful, the arm, if not the throat.

I stuffed it, though, that lump, and pulled it together because to give this fine person whatever amusement I could give her would be an achievement, the very stuff to start my new life with.

I was actually *trying* to get laughed at now.

"I was going to ask you if this was the same tour you gave us in the previous group, because there is no way I saw that chapel before. And I would have noticed a thing like that no matter how many misty mountains surrounded us. And that other thing behind it. That was a *yurt*, is that correct? Because, again, no *way*. If this is the same route, then somebody definitely erected that thing in between the two tour runnings, because it was certainly not there before."

Lord. Oh my, but this was glorious. My cheeks bunched up and the corners of my smile strained hard to try to meet up around the back of my head. The sound of Joyce laughing, the sight of her, tickled me so much, in a way I had not experienced in . . . some time. I did all I could do not to perform that little-kid thing of wrapping my arms around myself and squeezing to try to quiet the rowdy butterfly gang inside me. My neglected and soft abs would offer them no protection if I squeezed hard enough.

"Are you just pulling my leg with this daffy routine?" she said just before we reached the admin building. She was guarding her great generous laughter and her big open smile now, trying to figure whether I deserved them or whether I was just playing the dunce for show. Her suspicious face was a sharper, harder beauty of a thing altogether, and I knew already I didn't want to see it any more than necessary, beaut or no.

But guarded or not, suspicious or not, every look she showed had those same soft chocolate-brown eyes. The eyes that looked like they knew me, my *best* me, and I was already completely gone, melted right into those chocolate eyes.

"No, no, no, I swear," I said, more panicky than perhaps a normal person would be in this situation. "This is a genuine certified fool you're looking at right here. I would not be putting you on like that, I promise. I was just trying to stay totally engaged, not waste your time like I did earlier. I mean, you volunteering to help out the likes of me, I should have more respect than to spend the whole thing with my head in the clouds. That's just bad form, bad manners, a poor reflection on a guy's home training, and altogether inexcusable."

Now, as much as Joyce was pondering me and trying to work me out on the nonsense joker scale, I felt like I was getting the full range of her very articulated facial expressions in a crash course. It was a little disconcerting, and a whole lot of distracting, and if the rest of my courses turned out to be this mesmerizing, then I was going to do spectacularly well at Carnegie College.

Joyce held the door to let all her charges file in ahead of her, and I stood by, helping, I suppose.

"See," I said, pointing at her face in case maybe she didn't know it was there. "That head-tilt, the quizzical expression that seems like it's asking lots of questions or even just one or two heavy ones? I mean, I'm kind of shredded about it, because I think it's lovely, honest, but it worries me a bit at the same time. Like I would enjoy standing by and watching you make that face at something else, so that way I could just appreciate it and not be unsettled by it."

The two of us were standing there, teaming up to hold that door mightily open long after anybody needed us to. Whether she was doing it on purpose or not, Joyce just drilled me then, with that bewitching, probing look. She held it, and me, until I couldn't bear it anymore. I just involuntarily snapped my gaze away from her the way a dog bails out of a staring contest. I turned to look up and off in the direction of my friendly misty mountains.

"I see you now," she said while I held my mountainward position. "You are a *charmer*."

It was unmistakably not a compliment.

"No," I called after I felt the small breeze of the door closing behind her. "No, I am absolutely not." I yanked the door back open and scurried after her. "I promise you I am nothing of the kind. Ask anybody . . . Well, once I know some people here, you can ask them, and I am certain they will vouch . . ."

wherever you go, there you are

One thing that has not changed, that will never change, that has no chance of changing, is that I have no urge in me to hang out, to be part of some core or corps or tribe or gang or pod of guys who are always seen together and seem to like it that way. Not that I'm a recluse or a hermit or even opposed to this kind of thing. I like parties, sometimes. I like folks, people, much of the time. But to be honest, I mostly liked most of them from a little bit of distance.

Carnegie represents a complete scratch-start for me, a reboot of my whole existence. But while I will always be friendly and polite and cool with whoever I can manage, there is no way I'm going to start cultivating a social circle around me or *pursuing* friendships now that I've resettled. That always struck me as one of the stupidest notions anyway, *pursuing* a friendship. Not that I'd be called up as any kind of expert on the subject, but the thought of hunting or chasing somebody down could not possibly be further from any valid definition of making or being a friend to anybody.

I would not be averse to pursuing Joyce, though. The thought keeps crossing my mind. But there will be no such approach unless and until she makes it blindingly clear that this would be acceptable and desirable. I'm already preparing myself for this not being the case. I could be alone and be all right. I could handle that. I've spent enough time already thinking of my life in those terms. I've never minded being alone.

I suppose this would be the explanation for how I could have gone deep into my second day of preseason workouts, prior to the first day of classes, without really meeting any of the guys on my team. Like Coach said, I'm behind everybody else, so maybe I would have benefited from introductions and greetings when they were being done more formally. Or maybe not. There are still opportunities, names being passed around from coaches to players, from returning players to new guys, from one new guy to the next one, and ultimately into one ear and right on out the other. For whatever reason, for lots of reasons, I feel very much on the outside of something.

Which gives the shock all that much more of an electrical jolt when it comes.

We had probably seen each other up close-ish, passing within six to eight feet of each other a dozen times before this, and nothing, blank. What it finally takes is a bump-and-run. He's a receiver, in a helmet and no pads just like ten other guys lined up with him. I'm a defensive back, playing corner even though I was barely mediocre there compared to how well I'm suited to playing safety. But the respective backfield coaches decided to give everybody a look-over by running through a few pass plays, and now we're lined up across from each other.

You are taught, if you are taught well, to make eye contact across the line. Get the guy's attention if you can, and if you can, then use it. Show mercilessness and bloodlust you possibly don't have but *show it* if he dares to lock eyes. Then, on a bump-and-run, forget about "bump," which is a word that has no place in football and is only there to make the game sound more puppyish than it is or ever was. "Bump" is window dressing. On the field, "bump" means "bang." That's what we were taught, d-backs and receivers alike. Take no shit, dish it back out, make it unpleasant.

So, at the hike of the ball, with this guy and me full-tilting at each other for three or four strides, you could anticipate a mighty crack as we collide like blind fiery meteors. Because his eyes had indeed met mine and they told me indeed he had been taught like I was taught, not to look away, not to shy away from contact. . . .

Because we were taught by the same people. At the same time. At the same place.

We never collide because we recognize it before that can

happen. Also because the play goes to the opposite side, my guy was just a decoy, and it's called dead when the quarterback throws the ball ten feet over his real target's head. And because we are both just too stunned to follow through properly.

"What the hell are you doing here?" he says as we stop short and stand shaking hands. In the place where I wasn't supposed to know anybody and, more importantly, vice versa.

That is a question I would never have prepared for. It's as if I've parachuted behind enemy lines like some kind of a slimy rotten spy.

Two assistant coaches come onto the field to wildly wave these units off and give the next bunch a shot.

I pick the conversation up on the sidelines. "I am an enrolled student-athlete here, is what I'm doing here."

"But, here? You're not supposed to be *here*." His look is a strange swirl of intensity, astonishment, and at least a bit of anger. "Everybody everywhere knew you were going to Norfolk for, like, months already. I knew I was going to be on my own coming here, and that was cool, and it was not shocking and maybe it was part of what I came here for, and . . . Jesus, what the hell are you doing here?" He's laughing enough, now that astonishment is becoming the dominant element, that I have no choice but to join in.

So I laugh with him, because it feels great, and because it's so absurd, and because, could you believe it?

"I was forced to make a last-minute decision," I say, "because of . . . circumstances beyond my control."

"Ah, yeah," he says. "Everybody knows about the circumstances by now. And the control. Or the lack of it."

The laugh we shared seems like a long time ago already. Because in one short statement he's wrapped up the whole issue of what I had to get away from and what I would obviously never be able to get away from. Not without putting a fat chunk of country between me and all the wrong stuff, but I never figured on being followed, being reminded, being suddenly and weirdly yanked all the way back into the worst things. And frightened by it.

He's reading me, over my silence.

"Listen," he says, "I hadn't planned on having this conversation, here and now, any more than you did. Fair to say we're both still in shock. But I'm not inclined to go rocking any boats unnecessarily, if you're wondering. So relax, Killer."

It hits me like a head butt. There were a few times on the playing field when I got my bell rung by a helmet-to-helmet collision and the lights went dim, my coordination got all short-circuited. That name, out loud, right now, after *all*, feels just like that. Damn it all to hell.

That was of course something I was wondering, about him making deliberate mischief with this. But if he thinks that calling me Killer, a reference to the other great dark shadow that loomed over my life at one time, is not rocking any boats, that's a problem.

"Could you not call me that?" I say crisply. It sounds maybe a little more aggressive than I'd like, but this is serious.

146

"I'm hoping for a fresh start here. And I don't think a nick-name like Killer, and all the questions that will come along with it, is going to be a big help with that."

He frowns. "You're a football player. No football player in his right mind would ever decline a nickname as badass as Killer. You'll be an instant legend."

"Hmm, yeah, I don't want that. I want to be known as a good player, just another good guy on a good team. That's my dream, so if you don't mind, can we lay the Killer to rest right now?"

He huffs, as if I have taken something great away from *him*.

"That's the boringest dream I've ever heard of."

"Well, I am sorry about that. But a guy's name is his property to use his own way."

Good thing he can't read that I'm also wondering what his damn name is. I went to school with him for four years, played football with him for two of those years. We were on the freshman squad together, and again on the varsity as seniors, once he finally made it above junior varsity.

It is right there, though. I can just about taste it . . . begins with B . . . C . . . D . . . E . . . What the hell is my problem? What the hell is your problem, Keir? How could this be? What kind of person lets this situation come to be? F . . . G . . . H . . .

"Kelly," he says, laughing at me and then clapping hard at a nice one-handed catch by one of his competitors at wide receiver.

My first thought is, no, that's not it. "Damn," I say, causing him to laugh again. "Billy Kelly. How you been doing? How was your summer?"

"Great, excellent, Keir. Thanks for asking. Oh, and Kelly is my first name. Kelly McAvoy."

I stare down at my shoes, the only thing to do in this situation. At least I know that much.

"So sorry, Kelly. I am a shit."

"Well, the polls haven't closed yet, but *shit* is starting to look like the consensus choice."

I look back up into his face. "Sorry. Really sorry, sorry, sorry. There is no excuse for forgetting a guy's name—but my excuse is that I have had . . . a messed-up, stressed-up year and that's maybe affected my thinking sometimes, and my memory. But I did know your name, you know that. It would have come to me in another minute."

"No, it wouldn't."

The certainty he puts into that statement cannot be good. "It wouldn't?"

"Uh-uh. Because on the odd occasion when you ever talked to me, you called me *Kerry*. Every single time."

My chin drops so heavily to my chest that I get a pulled muscle instantly in the back of my neck.

"McAvoy!" one of the assistant coaches hollers as one of the other receivers comes limping to the sideline. He prepares to take the field, and I look up to watch him.

"Look at that," Kelly says, slipping his helmet back on.

"He knows my name, and it didn't take him anywhere near four years to learn it."

"Ughh . . ." If you were standing nearby with your eyes closed when I made that sound, you'd've thought I just took a helmet to the chest. My eyes are shut tight, and that's how it sounded to me.

"Don't sweat it," Kelly says. After he gives me a big slap on the shoulder, I open my eyes to see him running backward onto the field. "That's all in the past now, right? Ancient history."

"Right, history," I say, and then he turns to jog away. "You were coming here all along? Kelly? How did I not know that?"

He half turns, palms up to the big, big sky smiling down on Montana. "Don't know, man. No idea how you could have not known that."

What kind of a guy would not know that? You shoot your self-rocket across the sky, across the country to hit a target as small and remote as Carnegie College without knowing that a high school teammate of yours was already planning that very trip?

I would say, a stupid guy. A myopic guy. But that would be partial and obvious and letting myself off too easy. And it would never amount to anything like a good excuse.

glacial erratic

I was doing my running. Winding and climbing my way through the network of trails. The walkways that zigzagged through the Carnegie campus every which way. You could not go wrong taking a run anywhere on these grounds because you could tailor it to yourself, gentle rolling course, hill climb, flat and fast, any combination. Best place I had ever run, that was for sure, and that was even before I caught sight of the lovely Joyce coming down the big hill away from the admin building, just as I started my climb upward.

"Hi," I said as we approached each other.

"Hi," she said. And if there was anything other than sweetness in her tone, I couldn't detect it.

Way too soon, we had passed each other, and with every step, I thought, we'd have put two more steps of distance between us.

So after a very, very brief climb I made a hard, looping, shameless turn back down, making airplane wings with my arms as I did it too.

"So, did you do your research? Check up on me like I said, to see if I was a 'charmer'?"

She leaned a bit in the other direction when I jogged up and brought my testosterone musk maybe a little too close to her, and started walking. She bounced back into form quick enough. "Hey, there's a real man, I just passed him, running properly *up* this hill. If you hurry, you might be able to catch him."

"What?" I said. "A real man? Why would I ever want to run and catch one of those?"

"Yeah, I see your point. Anyway, I was lying. Even if you hurried, you'd never be able to catch *him*." She went all dreamy-woozy, fanning herself with a folder and blinking a lot.

"Really?" I said. "That good, huh? Maybe I do want to catch him."

"Ha," she said, pointing at me for emphasis.

God, I loved this place. I reminded myself hourly of that, my great good luck on this one. All for the best, in the end, and who ever would've thought we could get here from there?

"So, Joyce?" I continued.

"Ah, yes, I did my due diligence, and it appears you are not remotely a charmer. And I checked, asked people in the street, checked databases, FBI files, all coming up empty. So

151

it appears, mystery man, that you are totally clean, utterly charmless. Congratulations." She even shifted her backpack to free her hand to give me the official shake.

Then she shook me entirely, by slanting down the footpath, to the stairs, to the library. The Andrew Carnegie Library of Carnegie College.

"That is maximum Carnegie right there," I said, and she jumped with a fright.

"Jeez, Keir, don't sneak up on a person like that."

"I didn't. I swear. I'm sorry. I didn't sneak up because I never left. I stayed right with you, because you didn't tell me not to. Was that all right? You didn't, did you? Tell me to go, and I somehow didn't get the message?"

"Oh, come on now, relax," Joyce said, and my whole cardiovascular system powered right down in obedience to her.

"Okay," I said, "done. Anything else?"

"No, that'll be all," she said with as much faux snoot as she could manage. Which was not much, because this was a girl with nothing artificial or put-on about her whatsoever.

A few seconds later it got awkward again. Well, I did, but the result was awkwardness all around.

"Um, Keir?" she said right up into the big carved walnut front door that well represented the Andrew Carnegie Library of Carnegie College. She was talking to the door because she had been talking to a wall when she told me *that'll be all.*

"You weren't thinking of coming into the library, were

you?" she asked. She fidgeted a bit, because I was an oaf and hadn't unpinned her yet. "Keir, could you back up a little bit? Please?" She was sounding agitated now, and I leaped back, just about toppling over the box hedge framing the entrance area.

"Sure," I said, revving right back up again. "I haven't been in the library at all yet."

As I powered ahead to go in, she suspended patience and niceties—or I exhausted them—and stiff-armed me to a halt.

"No, you can't come in. They have a no-sweatball policy. Another time, Keir," she said, giving my chest a hearty slap, then dashing inside before I could do anything else disruptive.

Sweatball? How was that at all possible, since I hadn't been running for even five minutes? I was not a sweatball, and I was going to make it my mission to get Joyce to stop seeing me as a perspiring dumbass jock and start seeing me for me.

Then, as I was about to turn, and as the heavy door slowly thunked shut, my eye was pulled by the poetry quote carved deep into the wood in letters three inches tall.

> *O wad some Power the giftie gie us*
> *To see oursels as ithers see us!*

"Pshhhh, gibberish," I said, wiping a bit of cool clamminess from my forehead and heading away. "You'd think to get on the library door, you would at least have to be able to spell."

· · ·

Joyce had told me on that first orientation day that she would be happy to show me all the off-tour, but no less essential, ins and outs of the campus that would be home for the next four years. She gave me her contact details on the inter-Carnegie-community-bulletin-board-whatever that she knew would be a test just for me to navigate. I could have asked for her phone number to simplify things. But that felt aggressively forward, and I wasn't nearly that confident with this situation. She could easily have said no. I couldn't have dealt so well with the directness of no. Better if the no got dissolved in the faceless world of the community bulletin board disembodied rejection.

We had also now eliminated my casual, running-into-the-girl-somewhere-on-campus approach as being at best unreliable.

And since I always left my phone behind when I walked out of my place and into the world, requesting a phone number could quickly lead to sensible inquiries with sensible answers that nonetheless I might not have been up to discussing. Why don't I carry my phone with me? *I don't want to be reachable*, is probably not the kind of thing to make a new person relax about you. Even though it is a perfectly reasonable position to take, in my opinion.

So, all things considered, I am pretty pleasantly surprised to check in with my Carnegie mail and find that she has replied. And that we have a date to finish that campus tour.

I am right where she told me to be, fifteen minutes before she told me to be, on the bridge spanning the duck pond. I am already considering thinking of this as *our spot*.

"Well," she says, as I watch her approach, "you are punctual, which is always a pleasant surprise in a guy. Even a normal guy, so in a football star it's kind of phenomenal."

I am kid-like excited at the sight of her, at the graceful approach of her, regardless of the trash talk. Then she reaches the crest of the arching bridge where I stand against the railing, and she continues walking right on by.

"I haven't even played yet," I say, scurrying to catch up to her. "So I can't be a star, and even then I won't ever be a star, just because I'm not. So, as a matter of fact, I *am* a completely normal guy, which is all I want to be. But, yes, I am punctual and quite proud of it."

"Okay," she says with some finality, as if I have made my case and it has been accepted. She seals it, and shocks my socks, by taking me by the hand without breaking stride. Right by the hand.

I think for probably the whole next half hour or so, I shut up completely, concentrating on holding the lady's slender strong hand. Meanwhile Joyce shows me the sights only a grizzled sophomore would know. Like, the mailbox. And a *second* mailbox. Mailboxes never even occurred to me. She shows me the campus store that is to be avoided because of the chicken wrap/salmonella scandal, and the one just on the edge of the campus that has only one brand of any item but is still honest and clean and open practically any time of day or night despite having no posted business hours. From that point, on the outer boundary of our college village, we turn back inward, weaving through man-made, Carnegie-made paths that diverge from the main road through the woodsy flank of the grounds. The footpaths are rough-cut enough to be natural but so smooth and easy to walk, even as the dusk starts settling over us, that clearly there is attentive groundskeeping at work in this fine place.

Still, Joyce leads me by the hand over the gentle terrain as if she is the only thing keeping me from the dangers of the forest.

"Thanks for this," I finally say.

She stops and turns, bringing her face right up to mine when I fail to stop in time. Some failures aren't so bad.

"For what?" she says.

Funny but I don't immediately have the words for that, even though I was the one who started it.

"You mean for showing you around?" she says. "Pah, I take all the new good-looking guys into the woods. Before they get a chance to hear about me, and then that's the end of that."

My heart is very excited by this, by Joyce and her way of being cool and fresh and provocative. My heart wants to tell her as much and is banging on the interior walls of me so fast and hard I am already deeply embarrassed that she can undoubtedly hear it. That she can feel it, we are that close.

"Are you not going to talk now?" she asks me. "That was some pretty saucy stuff I just came out with there, and nothing. Are you horrified? Are you scared? Are you that gullible? All those things are fine. Just tell me because I am about now running out of all my boldness and am getting to feel a little bit stupid."

"No," I snap. "Don't do that. I wasn't saying anything just then, because I was struggling to keep up, I think. But while I probably am gullible some of the time, I don't believe at all that you take the freshman guys one by one into the woods. And what I was thanking you for was just being so nice to me. Nicer than you have to be, that's for sure. So, thanks."

I can see, in the crinkling, mostly smiling, partly probing eyes, that she is again—or maybe still—wondering if I'm playing her somehow. I am very much looking forward to not seeing any more of that look. Every single other possible look she possesses will be welcome anytime in place of that one.

"I still don't know if I can work you out, Keir," she says. "Are you a wide-eyed innocent, or are you a player?"

She has not moved one inch away from me, which I have to think is a good sign. She's not worried or anything, or she would not linger in the woods alone with me.

That thought makes me feel . . . better than anything has made me feel, about myself, about the universe, in a long time.

"I am a good guy," I say.

She nods. It's nothing definitive, and in fact I don't even know for sure what it's supposed to mean. But a nod is still better than a wide range of other possible responses. She is a cautious girl, seems really smart and like life won't sneak up on her very easily. She seems older, in a way, older than me, of course, but older than a sophomore, too. I like this about her. I want to touch this, the smartness, the knowingness. I want to be a part of it. It's a beautiful place to begin a new everything.

We suspend the conversation two minutes, three minutes, just being there close and gathering whatever two people can pick up from each other without words. I have no doubt that Joyce knows something about what those things might be. I'm happy just to go on breathing her in, because that is plenty of Joyce and I'm grateful to get it. If she has some gift for inhaling whatever the essence of me might be . . . well, I hope she does. It would be sweet, finally, for a girl like this to know my essence. My essence would love to be known.

Then, before I can quite register movement, we are mobile again. She is leading me by the hand once more, and with a clear sense of purpose. Five more minutes of serious striding, through woods that grow continuously denser, making the evening ever darker, and a clearing abruptly shows itself. And in the center of the clearing is a magnificent brute of a boulder, as big around as the Yurt times six, and about four Yurts tall. There are mosses and lichens, sections that have some sparkly mineral content that picks up and reflects back all the weak remaining light, making the modest bit of clearing seem luminous in contrast to everything else around.

"Wow," I say, "I wasn't expecting this."

"It's my favorite spot on the whole campus," she says, walking up and placing two hands flat against the rock like she's going to try to roll it. "Getting to be my favorite place on earth."

"It doesn't look like it even comes from earth."

"Yes," she says, turning to me with excited eyes glistening. "But it is, just not from this part of the earth. It's a glacial erratic, which means it was carried and dropped here by a glacier millions of years ago. That's why it doesn't have the same composition as anything else in this entire region. Is that not thrilling? I think about that all the time, this massive chunk of a thing, bobbing along its icy glacial path for God knows how long, just bumping along, when all the time, it had a destination. It had a destiny almost, and that brought it right here, from thousands of miles away, away from its home, because it was somehow supposed to be here. It's mad randomness when you think about it, if anything is ever even really random."

I feel myself grinning hard, mirroring Joyce's joyful broad smile. She's irresistible, and it's, y'know, only a rock. I could believe in this rock, though. I could believe in anything that somebody else believes in this intensely. Depending on the somebody, naturally.

"Are you laughing at me?" she says, dropping her arms to her sides just as she approaches me again. She stops about two feet short and stands rigid like some kind of glacial erratic security guard.

"Oh, Jesus, no, Joyce, not by any means would I be laughing, I swear."

"Hmmm," she says. "You looked like you were laughing. And there's only me, you, and the rock here. And the rock's not funny. This is special to me, I want you to know. I never bring anybody out here, and now because I think maybe I see something in you, I take a risk and I do this and . . . there, you're doing it again. Right there."

She takes the step forward to bring her pointing finger right up close to point at my teeth. This, of course and unfortunately, causes me to splutter out what is undeniably laughter.

Joyce's eyes go bulgy with mortification, and she is completely justified in feeling that way, except that she could not be more mistaken.

Alarmed now myself, that she will flee the scene before I can make it right, I instinctively reach out and seize her hand out of the air between us just before she can withdraw it from me.

She stares for a confused few seconds, at my big claw hand imprisoning her fine and slender one. It is a bad and wrong moment and will be for as long as I fail to correct it.

I act. I lean in, slowly and gently. And I kiss the back of her hand. I linger, breathing in the warm skin scent and thinking this is the first hand I have ever kissed. A hand. I have never kissed a hand before, never came close, never even considered the possibility. When I look up, she is watching me intently, suspiciously. At least it feels like that.

"You are really beautiful, Joyce. And I'm not talking about your insane attractiveness to the naked eye, which you are surely sick of hearing about. I'm talking about this, the geeky rock-loving thing that is so batshit it's breathtaking. And you just came right on out with it, which . . . I can't even tell you why it was that wonderful to me, I'm not even sure why. But it was special, and it definitely was not me laughing at you. Okay, right, except that very end part, which I suppose was that. But still, it was the best kind of laughing."

I am still holding on to her hand, and I am watching my hand now, as it is squeezing her hand. I should be looking at her reaction, her eyes, her face, but I can't seem to tear away from staring at her hand, and at my desperate worried grip on it. It is a warm, well-intentioned grip just the same.

Then her fingers start wriggling, her wrist turns, she is pulling her hand away, or at least she's trying to.

"Let go, please," she says. "That kind of hurts."

I look up at her, surprised, a little offended, a little ashamed.

"God, I'm sorry," I say. But I haven't let go.

"You don't know your own strength," she says, reaching with her other hand to help the letting-go process along. And that's easy now, the tension I felt before dissolving instantly at the touch of her fingers on mine. My hand comes away from hers as easy as a peel from a banana. I am moved by how gentle she is about it, and how warmly she now looks at me. We're good. We are both good.

She reaches in with authority and yanks me to her side. She has my arm linked tightly to hers as we turn up the path toward the center of campus again.

"I'm not a geek," she says casually, playfully. "I am an earth science major, with a concentration in geology. I love the earth."

"The distinction is duly noted," I say. "And, might I add, the earth absolutely loves you right back."

"Uh-huh. Flatterer. So, Keir Sarafian. I guess I've sort of told you a little about me. Now, other than being our mother planet's authorized spokesperson, is there anything I should know about you?"

I almost have the answer out before she's finished the question.

"Nope," I say.

She laughs, and tugs hard on my arm, which is good. Because I don't know how I would explain my sudden quick, choppy breathing without her breathy breathtaking laugh to smother it.

"Okay, strong and silent," she says, and I try to join in the laughing, try to cover up my sudden nervous-pervous panting. "You just take your time. Talk when you feel like it."

"Ha," I say, chopping out an off-key, out-of-place sort of laugh. She doesn't appear to notice, and for that I feel even more helpless, hopeless affection toward her already.

162

special teams

Coach wasn't joking.

When I finally get to break away from the mortal combat that is defensive backfield training, my spirit is lifted on the thought that I will now be where I belong, proving my true worth without risking my life. There was never any doubt that I could kick a football high, and far, and straight when I was called upon to do so. And the thing that really separates an exceptional kicker from just another guy with a strong leg is doing it under the most intense pressure. *Boom!* You could hear it from the next state. Like somebody shooting a moose. Or a moose hitting a speeding car. The sound of a perfectly struck football makes a gorgeous, full explosive noise way beyond what should come from anything that can sail through the air so lightly. And sail it does, thirty, thirty-five, forty, forty-two yards, beautiful arc, and then zip, through the uprights. If it was radio remote controlled it could not have gone more flawlessly than that ball did.

I stand there with my eyes still stuck up toward the clouds, toward the apex of the trajectory of that highlight-reel kick. I can still see it there lacing across the sky, that flight path, that vapor trail connecting the dead ball lying peacefully in the end zone, and the walk-on, soccer-playing sonofasomebody who just kicked it.

And there's another one just like him waiting to tee it up right now.

This was never part of the plan. This was never part of any plan.

"Hey there," says the second guy, holding a ball as he comes to greet me. "Keir, right?"

"Right," I say.

"I'm Christian," he says, smiling warmly and shaking my hand vigorously, the way you would if you were meeting a real somebody.

"Hi, Keir," the first guy, the man attached to that mighty boot, says. I walk up to the spot where he is now crouched into holder position for the next kicker. He reaches up to shake hands from that position. "I'm Tory. We've been hearing about the surface-to-air missiles you're known for routinely booting. Back East. Jeez, with the air up here, they're going to have to start altering flight patterns with you around."

It would be a good idea, and probably healthy, if I could

work up a nice seething hate for these guys, with the competition between us an unavoidable reality. I'd seem to be off to a good start, with the first guy carrying a whole religion in his name and the other guy saying complimentary things that could only make sense as sarcasm.

Not to mention that whopping great kick that introduced us in the first place. A blistering, motivating hate shouldn't be a problem.

"My kicks?" I say, pointing and tracing the line of flight Tory's ball took just a couple of minutes ago. "That one kick right there would have earned you a scholarship offer from most of the recruiters who scouted me."

"Ah," he says, waving me away. He puts his head down and concentrates on the fine point of perfectly positioning the football for the other guy to make good. "This is easy. You've done it in the heat of real games. That's a whole different beast. I don't know what I'd do under those conditions."

"Me neither," says Christian, who is lined up several yards off the ball and looking at it like a pre-pounce cat zeroed in on its prey.

Well, he might not know what he'd do under *those* conditions. But under these ones he blasts the football with such a full-body assault that he is already facing in the opposite direction when the ball screams through the goalposts. It's more like a line drive hurrying to exit a baseball park than anything I have ever seen happen to a football.

"Jesus," I say as Tory stands up and the three of us admire

a job pretty damn well done. The second ball wobbles to a stop just a few yards' distance from where the first one is still playing dead in the grass, nursing its bruises and catching its breath.

"This is going to be some fun," Tory says.

"I know, right?" Christian says.

A line drive, practically. From over forty yards out.

"Are you seriously telling me that neither one of you guys ever played organized football before this?"

"Never," Christian says, arms up like a surrender.

"Never," Tory says.

"I was all about soccer," Christian says, "until I tore up my ankle and came back slower than our mascot. And we were called the Jumbos."

"Same here," Tory says. "I was all about soccer too. Until I sucked. I was a goalkeeper, so a bunch of times every game I was in a position to just punt the ball as far downfield as I could. I mean, just *ka-blam* it. It was a lot of fun. Except when the other team would bring the ball back upfield and put it in our net. Repeatedly. People in the stands started to make that *whoosh* sound before the ball was even behind me. I think I learned to blast the ball just out of frustration. I still can't believe you can have a spot on the football team just for doing this one single, fun thing."

"Exactly," Christian says. "That's exactly how it was for me. Hey, if they'd just let me use a round ball here, I could *really* get some distance going."

"Yeah, right?" Tory hoots, and the two of them high-five in

a sort of awkward way that I suppose soccer players do, or they do when they're trying to simulate football behaviors that they have seen on TV but have not yet gotten natural with.

And yet, in reality I am the unnatural one here. I'm the one who is struggling even to hold up the undemanding tail end of the banter, because all I can say to the guys is, "So, you both do punting as well as placekicking?"

"Well, yeah," Christian says, looking the slightest bit embarrassed for me, "but, I mean, what's the difference, really, right? It's all kicking."

"It's all kicking," I say, as Tory starts jogging down the field to retrieve the many footballs they have already deposited into the end zone. Christian tugs me playfully by the shirt and starts me running alongside him, like a true teammate, behind Tory.

What's the difference? If you happen to be great at both individual kicking specialties when coaches are deciding who makes it onto their special teams?

Probably it's the difference between getting a spot on the final roster, and getting cut.

This was supposed to be the easy part. I was *money* at this, which was why kicking was the very centerpiece of my plan for the perfect life at Norfolk. And when that didn't work out, kicking figured to be even more of a meal ticket when I adjusted my sights down to small-college ball at Carnegie.

And now. Now the kicking game turns out not to be easy

at all, just like nothing is turning out to be easy at all the way I expected. And everything I thought I knew is completely confounded into my not knowing anything now and probably I never did.

I spend the rest of the day with these guys—the *soccer* guys, can you imagine? These are the same guys me and the rest of the *real* football players just one year ago would have been tossing around like orcas do with seals before tearing them into bite-size edible scraps. But I'm not tossing anybody around, and I'm not easy-breezing into my comfortable starting kicker position, because the truth is I am kicking my ever-loving guts out just to keep up. It is a straightforward competition, a process of three guys kicking one football over and over in turn, from different distances, with different holders, in front of different assistant coaches until we are eventually kicking in front of the big man himself. And suddenly everything is on the line, where I had previously assumed there wasn't even a line for me to worry about.

As the afternoon wears on, the kicks mount up, and my lack of training starts to show.

And I start *trying*. Then trying harder. Then trying everything, everything I didn't used to have to try because I just always knew the big kick was going to come when I needed it because it always had.

"Just ease up on it a little bit," Christian says, startling me by patting my back when I peel off to the sideline. I'm frantically trying to massage the elasticity back into my right hamstring and force the searing pain right on out.

"How am I supposed to ease up?" I say, to the sound of Tory's latest tape-measure-job of a punt. "The harder I try, the less distance I'm getting with every kick. And every yard I lose seems to somehow find its way into *your* results, and Tory's. If I ease up now, my kicks will be going backward over my head by the end of the day."

"Nah, you're just pressing. The coaches can see that. Everybody knows what you can do, because you've done it. It'll take more than a couple of squibs and shanks for them to forget about a talent like yours."

Jeez, the squibs and the shanks. I botched more balls off the outside of my foot, or my toe, during this one tryout than in my entire high school career. It's painful to even hear Christian say it.

But he doesn't say it with any jerk in it at all. Like a lot of people would.

I straighten up when I hear Coach Muswell screaming for the competitors to get their asses on the field pronto unless we were just planning to concede both of the two kicker spots on the roster to Tory, which would be just fine with him if that's what we wanted.

That is of course not what we want. What I want badly, what I have more or less always and only wanted, is that placekicker's job on the college football team and the life that comes with it.

"Cut that out!" Coach hollers when he sees Christian doing the Christian-like thing and lending me a helping hand while I limp back toward the action.

169

"It's okay, thanks," I say, nudging his hand away.

"You sure?" he says, still walking close by. "I don't mind getting yelled at."

I'm shaking my head and clutching at my screaming hamstring while I struggle onward.

"Christian, I mean, thanks. But why are you being like this? It's kind of a dog-eat-dog situation we've got going here. Supposed to be merciless. Why would you want to bother with helping me out, me being the competition, after all?"

He holds up his hands, laughing a little as Coach bellows for him to get over and kick that goddamn ball right this goddamn minute.

"It's only football, Keir," he says.

He pats my shoulder and runs to the spot on the field where our mighty head coach is very, very specifically pointing, as in, crouching down and possibly making contact with the grass with the tip of his pointing finger.

Tory also rushes to that pinpoint spot, squats into position, and plants the football precisely, as Christian strides up and blasts away, perfect form, kicking right *through* the ball the way they always tell you to do.

I'm just standing still, watching the flight of the ball with admiration, same as everybody else.

It's only football, Christian says, and he is right. But he could have just as easily said that I wasn't really his competition, either.

clean break

Joyce shows up unannounced at my door, or at least it was unannounced to me. Fabian is suspiciously flow-going about it. For a guy who monitors the weather forecast for a week in advance just to line up appropriate clothing, there is no such thing as a pleasant surprise.

"Here you go," he says to her, dragging me by the arm to the door. "Stay out as late as you like, kids. I won't wait up."

Joyce finds it very funny when Fabian slams and bolts the door behind me. Joyce finds it funny pretty much whatever Fabian does.

"So, you've been driving your poor roommate insane," she says as we walk along at my slow, sore pace.

"He was already insane when I got here," I say.

"Fair enough," she says as we reach the duck pond, "but you weren't. As far as we know. Hmmm, *do* we know that? I probably should have asked that earlier."

"Yes, Joyce, we do know that." We do. We absolutely do.

"Great. I'm glad that's established. As for today, though, Fabian's a little worried about you. Ranting and slamming things around, that's the kind of stuff that freaks people out, you know. Confidentially, I think he's a little worried about his own well-being, too, ya big brute. Like he doesn't really know you entirely yet, and if you wanted to decapitate him or something, there wouldn't be much he could do about it with just the two of you trapped in that cell of yours."

She says this so matter-of-factly, the same way she pointed out the campus's two mailboxes, that I have to treat it just as casually or expose one or the other of us as maybe psychotic.

"True," I say. "He's got these little arms, like linguine. There'd be nothing he could do."

As we reach the bridge that crosses the pond, I bend to gather up a handful of stones. "Bend," though, is possibly not accurate. With my right leg burning from pain and calcifying to the point of uselessness, my bend is more like a mechanical flamingo maneuver, the petrified leg sticking up skyward while my upper body pivots groundward over the other hip.

When I eventually right myself again, Joyce has both hands covering her mouth, trying desperately not to laugh.

With basically nothing else left to lose, I go for the dignified approach.

"Did I miss something funny?" I ask, blinking repeatedly and clutching my rocks.

•

She no longer feels the need to try, and bursts out laughing. "You did, you *so* did, Keir."

When I heroically continue with my silent blinking, she shakes her head and clutches my shoulders.

"And from the look of you," she says, "you're *still* missing it. Come on, now."

I walk ahead of her up to the crest of the bridge. There we both sit, extending our legs through the metal bars of the railing, our feet dangling a few feet above the still water. Neither one of us says anything for a bit, which is not a bad thing. I toss stones, one every half minute or so, and watch the ripple rings expand and disappear again. My leg feels much better in this position. I could plunk rocks like this for a good long time, I think.

"But it *is* only football, you know, Keir."

Plunk.

"How can football be *only* football, Joyce? Football is what got me here. Football is the main reason I'm here at all."

"Is it? I don't know that. How do I know that? For all I know, you could be here for a whole bunch of reasons. In fact, I think it would be bizarre if you were not here for more than just the one reason. That would be sad, frankly. I would think there would be more to you than that. I would certainly hope so."

Plunk.

"Yeah?" I say, in a voice and an attitude that I regret and already wish I could undo. "Maybe you wouldn't."

"What's that supposed to mean?"

I'm out of stones.

"I'm out of stones," I say, allowing my arms and legs to hang limply dead over the water.

"How can you say that, that I wouldn't hope to find more to you than just a football player? Are you saying that you're a nobody beyond your identity as an athlete? I don't believe that for a minute. Even if you were crazy enough or brainwashed enough to believe it yourself, I still wouldn't buy it. It's obvious you're more than that. Of course, everybody is more than that, right, of course. But to be honest, when it comes to college football players, if most of the ones I've met wanted to claim they were all ball and nothing more, I'd say, yup, I see what you mean. Do you really wish you were like that?"

I very, very almost do. What a straightforward life that would be, simple, comprehensible, unapologetic.

"Being a kicker on a football team, and doing it very well, is who I was, Joyce. It was the easiest, most reliable part of being me when being me was kind of not bad. And not difficult. It was the only thing I felt like I could count on when I made this massive leap of life to come to Carnegie. Now I find out there are at least two guys who do my best thing better than I do. That has my head spinning right now, it really does."

She hops right up to her feet and starts helping me get up as well, even before I've decided I want to.

"Take it easy, please," she says. "So you just ran into a

rotten bad break. There was no way of knowing the only two guys around who could outkick you would suddenly decide to come out for the team."

We pick up our slow, gimpy walk where we left off and trundle down the far slope of the bridge. "I don't even know that much," I say. "Those are the only two guys I've seen kick since I got here. Maybe everybody in the state kicks better than I do. You could very well punt a football twice as far as me, for all I know."

"Well," she says, holding my elbow the way you would with an elderly person, "I've never tried, but from what I'm seeing with that leg, I like my chances."

"Fine," I say, "that's just terrific. You should show up for practice tomorrow in my place. Then at least one of us will have a chance of beating out *Christian* and *Tory* and send them packing back to soccer where they belong. *Soccer.*"

She is honestly trying to help me get over this, get over *myself* is probably what she thinks.

"Are they really jerky?"

"No," I snap, throwing my arms up and causing her to pull away from me. "They're excellent guys, actually. And they just kept getting more decent as I got more pathetic. Which makes me *completely* furious."

I must sound in dire need of therapeutic care now, because Joyce wades right in through the fog of idiocy I'm casting and puts a firm arm around my waist. I'm so stunned by this that I find myself staring at her hand on my hip for several strides.

"You, Mr. Sarafian, are a pretty wound-up guy, I'm starting to realize."

"No, you're not," I insist. "And I'm not."

"Well," she says coolly, "then I guess you're not. My mistake. All the same, I wish they weren't such sticklers about carding up at the student union there, or I'd buy you a nice relaxing drink right now."

We're passing the complex where the college's social scene is clustered: the union, arts center, movie theater, post office, pharmacy.

"That's a very thoughtful gesture, Joyce, thank you. But I don't drink anyway."

"Ah," she says in the politely confident way she says most things. The way I wish I could say anything. "You're of the 'my body is a temple' persuasion then?"

"Well, yeah," I say, "that's pretty much it."

"Too bad. I'd say if anybody could benefit from a medicinal tipple or two, it would be you. And I do have some wine up in my place."

Ah, now look at this. The new life is, seriously, throwing up a lot more challenges than I was planning on. It was supposed to get simpler here, much simpler, was the very soul of this plan, a good plan, a good soul.

"Well, what I was meaning by that, anyway, Joyce, probably I could have done a better job saying what I mean. I could, probably, always stand to be more precise with my words than I am. . . ." I almost wish she wasn't up against me like she is, her arm around me, my arm over her shoulders. It's one of the berserkest things I ever almost wished, but it's because I'm worried she must be able to feel me trembling with overexcited nerves. "I'm not a freak, is what I mean to say. I'm not a fanatic or whatever. And yes, uh-huh, a glass of wine sounds like a tremendous idea, thanks, I would love to . . ."

Tremendous? Sheesus, Sarafian.

"Great," she says, giving me a quick hard pulse of a squeeze. "I believe that's a wise decision."

"It feels wise," I say.

"Indeed. I think even your limp is suddenly cured. Look at that."

She's right. There are, I'm sure, perfectly sound physiological reasons for this miracle, reasons that don't at all suggest I'm a fraud or a wimp or a simplemind or a hypochondriac or a lying conniving manipulator, but I have no idea how to even begin that discussion. But I do know I need to fill the space with better thoughts than those.

"Yeah," I say breathlessly. "That's amazing. Listen, as long as you have those kind of magic powers to take away pain—which I totally believe, by the way—would you mind while you're at it just kind of rerouting that pain to those other two guys for me?"

"Charmer," she says. "Comical charmer."

Better things. Those are better things combined in those words, way better than the worst things somebody could think about a guy if they chose to.

"Just see what you can do," I say.

"I'll see what I can do," she says.

I have to fight every impulse inside me that's dying to say I'm already seeing it, what she can do.

She can do so much by doing just a little, and she has no idea.

"Keir?" the warm Dream Voice says, the way the Dream Voice always says.

"Mmm," I say back, the way I always say back.

"You're very strong," she says, "and this is so great. And I could do this all day. Except that I can't. And you can't either. We have things to do. Keir? You have to let go now. We both have places to be."

It takes minutes, and layers of thought, to work my way up out of deep perfect sleep, to shallow perfect dreamy-woozy, to real-world realization.

And the realization is better than the dreams.

I am lying on my side in the bed of the girl. I have both arms wrapped decisively around her and can think of no reason to ever do anything else.

Joyce, unfortunately, can think of reasons.

"I'm having trouble breathing," she says. "You're squeezing too hard." When I fail to take the hint, she grabs my hands and forcefully pries them off her rib cage. Then she holds on to the hands, which is a fine trade. "Also, I have an appointment to meet with a professor in twenty minutes," she says.

"Professor who?" I say.

She is already wriggling because I'm working to reestablish my python grip on her.

"Professor Not-Your-Concern," she says firmly. "And are you not supposed to be lining up right about now for your last chance to show the football staff what you've got? Or was that just you talking big stuff last night?"

"Shit," I say, releasing my magnificent captive exactly according to her plan. I scramble off my side of the bed as Joyce scrambles off hers, and I pray to whoever still accepts prayers these days that she isn't already longing for the time when both sides were still hers.

"Go get 'em," she says kindly, shoving me out the door.

It's hard to tell exactly, whether events—Joyce-related events—have improved me physically to the degree that I am bounding like a wild mustang across campus, but that is just how it feels. I'm covering the yardage between her place and mine with such speed and power and agility that there is no way anybody beats me out for any position once I carry this over to the playing field.

"Are you better now?" Fabian asks as I burst through the door.

"Better than *what*, Fabe-u-lous?" I ask loudly, stopping to sandwich his concerned face between my hands.

For once, he's caught semi-speechless, but quickly catches up. "Better than yesterday," he says, like an accusation. "Better than—"

179

"You can stop right there, my good friend. Because the answer is yes, regardless. I am better. Better than ever, better than everyone, better than . . . everything. What you got? Whatever it is, I'll better it on this fine morning. It's a fine morning, isn't it, Fabian?"

I go to my closet and pull out my sweats and throw last night's clothes every which way.

"You know, Keir," Fabian says, standing by close enough to give me the eye of disapproval.

"I know," I say. "Whatever it is, I don't know, but I know."

I see out of the corner of my manic, lucky eye that he is following the flight of every item I throw. And I know that he's going to collect everything and put it all right after I'm gone, and I know that I don't deserve him.

"Yeah. And now I'll say the thing I was actually going to say, whether you know it or not. Which was, you know, Keir, a guy like me would think . . . that is, a guy like me is rather shocked, that a guy like you, stud-ish, football jock, one of life's obvious *chosen ones*, should get all discombobulated over some attention from a girl. Or, like yesterday, that you should get all rattled because there's some competition in camp. Isn't this what you guys are all about? Isn't this exactly what makes you guys *you guys*, as opposed to us? I mean, frankly, I was expecting some sterner stuff, a little bit of love-'em-leave-'em kind of business that I could at least, for once, *witness* if not, you know, ever personally experience."

This takes me completely by surprise, and I go rigid. I'm

not even sure what it is that gets me. His nerd's-eye view of life on the other side is probably pretty common, so that couldn't be it. Maybe because he is so, so, so wrong about me? Again, not an unfamiliar situation for me to find myself in, so this shouldn't completely immobilize me either.

"Keir?" he says with what I think is deep concern in his voice.

That's it.

"Keir? Are you all right? Should I do something?"

That's it. That's exactly it.

"All right, Keir, you're creeping me out now. If you don't tell me to do something or not to do something immediately, then I'm going to do something. I don't know what I'll do, but it'll be something."

I reanimate, just for him. I turn his way slowly, taking in the decent, goofy-ass concerned look on his face. "Don't do something," I say, clapping him on the shoulder. "Everything's cool."

"Okay, well, if it's all cool, don't do that upright rigor mortis thing again. Deeply unsettling, that one . . . Are you laughing at me? Stop laughing at me."

"I apologize, Fabian, sincerely, man. Sometimes my face, and my voice, and my body language and whatever, they don't come together and say what I really mean. It only sounded like laughing at you. What it was in reality . . . right, I don't know if there's even a name for it. But . . . here's the thing, the point, what I'm still . . . It's phenomenal to me . . ."

He checks his watch, being very obvious about it, tapping the crystal and everything.

"You *think* about me. Like, when I'm not even here and all. I still, you know, exist for you after I'm gone, before I return. And it's not the kind of thinking people probably mostly do when a guy leaves the scene, like what a jackass, what a whole lotta hole that guy is. None of that."

It seems like I've got him pretty well puzzled by this point. "No, of course none of that. Why should I think any of that? You're my friend."

It's a big thing, probably a bigger thing than it looks, that he is causing me to lean in close. To study his honest good-guy face. He is an honest, good guy. And I'm his friend.

"It just kind of boggles my mind, is all," I say, and I hope the grateful I feel is there in my voice.

"Well," he says, "at least now we know what's boggling it."

And even though I am aware of being late, I am likewise aware of not, at this moment, caring much. It occurs to me that this is one of those times when a guy should slow down, take the extra minute or two to breathe in and appreciate good things.

I don't even close the dresser drawers or my closet door on my way to stretching out on the bed.

"That's my bed," Fabian says.

"Man, you do get hung up on silly things. What, are you afraid I got cooties or something that you might catch?"

"I've got no idea what you might have. But if you don't mind, I'd prefer to catch it the fun way, like you did."

"Ha," I say, "you make a good case, my friend." I get up off his bed and take the five-stride glide over to my own, beneath the window. The view out there, the mountains rolling under a clear bright sky, is one of the three fine things I've lucked into here at Carnegie. It fills me with a kind of awe that I never quite found . . . anywhere else. I think that if I ever lose that awe, that's when I'll be worried about myself.

"Your father really misses you," he says, striking thunder and lightning through the flawless day I can see right in front of me.

"My life isn't like that, you know," I say instead of whatever it is he wants me to say.

"Did you hear what I said? He just wants to talk to you once in a while. To hear your voice, know you're okay."

"I never even had a girlfriend. Not ever. Are you surprised? Well, it's true. It's true and it's because. Because I was always in love. Always, from the beginning of time, I'd say. I was too much in love to ever even try to have a girlfriend."

"Um, yeah, I guess I'm surprised. It's kind of nice, I think. Weirdly noble? Nobly weird?"

"Let's go with the first one there, huh?"

"Okay, Weirdly Noble, how about calling Ray?"

"Okay, well, how about *not* calling him Ray. You're not his son, so you're not allowed to call him Ray."

"I might not be his actual son, but at least I talk to him."

"Dog and bone, dog and bone, dog and bone."

"And he's an excellent guy, by the way. A really lovely guy to talk to. *I* look forward to his calls."

"You have to stop answering my phone. And if I turn it off, leave it off," I say, forcing myself to stop looking at the sky in order to give him a glare, and all the more irritated as a result.

"Carry it with you then, like I keep saying."

I spring up off my bed, bending right into the crucial task of stretching out my hamstrings. "I have to get going," I say, hopping in place, toggling my head around to get my neck muscles loose. "I have an important morning in front of me, cracking heads and taking no names. I have to show these guys some of the old stickin', because I won't be doin' no kickin'."

"Good luck," Fabian calls as I stomp across the room and out the door. "Don't get killed or anything."

He has no idea what he's talking about, and I have no interest in educating him. Because right now I'm already someplace else. Someplace very much else.

The field I am approaching now is already wild with football intensity. As it should be. The last chance for guys to show what they've got before the final roster cuts, and I felt the buzz of desperation energy basically the instant I stepped out the front door of the residence halls.

"Coach Muswell," I call, running faster as I get closer to the action.

He and several assistants are on the near sideline, with their backs to me as they face onto the field. If Coach hears me call, he doesn't show it.

"Coach," I say, stepping right up in between him and the assistant closest to him.

He doesn't even look at me. "Late, Sarafian? For the very last session before final cuts? I thought you were supposed to be smart."

"I am, Coach, I am smart. And I really want to get a chance to show you. I'm sorry about being late, it'll never happen again. It was my roommate. He was having this crazy insane mental crisis, and he woke up screaming and I had to get him down to the clinic because he couldn't calm down and I had to phone his dad, and I knew it was going to get me in hot water with you and possibly cost me a spot on the team ultimately, but while I did take all that seriously into consideration, I had to make a tough call under pressure, and I decided risking the consequences on the football side was going to be secondary to doing the only right thing and getting my friend the critical care he needed."

He turns just his big Coach head, like an owl with a baseball hat on. He blinks at me a few times, curls his lip, and says, "Get some pads on."

When I return in no time all geared up, he makes things plain for me, and I welcome that.

"Keir, here's where we're at. You are unexpectedly on the bubble. I honestly do not know whether I am going to have a Sarafian on my roster to start the season or not. I am sure there are many reasons for why we've gotten to this point, but the only thing that matters is that it's happened and neither one of us is happy about it. Unless I'm mistaken and you don't particularly care, which, frankly, is how you have looked on the field a lot of the time."

"No, sir, Coach!" I bellow like a lunkhead, like they taught us the first session of the first tryouts for freshman football back in high school. Coaches love and admire the lunkhead bellow, and I can produce a quality one when required. "I am not happy about it. I'm gonna show you today. I'm giving you everything I got, leaving it all out there on the field so when you make your decision, you'll know it's the real me you're getting."

"Good," he says, nodding approval that I'm at least singing the song. "That's good, son, because as I told you before, these scholarships are very precious commodities here, and so far you haven't given me a lot of cause to believe that I spent this one wisely. And by now, I think you've already become aware that you'd be no better than third on the depth chart as a kicker—where the depth chart doesn't really extend beyond two."

"I do realize that, Coach. Those two guys are otherworldly."

"Damn fine boys too. I rate that highly, you know. I want fine young men, strong character types, good students who represent the Saints proudly at all times."

"Yeah," I say flatly. "They are awesome inside and out."

"Well, now's your chance, and I suggest you be likewise awesome inside and out. Now, the assistants are running the show. There are a whole lot of different schemes and situations they'll be testing you guys with, so be prepared, be smart, listen to audibles, be prepared to make changes on the fly, and finish your tackles. You'll be on at cornerback with the defensive B squad."

"Coach?" I know this is the worst time imaginable to be interrupting him at all, never mind daring to give him suggestions on strategy or personnel. But if I don't, I'm going to fail and none of this will matter anyway.

"What?"

"I'm not a cornerback."

He sighs, the way a police dog would sigh. "Yeah, I think we had this conversation once, back at the beginning. Well, guess what? You're not a kicker anymore either."

"I know, I know. I'm just saying, back at school, when I was at my best, aside from the kicking, I was a free safety. I got by when I was needed at corner, but I'm not great at man-to-man, and I'm not blazing fast, especially not at this level. I'm afraid I'd get exposed pretty quickly.

"But what I did, what I got kind of famous for, was playing in the middle, facing the play. I can read an offense, Coach. I can be in the right place at just the right time, and I can hit. When I really commit to it, I can hit as hard as anybody you've got. I was renowned for my ability to deliver a hit."

He's giving me a funny expression here, his lips pursed

and pushed out in either a contemplating mode or maybe preparation to blow me raspberries.

Then he points at me with a football-for-life finger that is so gnarled it looks like it has knuckles in four different places. "Free safety."

"Yes!" I hoot. "All right, Coach. I won't let you down."

"I will expect you not to. Now, Keir?" The finger is sort of wagging, more like chopping. "Focus. Commit. Read and react rapidly. And I cannot emphasize this enough: *do not miss an open field tackle, not once.* Players who miss open field tackles play for somebody else, because they don't play for me."

"Can't be fairer than that, Coach," I say, popping my helmet on my head so aggressively it could be the hardest hit I take all day.

That's not how it turns out, as it happens. Because that's not football. And I am so glad for that.

I'm reborn at safety. It was true, every word of what I said to the coach. Every word, that is, after I stopped turbo-lying about why I was late. I can see the field, and every single play the offense tries to run, so clearly it feels as if I am watching the tape replay of a game I already played a hundred and fifty times. It's as if I have inside information, like when one team manages to steal the opposition's playbook and gives them a mauling, come game time.

No disrespect to Coach Muswell, but to be honest, his sets and schemes and play-action tricks are not as hard to decipher as he seems to believe. As a consequence, I am not far off the ball at the end of almost every passing play they attempt. And as for the running plays, I'm there on all of them.

Bam! Our fullback, who isn't massive but sure is one solid squat block of granite, erupts straight out of the backfield and right up the middle. It was a broken play, where the middle of the offensive line was supposed to have opened up a hole for him to squeeze through. But they got stuffed and manhandled by our two gigantic defensive tackles, so the hole isn't there. Until the fullback makes one for himself. *Blam!* Big guys from both sides of the line bounce and stagger as the ballcarrier shoots through like a cannonball. Our middle linebacker was caught out of position but makes up ground fast. He catches the guy, almost strips the ball off him as he gets a grab on him from behind.

That slows him down just enough, and I have him lined up from twenty yards away. He's grappling, looking down as he tries to maintain control of the ball, and that's where I get him, *carraaack!*

I'm so torqued up and tuned in that I am aware of every gasp from the sidelines and on the field. I bounce right up and bash my chest with my fist once as the fullback gets slowly up, and the ball finally comes to a stop in western Canada somewhere.

There is a lot of woofing going on because this is football, and that is the football that football players like. A slap on the ass here, a smack on the helmet there, and I am lined up once again in my spot, at my position, where I belong.

A bunch of running plays follow, and every single one of them is directed through the central highway, the stretch of the field that runs between the hash marks. That's the zone, our zone, where the middle linebacker patrols ten yards in front of me, and after that I am the only lawman left between the ballcarrier and the goal line border he needs to cross to collect six points over my dead body.

As a unit, we are not bad, the defensive B squad, and the running game is not getting much off us. A yard or two per carry, then one goes for seven, then the quarterback gets cute and fakes the run, dumps a quick short pass to the slot receiver, who's gained eight yards just by making the catch, but he's not getting a single yard more.

I actually sprint right past the linebacker who's going for it, but I get there first. I hit the guy just at the point where he's collected the ball, tucked it in, and turned upfield. But there is no upfield for him as I crunch him with all the strength and desperation and kinetic malevolence I had generated from that full-tilt run from those twenty yards out. And from a long way beyond that, too.

It's a deadly, textbook hit, but so is the catch and hold. He's lying on his side as I push myself up off him with both hands on his rib cage. "Good grab," I say, offering him a hand up. "Way to hang on."

"Thanks," he says, ignoring my hand and hopping to his feet. "I never drop." He gives me a sly grin that I recognize from thousands of competitive moments with hundreds of competitive guys.

The grin says, *That didn't hurt*, and *Show me what else you got*, and the grinner is Kelly McAvoy.

There are some guys who can make that face, who are so masterful at it, they make you feel like you'd run across eight lanes of highway traffic, through razor wire and a plate-glass window to hit him again. Kelly McAvoy is one of those guys.

It's a thing of beauty.

"And all that time, I thought you were a big hitter. Huh," he says, turning his back to me and jogging back to his squad.

Oh. Oh, yeah. He's good. Good for me, especially.

I think I forgot, sometime fairly long ago, how much fun football could be. I won't be forgetting again, not if it keeps going this way. This is the right way. I'm playing the right way, I'm feeling the right way, and when you've got that going, life should cooperate. Life should be fine, and it is fine, today, the finest day.

They have switched their approach. We came off the field for a good, long, welcome breather while the A offensive and defensive lineups took over. Now we're back on the field, and the coaches' strategy is picking up right where it left off. Having tested our mettle against a primarily running attack, they are mixing it up now but favoring the passing game heavily. It's a much more demanding task than it was, as the quarterback is doing an excellent job of spreading the field, throwing short passes and long ones, across the middle and straight down the sidelines. He's using all his weapons, releasing his halfback to catch a pass, connecting with his tight end after sending both wide receivers flying downfield and drawing all the coverage that way. Including me. By the time both myself and the strong safety recover and scramble back into the play, the end has picked up twenty-five yards—twenty-five of *our* yards, specifically, as he gallops right along through the very heart of my patrol zone.

"That was your read, Sarafian!" Coach roars, making sure I know what he's noticing, that what I was promising I'm not now delivering.

I think I am overall having a stellar session. I'm making reads, making hits, hitting my spots. I don't know what he's thinking, but whatever I'm doing, I have to do more of it. Do it stronger, do it better, do it more ferociously. Because I hear him. Maybe it's my imagination, or maybe it's not, but I hear Coach screaming me out, a lot, and I don't hear him doing it to anybody else.

I have to turn it up, several notches.

I'm thrilled every time they put the ball on the ground, because I am totally locked in on the running game. I sniff it out, I get a ridiculous jump on the play, and before the runner gets more than a few yards past scrimmage, I am there to stop him, sometimes with the help of my slower-reacting teammates, sometimes not. Several times, many times, I find myself sprinting right past our middle linebacker to make a tackle he should have made. He is a senior, one of the team's defensive captains, and because of his position at middle linebacker he's supposed to be sort of our general, our mastermind, our quarterback leading the B-squad defenders. He is not a B-squad defender, and he can't be getting shown up by one.

After one of those plays, one of my best plays all day, I am running past him to get back to my position when suddenly his shoulder surges forward, crashes into me, and I am flat on my back looking up at his angry mug.

He doesn't say anything, just glares at me with glowing orange eyes through his face mask, trying to stare me down.

Notwithstanding how clearly down I obviously am, I'm not having this. I don't say anything either but spring to my feet, bumping my face mask with his as I do, then spin back in the direction of the free safety's home office.

However, I don't care. I don't care how big he is, or how fearsome he is or how established on and within the team he is—the answer to all three, by the way, being *extraordinarily*.

If you don't do your job, then somebody else will do it. Too bad. I have no time for you, pal, no sympathy, and, regardless of how much you try to intimidate me, no respect. It's just too bad.

"Too fucking bad," I call to the back of the linebacker, my teammate, my supposed leader, just before the snap of the ball for the next play.

It's a pass play. It's a quick release to the sideline way to my right, and I am hauling full tilt in the direction of the play, along with everybody else. The receiver makes a nice jumping one-handed catch, pulls the ball in, and immediately fakes the cornerback right out of his socks with a slick shimmy move. Strong-side safety is right there as the receiver cuts to the inside. He's got him lined up, but the guy cuts again to the outside, which nobody was expecting, and our safety loses a step, lunges and bounces harmlessly off the guy, who sprints away like a racehorse, never to be troubled by any of us again.

I continue the pursuit anyway, because that's what you're supposed to do, probably forty-five yards in all. By the time he crosses the goal line, there is about fifteen yards more space between us than when I started chasing him.

I am utterly winded, with my hands on my hips, as I make the long trip back to the sidelines while the kicking team comes running out for the point-after attempt. I see both Tory and Christian running out, both with a weird high-stepping leg motion where they're practically kneeing themselves in the stomach and could only have come from soccer. I don't even want to know which one is going to be kicking and which one is the holder.

"Looking good out there," Christian says, slapping my stomach as he passes.

"I know," Tory says. "He's a new man. Somebody must have got laid last night."

"Ahhh, ha-ha," the whole of the point-after unit of the special teams bursts out laughing. They seem to have bonded together into a close-knit bunch already.

Would I be part of that now, if I had done a better job kicking?

Or would the whole thing be totally different if I were part of it?

• • •

When I trot onto the field with the B squad again, I'm feeling it, and the *it* I'm feeling is not what I was feeling earlier.

I'm fatigued, and I'm sore. The passing game is running me ragged, trying to figure it out mentally and keep up physically. I know the situation is deteriorating when I find myself starting to guess. That's the worst, when your instincts go fritzy so you can't read the play, and your legs are quitting on you so you can't cover up mistakes by finding that extra gear.

Except, I find that extra gear.

I am borderline insane with the awareness that my whole new life is on the line right now. Very few people get a second chance like I got, and I'd bet nobody gets a third. As the notion hits me that it all could come apart in the next half hour, I get a surge of maniacal energy.

I still feel the strains and bruises everywhere, but now I like them. They are welcome, because the contusions *are* football, and they keep me company like old teammates and pals.

Right from the go, the offense is targeting me now. Every pass play, every run, is either coming straight up my alley or faking one way before slanting in my direction.

Good. I'm dead on my feet, but good. Coach wants to know if I'm for real.

Bam!

I catch a receiver getting cute, about to lateral the ball to the tight end three yards away, and I absolutely level the guy. I hit him so hard there's a sound like a fire alarm sounding

195

from inside my own helmet. I don't even know if the tight end received the ball, scored a touchdown or not, but in this instance that was not my problem. My problem was this guy lying on the ground in front of me, who will never again try a gimmick with me chugging full tilt at his chest.

That's what I needed to do, that's what the coach was looking for me to do, and that is what I did to perfection.

I extend a hand to the guy as he spends an extra several seconds on his back. He declines my sportsmanship, so I turn to walk away.

I bump right into Kelly.

"Tone it down, man," he says.

"What? You know how this works, Kelly. Nobody tones anything down, not at this point. Especially guys who are on the bubble."

But I was never supposed to be a bubble type. This was not the way it was supposed to be.

"A lot of these guys are gonna wind up being your teammates, remember."

"If I don't keep popping these guys, I won't be anybody's teammate. And if they can't take it, maybe they won't either."

He gives me a strangely offended look as he backs away toward the offensive formation again. I don't know if maybe Kelly lost his edge between high school and here, but that's for him to deal with. But it's not going to happen to me. I'm not going to set any sprint records on this team, so I have to show what I can show. But if they have some kind of Richter scale for registering the magnitude of hits, that's a record I'm going for.

And for the rest of the session I do exactly that. I stomp and crash around the field as if the whole place belongs to me. I play smarter as I get more tired, old tricks coming back to me from when I played DB regularly. I hedge this way or that to get an early jump on a play I sense is coming, because otherwise I won't have the legs to catch up. I don't guess right every time, but I do well enough to look like I belong.

And, most of all, I make sure that when I am in position to make a tackle, I *make* that tackle.

A few times Kelly is my man, and I do stop him but not always without help. I hit him first, but he absorbs it, fights through it, pulls me along until one, two other defenders come along and drag him down.

He's bigger than I thought he was, and he is in beastly shape. He plays a sort of hybrid receiver–tight end, and he will give a lot of teams fits trying to match up with him because of his speed-size-agility package.

"Man, you bulked up over the summer," I say as it's his turn to offer me a hand up after a collision. I, however, accept the offer out of good sportsmanship and a concern that I might not get up otherwise.

"Not really," he says, and goes back to work.

How could I not notice that I was playing on the same team with a specimen like Kelly McAvoy? How was that possible?

I have to admit that generally the players here are bigger, stronger, faster, and quite obviously more committed to training than what I encountered regularly in high school. This was to be expected, so why do I feel like I wasn't expecting it? Where was I? Was I thinking I was just about good enough to hold my own at Norfolk? And that small-school NAIA Carnegie was going to be such a step down that the whole thing would be a stroll for me?

I hope I wasn't thinking that. I don't think I was thinking that, and I don't want to think that, because that guy, with that thought, would be a grade-A shithead. These players here, and naturally, players at decent well-run programs all over the country, are legitimate athletes. It would be like, if you took the top tier, the very best half dozen or so guys from every team I saw in high school, including my own, took all the best guys, the guys you stopped everything to watch, the guys who could do the spectacular things like lifting houses right up off the ground, like running a lap of the school's four-hundred-yard oval track so fast it was earlier when they returned than when they left, stuff that normal *players* couldn't do and that normal people in the street couldn't even dream of ever doing, it was like if you skimmed all those guys off the top of the athletic cream, those would be the guys who wound up at all levels of all kinds of college programs all over America.

Those are the guys I have to compete with for a spot on the team, for the privilege of playing against all those same guys every week in games that count. I'm no dunce. I'm not a chump or a dreamer. I knew this was what it would be like.

I also think I more or less know what it would be like to

have a surface-to-air missile shot through my stomach. You can *know* every damn thing there is, but until you get hit by it up close and murderous, you don't know shit.

But right this second all that matters is that one of those guys is motoring straight at me, having caught yet another pass going right across the middle and into my area of responsibility. I have plenty of time to see him come, and he's making no move to avoid me, so I do what I've been taught and I plant my feet, start my surge forward, toward him before he can get me first and send me hurtling backward like a tumbleweed. When the impact comes, it's not like it was two or three or six years ago when I discovered that the well-executed tackle does not feel like anything at all no matter how hard you crash it.

No, this one I feel, in every last one of my body's bones. I'm sure if I had the time, I could even count all of them, as they individually crackle and squeal.

At some point this became a man-to-man competition between Kelly and me. We are isolated, play after play. Even when he is not the target receiver, he's coming at me as a blocker, and we spend practically the whole time in what has quickly become a war. I have been hitting harder than he might have been expecting, but too bad. He should have been expecting it or he's a fool. Behind the face mask, his face has been getting redder, his eyes more bulgy, and this just makes me happier because it means I'm doing my job.

This time, though, despite my perfect planting of the feet,

I get blasted by him. I hurtle backward and roll like a tumble-weed. And this time, as he walks over me, he doesn't bother picking me up.

"What happened?" he says coldly. "I thought the Killer was supposed to be a famous big hitter."

"Do not call me that," I say, with multiple varieties of shame packed into it and a fresh sizzling layer of anger on top.

"Sorry, I forgot," Kelly adds, with me now up to all fours. "And maybe now you'll remember my name too."

He's trying to follow me. Fuck him, fuck this, fuck it. He cannot follow me here. The Killer. After all that, all this, after everything, he still thinks he can follow me.

And now I'm on my hands and knees on the football field, where the son of a bitch knew he'd find me.

"Are you all right? Sarafian. Sarafian, are you injured? Can you get up? Do you need the stretcher?"

Our team trainer is crouched looking at me from one side, the opposing squad's trainer from the other. A few play-ers are scattered about in the background, but it doesn't seem to have much to do with me, beyond my lying here clogging up their field.

"I'm fine," I say. "Just got the wind knocked out of me."

I got a whole lot more than that knocked out of me, but I won't be saying that to anybody around here.

With the last remaining vestiges of my old football game-ness, I spring to my feet in complete denial of any internal malfunctions I may or may not be enduring. I break immediately into a healthy jog to get back into position and wait for the next play to reveal itself. The day is almost over, as are any last chances to seize a spot on this team.

I'm begging the universe to send Kelly McAvoy and the football my way.

The universe obliges.

It's a stupid boring little dump pass, the kind you see a lot at the end of an exhausting workout. Kelly catches it with plenty of time to haul it in and square up on me.

But it doesn't matter. He's screaming with rage as he aims for me, and I see he is out of control, and I always knew how to turn somebody's failure of control into an advantage for me. I come at him straight, getting my sights on his thighs, going low, until he is close enough and I explode upward with pile-driver force.

I glance off his chest and catch him right up under the chin guard. He is completely rocked as his legs go out from under him and I come right over the top of him, before slamming him onto his back, into the ground.

"What was your name again?" I say as we are face mask to face mask.

I thought he was going to laugh, I really did.

I got that one quite wrong.

unreachable

Y our dad phoned again," Fabian calls as soon as I walk
in. It's late afternoon and the exact middle of the
limbo zone, twenty-four hours since the final workout, twenty-four more till they post the roster.

I've been too on-edge to talk about it with Fabian, or
Joyce, or anybody yet.

"Did you hear me, Keir? I said your dad called again."

"You answered my phone again," I respond. It's already a
thing, a routine, a kind of comedy sketch we've been honing.
Despite the fact that we've only been occupying this space
together a short while. My previous roommate and my current one have spoken to each other more times than Ray and
I have since I left home.

They achieved that already by the time they had spoken
once.

I know the question. But I don't know the answer. Of course I should call him. I should call him every day. He deserves that, and a lot more. He deserves better, way better. Better than me, is what he deserves.

"You know, Keir, you really should carry your phone. There are lots of good reasons. It just makes sound common sense."

He deserves Fabian. I'm glad they have each other to talk to.

"Sound common sense, Fabian? Like when a guy tells you, if you answer my phone again, I'm gonna choke you to death and so you then wise up and stop answering the guy's phone? That kind of sense?"

I don't know what I'd do if he really did stop answering.

He's chopping up fruit salad at his desk. He's got a skill there, no question. He's fast and makes no mess, and the shapes of completely unrelated fruits like bananas and plums somehow come out in the same rectangular cubes. And he always shares with me.

"That's not what you said. You said you would throttle me."

"I used the word 'throttle'? I don't think so."

"Possibly not. But can't you allow me to make little improvements here and there so I can pretend I didn't wind up rooming with a jock?"

I sigh, because this kind of remark also breaks no new conversational ground between us. But I like fruit salad. And against the odds, I like Mr. Fabian Delmonico as if he were my oldest, closest pal. And he seems to like me, too. Which helps immensely when two guys are having to coexist in a tight space when they have very different interests and no actual common history. One might be tempted to think that was exactly why they got along right out of the chute. He's an oasis of new and unusual for a guy wanting to unknow the familiar past.

Why should sad Ray have to be a casualty of that? Why can't he be a beneficiary of it instead?

He's not dead. I'm not a killer. I'm no kind of criminal.

"Fine, little improvements," I say. "But don't improve me so much I'm unrecognizable."

"Why would I want to do that?"

I drag my chair over to his desk and sit close to the fruit piling up in the bowl. I snag chunks of mango in between knife flashes, and he shows no effort to slow down or make any other allowance for the fingers crossing harm's way. That's the deal.

"So, you going to call Ray or what?"

"You're not allowed to call him Ray. I'm the one who is his son, remember?"

"I remember. Do *you* remember? At least I take his calls."

"But nobody asked you to. In fact, you've been asked not to. If I wanted to answer calls, I would carry the phone with me. I have no interest in being *reachable*." I chew the word out.

"Don't spit your contempt on the salad, or you will be asked to go back over to your side of the accommodation."

"I was just leaving," I say, standing, grabbing a fist full of mango and cantaloupe to mess with his carefully plotted distribution of colors and textures.

"Think of the *balance*, you Philistine," he snaps as I squeaky-drag my chair across the floor and throw myself onto my slab of a bed. I ease bits of orange-spectrum chunks of fresh into my mouth as I watch him redress the balance problem with a barrage of tangerine replacements.

Look at him. If there is one person who stands as a good example of just how far my life has mutated since only last spring, Fabian is that guy. He wears vests. It is just now striking me that he wears vests, every single day. He must have about eight in all. It's playing across my mind like a strange micro-fashion show, but it's actually the replays of the days when I was only half taking in the details. I'm noticing my friend now, in his details. Plaids, pinstripes, mostly not nutty colors or anything—though there's an all-silk royal-blue one that's really asking for it in daylight. Still, they're vests, so if they're worn as anything other than the anchor of a three-piece suit, then they don't need to be loud in order to be freakwear.

But the time or two when I was about to come out with some clever remark about the absurdity of whatever he happened to be wearing, he stopped me cold by reminding me with paralyzing sincerity that I could borrow any of his things anytime without needing to ask. I knew where they were all hanging, he said. I did. Cut me off at the knees when he did that.

And he has a typewriter and not just for show. A manual one, that I can verify he actually *uses* all the time as if it was a normal, functioning student aid to coursework and not just a prop for the journalism department Halloween party. Although he is planning to use it that way too, saying he's going as the ghost of newspapers past.

"What are you staring at?" he asks sternly, following my sight line closely when I wasn't even aware he was doing it.

"Nothing."

"Not nothing. You are lusting after my typewriter, I know it."

"No," I say. "There's only one freak in this room and you know it."

"No, actually, I'm going to be the bigger man here and admit that there are two freaks in this room. And one of them better keep his hairy football claws off my typewriter."

Football claws. They might not even be football claws anymore. If they aren't, what kind of claws have I got? I stare at them, turning them over and back again, looking for clues.

"No, actually, they both better keep off your typewriter. Man, that thing *clacks*. I can still hear it in my head way after you stop typing."

"Yeah," he says, and no, he isn't fooling, "it is a beautiful sound sculpture."

"No, it isn't. It's like living inside a tiny tap-dancing studio. It makes me borderline demented sometimes, just so you know."

He snaps his Tupperware bowl shut on the fruit and deposits it in his little fridge in between his desk and his closet. The fridge doubles as a plinth for the glorious typewriter when it's resting. "Just help yourself," he says, like he always says. Then he hops stylishly, like an old Hollywood dancer type, onto his bed. He's already in sitting position with his hands clasped around one knee when he lands.

"Listen," he says, "okay, I will try to be more conscious and considerate of the noise when I work on the ol' gal."

"Ol' gal?" I say. "You two go back a long way, do you?"

"Well, here's the story," he says, as he says when he's winding up to spin me a tale off a small and innocent inquiry. "The ol' gal and I do go all the way back, to orientation. I rescued her from this teaching assistant in the English department, who is always talking about *authenticity* in writing and saying things like it extends to everything, the clothes you wear and the coffee you must refuse to drink. And he says it with a really, really straight face, like, a pencil of a face is what he has. And so he's going to put on some kind of clinic of live, in-person, authentic writing at the front of the class because he was just too distractingly inspired by this typewriter he found at a yard sale the day before. Got himself all set up for some macho freewriting, which he was going to then subdue us with by reading when he got to the bottom of page one. So, to make a long story a little less long, there was a complete riot of laughter in the class as the TA was in a fury, sweat and hair

207

oil stuff streaming down his face because the *E* key was as much of a stiff as he was and fought him every step of the way, causing him to use up a solid fifteen minutes between abusing and coaxing the old mechanics into finishing just the one word 'steampunk,' before quitting and punching the typewriter repeatedly in front of everybody. And while I'm sure the ol' gal would have eventually come back to win the fight as well, I had to jump up and intervene. I was told to get the thing out and never let him lay eyes on it again. Didn't have to tell me twice, that's for sure."

"And *you* type something like a thousand words a minute on the thing."

He shrugs. "A little bit of the right grease in the right places, you can get almost any non-carbon-based life-form to do what you want it to."

I shake my head in a big mad-cow toggle of admiration. I flash for a second on how people I knew, somewhere and sometime back, would have smutted all over that greased-life-forms bit. And I thought of how Fabian, right over there staring back at me from the other bed—because in this mutated life I have a roommate such as this—how he would have been just exactly the type of character we would have taken wicked, rabid pleasure in hunting down and fucking up. Thinking up newer and ever more savage ways to humiliate him and expose the most vulnerable—

I stop myself. It was silent, just in my own head I was

thinking the words, and then I heard them, and they had to be cut off. They were wrong words, all wrong, and now they are stopped up in there, jammed up. My head suddenly weighs about an extra ten pounds, and I lean forward with my elbows on my knees and the heels of my hands pressed as hard as I can make them go into my temples.

"Keir?" Fabian says, sounding concerned. "Hey. Hey, are you all right?"

I can hear from the noise of the cheap creaky slats that he's coming off his bed to check on me. "No," I say—more like snap, unfortunately. "I'm good, though, man, thanks. Just really tired all of a sudden, so I'm going to, to lie down now." I promptly do that by falling straight back onto the pillow.

"Okay then," Fabian says, sounding not noticeably less concerned than before my assurances.

"Right," I say. "Thanks, that was a great story. Another one. You always tell such great stories, and you tell them with greatness. I don't know how you do it."

"Well, you know, English department. All we do is study the art of making stuff up all the time. Bound to rub off on a guy eventually."

"Excellent. It suits you. I will want to hear more, but tomorrow maybe."

"Sure, Keir."

"Would you mind, Fabian, if I asked you to turn off the big light?"

"Sure, Keir. Sure thing."

Sure. And then the *click* of that light, bringing on the darkness, feels like it saves me from something. An awful, horrible something.

"Thanks again, Fabian. I love your stories. I look forward to them."

"I'm glad," he says through the dark, in a strange old voice for a glad guy.

You cannot just *love* me, just like that, Keir."

"Why not? It sounds like a superb idea to me."

"I won't allow it, for one thing. It's a bit crazy. And, hold on, *idea*? It's an idea? Like something that occurred to you this morning when you got up out of bed and started planning out your day? Go to the gym around one o'clock, then, hey, here's an idea. . . ."

This is not at all the way it's supposed to go.

"Right, okay, sorry, I shouldn't have used the word 'idea.'"

"You shouldn't have used the word 'love,' ya nut. 'Idea' is a perfectly fine word, not terrifying at all, go ahead and use it all you want. 'Love,' my goodness, is a massive meteor of a word, a dangerous, powerful thing."

"Exactly," I say with more brightness than I feel, "so you do feel it too."

She sighs, stretching it out long enough for me to start wondering whether it's an exasperation sigh or a relief sigh and what it means for our future in either case.

"That's better," she says, clearing things up a little. "It's good that you can see the funny side anyway. Women can't resist a good sense of humor, you know. We'll keep it light for now, huh? Don't get so serious and scary."

My instincts in this area aren't incredibly trustworthy, but I don't suppose the whole love business is up for debate. I should be qualified to weigh in on the subject of me, though, right?

"I'll take serious," I say seriously. "But I don't think I'm especially funny or scary."

And in the latest twist in this long and winding road of surprises that maybe shouldn't be, Joyce seizes me in a warm full wrap of a hug. "Oh, Keir," she breathes right in my ear, which is now my favorite, luckiest of all my body parts. "If you could only see yourself."

I'm hugging her right back, naturally, and trying to gauge the exact right amount of pressure to use, to hold on with serious intent but without scariness.

"I'd really rather just see you," I say. "If I can see you, then that means you're with me. And if you're with me, then that means I must be pretty all right, and I have no need to see myself to know that."

"You are. You're pretty all right."

"And you're with me."

"I would have thought that was evident, but okay. Yes,

Keir, I am with you. I have to say, for a football player you're not exactly roaring with self-confidence."

Except that I am not a football player officially until I see my name posted on that roster in the gym in another five hours. If I see it.

And if I don't?

It's the last cut. It is, isn't it? The final remaining tangible evidence linking one guy and his open-sky future to another guy and his nonnegotiable past? That's the finality of it right there. But football was going to be the one link between my old life and my new one. Without it . . . I don't know if I could create another whole new everything without football to root me.

"Joyce, if I tell you that I'm scared, will I look like some kind of freak? Some kind of wimpy freak?"

She looks at me all leery, eyes flitting between me and all other directions for potential escape routes.

"Please, don't look like that," I plead.

"Come on, Keir, you're not exactly an open book with that kind of stuff. I should be allowed at least a look of moderate surprise."

I nod my head yes, and I hold up my hands—stop—but the words that will say it all much clearer come all sticky and slow, a molasses river.

"I don't think my confidence has been affected one way or another, but I'm not a football player anymore if a sheet of paper posted in the gym in a few hours doesn't tell me I am."

She smiles, broadly and knowingly. It's the kind of look

that should reassure a person, but I'm not able to get there.

"How could they cut you? They recruited you, for heaven's sake. That's absurd of them to give up on a scholarship athlete after such a short time. You are going to be fine."

"I can't think that way. They probably saw how desperate I was and cut me the minute I left the field."

"Oh, right. And you say your confidence is unaffected. . . ."

This is more painful than I thought it would be. It is laying bruises on me beyond what Kelly and the rest of them could manage in full contact down on the field.

"I can't remember a time before I was on one team or another. This thing, the games, the routine and discipline of practices and workouts, it was a big part of what helped me have an idea of myself. It let me identify me to myself when sometimes I would drift toward the feeling that I didn't know anything about anything. I'd see my teammates, lift weights with them, suit up with them, and they would remind me by the way they saw me. Slap my helmet. Pound on my shoulder pads. I would see the stats, see how many points I'd accumulated between field goals and point-after conversions. And there it would be on the sheet, complete, in plain numbers that needed no interpretation to tell me who I was and how good I was at it."

She nods, a big, slow up and down that says she understands and doesn't need—or possibly, want—me to say any more.

"I have to go," I say.

"Well, if you didn't say it, I was going to say it for you," she says, then rushes up to me before I can get the inevitable wrong idea. She kisses my cheek and squeezes my biceps. "You want me to come with you?"

"Oh God, no," I say.

"That's what I thought. Now, listen, I'm buried with coursework. But if you get cut—and you won't—then I want you to come back and stay here tonight. If you make the team, just send me a text. I don't want some macho overconfident jock coming over and ruining my studies."

My blood pressure decreases just slightly with that.

"I'm almost tempted to scratch my own name off the roster now," I say.

She starts manhandling me to the exit. "Yeah? Well, that would nullify the terms of the offer, leaving you with no football *and* no—"

"I won't!" I say, and rush out before I say anything else that stupid.

I pace like a madman, around and around and around the campus, killing time, slaughtering time, until the moment arrives and I march into the gym.

Some guys are ecstatic, hooting and barking, and the gym walls echo, making it sound like an old cowboys-and-Indians movie. Some guys are deflated, heads down and rushing out without making any sounds at all. Some guys make it very obvious that this was just a formality, like picking up the morning mail.

I stand for ages staring at the bland computer printout taped to the wall as other players come and go. I get bumped and jostled, I get backslapped by people celebrating their own good fortune, probably without even knowing who I am or what my outcome is.

Fabian was right this time, I should have taken my phone with me. I would love to stand right here and text the news to Joyce, but it'll have to wait until I get to my room. At least it will give me time to compose something clever and modest and not at all jock-y.

Most of the guys have come and gone, but I am still soaking it in, way more than I would have imagined. My own sweet celebration.

Christian and Tory appear, one at each shoulder as we survey the roster together. Not that there was any suspense about their fate, but one has to make it official.

"Super," Christian says. "You made it, Keir. So glad you made the cut. I would have felt awful knowing we made it, possibly at your expense."

"You might have even done me a favor," I say. "If it wasn't for you guys, I might never have found my old passion and been reborn as a defensive back."

"That's what we hear," Tory says, and slaps me firmly on the back. "Well done, Killer!"

"Yeah," Christian adds, "way to go, Killer!"

Dear God, no.

No.

I almost made my clean getaway.

But the Killer tracked me down.

team spirit

told myself I wouldn't react, never mind overreact. Take the high road, don't pay any attention, and it will die of its own no-big-dealism.

This is the beginning of all the better things I have traveled so far in so many ways to reach.

But as I stride across the field to begin my first full practice as a member of the Carnegie Saints football team, one after another of my new teammates on my new team in my new existence four thousand feet above sea level says the wrong thing.

"Killer!"

"Here comes the Killer!"

"Kill 'em, Killer! Kill 'em all!"

It's only banter.

It means I am part of the team, doesn't it? Doesn't it?

I smile ferociously as I stride with purpose and dignity straight into it. I smile harder and harder as I think about it, as I try not to think about it, about all the awfulness that comes here along with that name. I smile harder until I must look like Batman's Joker, because I am petrified that I am going to burst into tears because it is all coming apart, all at once, after all this effort.

I march directly to where the receivers and running backs are clustered, with Kelly in the middle of it, clapping and laughing like it is such a big happy joke that even I am going to love it.

And I finally get to where he is, still laughing away, and I'm still telling myself not to react, never mind overreact.

"Kelly," I say in a voice lower than I recognize, "tell them I'm not the Killer. Please, tell them there's no reason to call me that, because I am not the Killer."

The players who were chanting are now gathered around us and are totally silent. Kelly and I stand with about a foot of space between us. We can see each twitch of a face muscle and hear each quick shallow breath.

A smile unfurls across his lips, he gives me a gallant small nod, and then he calls out, "It is true, this man is not the Killer. But as a matter of fact, he is something else entirely. Something even worse than a killer—"

He cannot finish because I launch myself, fist-first, and punch Kelly McAvoy dead in the face.

He hits the ground like a felled tree but bounces back

up just as quickly and *bam*, I take a clean shot right in the mouth. Coaches must be catching on, because we're quickly separated and semi-covered by other players, who crowd around like nothing odd is going on.

They are assistant coaches, the special teams guy and the strength-and-conditioning guy.

"What's the story, boys?" the strength coach asks.

Lots of murmuring goes into denying there is any story at all.

"Right, then," the special teams coach says, pointing first at me, then at Kelly. "You with the bloody mouth, and you with the bloody nose, come with me."

He takes us to the weight room, then gets straight to it.

"Okay, you want to tell me what the problem is?"

"There is no problem, Coach," I say.

"No problem, Coach," Kelly says.

"Uh-huh," Coach says, checking his watch. "I thought as much. So, here's how it goes. I'm gonna leave you two here for exactly five minutes. When I come back, you will have solved whatever problem it is that neither one of you has. You solve it any which way you need to, but when I come back, it is solved. It is *not* to linger beyond that point, because that would be a threat to team unity. We cannot have a threat to team unity, or else someone is going to have to go. Understood? Good. Ready . . . solve."

"What if one of us kills the other one?" Kelly says as the coach walks away.

"That's easy," he says. "Problem solved." He slams the door.

"Why did you have to do that?" I blurt. "I told you I didn't want that name coming here."

"Too bad," he shouts. "It's a nickname, boo-hoo."

I take a breath, trying to rein myself, and this whole absurdity, back in.

"Listen, Kelly. This is probably a lot to do with my not remembering your name. You're right, that was awful, but we shouldn't let—"

"You want to know why you couldn't remember me? First, because you were a big shit, varsity for three years, and I didn't arrive till final year. You and your meathead pals were too good—"

"No, not true—"

"Entirely true. It was obvious, because you were the type of guys who wanted it to be obvious. And I wasn't part of your jolly thug crew. I was never big into drinking, I kept to myself, I was too quiet, and I know that kind of attitude is just, like, total alien behavior to the thug-life society."

"Hey, I was no thug. You know nothing. I was probably as much a quiet loner as you were. Sometimes I was a follower on this or that escapade, but it was all just—"

"Ha!" he blurts, sluttering spittle right in my direction. "Enough bullshit, Keir, all right? I was there. Were *you*? Sometimes I wonder what movie you were at. But the one you *starred* in was Keir Sarafian, Trouble's Own Master of Ceremonies."

"All wrong," I snap. "All wrong. You never even knew me.

I was at some stuff, sometimes, that got a little messy, but it wasn't me. You ask anybody and they'll tell you—"

"I don't need to ask, Keir. Did you forget again? I was *there*. Now, you can make shit up from now till the end of time for all I care. But you need to know that that is all ending here. You are going to have to put up *and* shut up for once in your life, Killer. Because you aren't good enough to be pulling this precious bullshit. You're not as good as you think, pal. Never were."

"I'm not precious. I just didn't want to be dragging old shit to a new place."

"Oh, really? Well, how do you suppose it felt to run into *you* here, huh? You think you invented the whole idea of a fresh start in a new place? Gimme a break. You would probably be the very last person from that team I would want to see here. Did you ever stop to think what the other guys thought about playing in the middle of that circus you were always bringing to town? I'll tell you what they thought, they wished you would just fuck off and take the circus with you."

"Nobody felt that way."

"Everybody felt that way. If it wasn't for a couple of hot streaks on field goals, being pals with Quarterback Ken, and the big reputation you got out of a major cheap-shot tackle here and there, you wouldn't even have been a big deal on our high school team, never mind being *here*."

"Shut up, liar. You're just jealous."

"Of what? You got nothin' I want."

"I made this team, didn't I? I made it by putting big hits on big boys like you, didn't I?"

"You did it the same way you got away with everything before. You picked your spot. You took a moment when you needed to, you threw yourself into the one practice or the one game or the one *play*, and you just mugged your way through it. Dirty plays and intimidation at the right time got you a long way, but you are gonna get found out now. You are gonna have to do it every day, with the big boys, because there's no kicking job for you to hide behind."

I start to storm out, but I realize there will be none of that. I'm trapped.

"Yeah, right," I say. "You're a jerk, Kelly, you know that?"

"I may be a jerk, but you, *Killer*, are a fake. And I can't wait to watch while everybody finds that out."

"I'm sure you'll make sure they find out, because you'll spread it around, just like with the Killer thing. Big deal, big man."

"I tell you what, Killer. Instead of trying to prove what a hard guy you are by starting fights with me, how 'bout letting your playing speak for you? How 'bout that, huh? 'Cause that's what I'll be doing. I'll leave you to it and won't say another word about you to anybody."

It's a reasonable proposition, and one any player worth his salt should be happy to live with.

I can only stare at him, because suddenly I have no words.

Coach bursts through the door. "Aw," he says with grand

mock disappointment, "nobody's dead. I guess that means you two have worked things out like gentlemen. Am I right?"

"You are right, Coach," Kelly says, and makes a big deal of extending his hand for me to shake.

"Right, Coach," I say. And I shake.

I let him do it to me, so it's my own fault. Kelly got inside my head, and immediately it started messing me up every which way.

Every last player on the team seemed to get bigger, stronger, faster, more clever with each day of practice. I lost ground every day, and it's my own fault because I let Kelly get into my head. It's the oldest, most obvious trick there is, and I let him get away with it.

The first day, I threw myself at everything that moved, I charged like a freight train full of malice, and I hit almost nothing. I was overthinking, was the problem. The only problem. I had to get back to playing naturally, instinctively.

Every day, the situation deteriorated.

Before the end of the first week of practice as a member of the team, I get the call to come to the head coach's office.

"What's the problem, Mr. Sarafian?" Coach Muswell asks from the other side of his massive oak desk. "Are you injured? You don't do anybody any favors, son, by playing hurt and not telling anybody about it."

"I'm perfectly healthy, Coach."

"Have you been studying the playbook? Because you look

lost out there. If you're not in the wrong spot, then you're in the right spot but about three seconds too late on every play."

"I know the playbook by heart, Coach. I'm just taking time to get adjusted to things, that's all."

"Well, Keir, I have to tell you, you don't have much time left for adjustment. Season starts next week, and if you don't raise your game significantly, I can't guarantee you're going to still stick with the team. Frankly, I had to cut a couple of guys who were playing a whole lot better than you are now. Where's that tackling machine I saw the day before cuts?"

"He's right here, sir."

"Is he? Well, okay, then. When you leave my office, make sure you take him with you. Because he's useless up here. We need him down on the field, understand?"

"I understand, Coach."

I don't sleep at all. I roll around, trying to shake Kelly out of my head, trying to remember the right things I did that I need to do again. I need to do it all again, and then again, and again, and again, day after day . . . forever.

I have to do it. I will do it.

I bring everything I have to the practice field the next day. Kelly is strutting around, full of confidence and chatter as if he knows something I don't, and it is making me demented. I see him sharing jokes with guys, making a big show of it, talking close into somebody's helmet, then the two of them laughing like donkeys.

That is motivation.

I feel it all coming back, all the right stuff, the toughness and the feel for the game, the lust for hard contact. Then, right from the whistle, I'm all over it.

All over the field, mostly. Aimlessly. I am somehow worse than any day so far, and I know it. I feel the humiliation and futility and I cannot even get it out by hitting hard, because the more I try to blast through it, the more foolish I look when I miss and tumble past the play entirely. So I gradually slow everything down, trade hitting for grabbing, and as the day winds down, I can feel everything winding down.

The clincher is a play I follow reasonably closely, a dump pass to Kelly, who then has a lot of daylight down the sideline where he can rack up one more touchdown on me and make his victory complete.

But shockingly I find myself gaining on him for the first time all day. Energized, I turn on the jets and make my last stand, running him down, dragging him by the shoulder pads and planting him on the turf ten yards short of a score.

The adrenaline from this one tackle is making me light-headed, and I'm sure I can build on this. I can come back, I can climb back up to where I ought to be.

I look down on him with at least this small bit of triumph and hope before I let him off the ground.

He gives me a big generous smile. Then he hollers, "Rape! Help me, someone! He's at it again! *Rapist!*"

I can hear scores of pounding feet like a cattle stampede,

over even the laughter, as players and coaches come running.

But at least Kelly isn't smiling anymore, and he's not yelling filth while I whale and whale on him, shutting that mouth up for at least this moment.

Coach Muswell tells me to come directly to his office as soon as I've showered.

put everything I've got now into moving along as if nothing unusual has happened. It is a college, after all, and people go to college to learn. I can learn.

When Joyce calls to see how I'm doing, it comes as a surprise. I haven't seen her since I made and then unmade the football team, and I'm afraid to find out what she might have heard about my behavior. We've exchanged a couple of texts, but that didn't tell either of us much about where we are at right now. Naturally, I'm not there at the time she calls, since I have statistics, Spanish, and English composition classes and yes, they all seem like they're markedly more difficult now that I'm an ordinary civilian post-athlete student.

But Fabian talks to her for forty-five minutes, so that puts the whole day in the win column, right? While everyone else in the world is playing football or talking on the phone, I'm listening to a stats lecture that sounds like Spanish to me, a Spanish class that sounds like an opera with the whole class suddenly in the mood to contribute all at once, all period, and an English class that I swear is nothing but the professor reading all twenty students their last rites one by one. The prof is lifeless, doesn't care who knows it, and only perks up when he tells us—again—how he got tenure on the first day that tenure was invented and hasn't had to work a day since. While my mind wanders, I come up with a prognostication, calculated in my head in Spanish, that everyone in that class is going to die two years earlier than they were supposed to just because of exposure to this man.

This is not what my mind should be doing. Joyce has her geology, and her devotion to it is a beautiful thing to behold. I can say for a fact that she has no issues with the word "love" when it comes to rocks. For a few seconds before I had anything to eat this morning, it occurred to me that it might be clever to point this fact out to her. Then I had a banana, a bowl of Grape-Nuts, and a glass of orange juice. This was followed almost instantly by the realization, coming up like a fiery sunrise, of the idiocy of revealing my jealousy. Of rocks.

Fabian has his "Transatlantic Literature from the Romantic to the Edwardian," which when I say it, sounds like I made it up to make him sound dweebier than he already is. But the way he crows it all loud and proud, you could almost believe there's crowd surfing in his classes.

As for myself and my concentrated area of study, I am a

committed undecided. Which I know doesn't help things at all. So much of me was supposed to be saturated in football. Is this all there is now?

"All righty, Keir, I have been seriously looking forward to seeing you," Fabian says as I enter the dining hall.

That is a greeting guaranteed to call me to attention, and I can't think of anybody else who would possibly say it these days.

"You have? That can't be good. If one of the high points of my day was seeing me, I would feel very, very sorry for myself."

"You already do," he says, shutting me right up and continuing on. "But we are not going to ruin date night by talking about that."

I look around me every which way to see if anybody possibly might have heard, though the curious stares I'm getting in return probably have more to do with my bug-eyed, swivel-head gawking than anything else.

I do want to thump him when he calls it that. We do this once a week now, meet for dinner after classes, to break up the monotony. And he insists on saying that, at least once every time, even though he knows it makes me want to thump him. *Because* he knows, is truer, and because of course I never do thump him.

He's plunked himself onto the seat across from me at the St. Lawrence Commons, the largest dining hall on campus, named for the patron saint of cooking, apparently, and more often referred to around here as LarryCom. He's clearly bursting to elaborate on his peculiar opening statement by saying something even more bizarre.

"Well, go on then," I say.

"What did you do today?" he says, grinning with the intensity of somebody who still believes that clowns only want to bring joy to children's lives.

I wait for another clue, but impatience comes quick and sharp.

"Is that a gag question? Because I don't even know where to go with that."

"Doesn't matter anyway. That's my point, that whatever you were doing, I'm betting I was doing the exact same thing, at more or less the exact same time. What do you think of that?"

"What do I think? Well, since I'm very hungry, I'll jump straight to the end. I think you're nuts. Your behavior is unfathomable to me. You're really happy and I don't know why, and you're bringing me into it and I don't know why—"

"I spoke to Joyce on the phone today, for *for-tee-five min-utes*."

"Yes, Fabian, you told me that. Remember? We crossed paths when I was on the way to Spanish and you were on the way to the *Yurt*. That's perfect for you, by the way, a yurt. What the hell is in there, anyway?"

"It's the Writing Center. But, Keir, I talked, on the phone, for for-tee-five minutes, to—"

"You told me. You were telling everybody, as far as I could tell."

"She is just, sooooo wonderful, though. I'm still buzzing from it."

"I'm happy for you, man, I really am. Good luck with that. Let me know how it goes."

"Awww," he says, and reaches over to give the back of my hand a fairly crisp slap. "Don't be stupid. You've got nothing to worry about. All we talked about was you."

"Really?"

"Of course. But that's not the point. Stop making everything all about you. The *point*, dear roommate, is that at forty-five minutes I clocked up more time on the phone, talking to a girl, than all the rest of my phone time with girls, my whole life, combined."

I'm happy for him and befuddled at the same time. None of which is helped by my being starving.

I go with the trusted fallback gesture that does the job when all else fails.

Double thumbs-up.

He doubles 'em up right back at me.

If everybody in LarryCom isn't embarrassed *for* us right now, then the building is devoid of any human souls at all.

"And I'm buying," Fabian says as we slide out of our seats. He's got a leer on him, made worse by a wink—dear God, the wink—that comes close to making me forget he is Fabian Delmonico. He made buying dinner and talking to Joyce sound somehow fused together and all wrong.

"You are like hell," I say.

We stand in front of the glass, staring at the entrees for a stupidly long time, since they don't really change very much from one visit to the next. Chicken Cordon Bleu is swapped out for boneless breast of chicken in a creamy peppercorn sauce. But that just sounds to me as if they took the CCB and pulled it inside out and there you go, more or less, there's your CCP.

Anyway, I always order the chicken. And I order it quickly. Fabian does things differently. So we stand, stare, linger in front of the entree display while he decides, and although there is no logjam of people being kept from their meals by my friend's indecision, this always makes the six-foot-three scowling food-service guy seem personally angry. He stands on his side of the entree divide, in his paper hat and his lengthy white apron, arms folded and hands clutching an oversize serving fork and spoon set like nunchuks.

Fabian is never intimidated by this, because he never notices it. For me it's like I get to come in on the most tension-packed part of the same martial arts movie over and over.

"Try the chicken," I say. I know he hates chicken, ethically. It's impossible for any human, even this guy, to hate chicken based on flavor or texture.

"I hate chicken," he says.

"Right, I forgot," I say, and start picking at my dish before it goes cold. The nunchuks man points a big warning fork at me, and I stop. This is almost exactly what "date night" is like every week. It's pathetic, and it's lame, and I'm starting to worry about what I would do without it.

"The whitefish?" Fabian asks me, or the guy behind the counter, or the crowd.

I'm the only one who answers, though. "I wouldn't."

I already know he is going to go for the tofu burger and green salad with sun-dried tomatoes and halloumi. I'm pretty sure the guy who's going to have to serve it to him already knows too. But this needs to run its course, and where do any of us have to go anyhow?

"Was that your whole story back there?" I ask. "That's what you were all excited about, telling me the same story about the same phone call that you already told me about six hours earlier?"

His nose is just about to make contact with the glass. "Shush," he says.

"Shush? No, I won't shush. You are boring the pants off me, my chicken with creamy peppercorn sauce is right now transforming itself back into its Cordon Bleu state just for something to do, and I think the least you could do is continue a conversation that *you* started, while we all wait for you to order the stupid tofu burger and green salad with sun-dried tomatoes and halloumi."

For the first time in quite a while, he straightens up and looks at something other than the food. He looks at me.

"I don't always get that."

"Yeah, you do."

"No way. I am not that predictable. Nor am I that lacking in imagination or spontaneity."

"Uh-huh. What did you mean, you were doing the same thing I was doing at the same time today?"

He is completely distracted, trembling with the tension, squeezing his two fists tight as he stares at that tofu burger like nobody has ever stared before.

"How are the Swedish meatballs?" Fabian asks in such a fantastic, pathetic squeaky squeal that the guy behind the counter doesn't even bother answering.

I scooch up right beside him, two little boys mesmerized by an aquarium, or a bakery.

"That is some unusually luscious-looking tofu, I have to admit," I admit, even though I don't at all have to.

"I do not need to get that burger," he says.

"What were we doing the same today?" I ask. "Was it this? Maybe you were having some kind of psychic vision, and what you saw was the two of us both staring at a tofu burger together, when neither one of us was going to order it."

"I'll have the whitefish, please," he says, and it's that voice again, only louder and more strangled and metallic, and it's such a glorious thing that the scowl melts off the server's face while he laughs and I laugh, and I put my arm around my nutty deter-mined pal's shoulders because, I guess, that's what you do.

Fabian manages to have a little laugh at his own expense, even as the fish makes him wince already just by arriving on the counter.

I am paying for our food and drinks when he says, in a whole other voice, not the squealy one, not the excited happy one. It's a voice that feels like it is just for us.

"I was going to make a joke," he speaks, "about how we were doing the same thing because we both spent our afternoon concerned about nothing but you."

I take my change and stare at him.

"Cold," I say, walking by him. I didn't say "untrue," however.

"Yeah, you're right," he says. "So I'll leave the joke out but still tell you that I spent the afternoon on you. First, talking to Joyce. Then Ray. Then, Keir, the athletic director's office called. And the bursar's office."

It's as if the entire big dining hall is controlled by one dimmer switch. And it's dimming. I feel somewhat like I felt on a few occasions on the football field when I took an especially cracking shot to my head. It's all a bit fuzzy, and I wonder for a few seconds if the darkness is going to keep on darkening and maybe I won't make it back to our table first. "Keir, okay?" I hear Fabian as if he is half a mile behind me. "Keir, okay?"

And the answer to that is most definitely no. Until we do get within reach of our table.

And Joyce is sitting there. She is smiling her broad brilliance the entire width of the table, and the surrounding tables, until she relights the whole place and the answer becomes most definitely yes, I am okay.

silver lining mining

have my head under the pillow because Joyce is trying to talk to me and spoil the bliss.

"But come on, Keir, you didn't really think they were going to go on paying you a football scholarship for four years without you playing any football."

"A half scholarship," I say.

"A half scholarship. Still, the point remains the same. Take the pillow off your face, will you?"

Reluctantly, I do. "I traveled forever. I came such a long way to be here. It can't just all fall apart so quickly."

"You're taking the total doomsayer position, Keir. Don't let yourself get so down. They can't be completely heartless. I cannot believe they would do that. Something can be worked out. Just go to the meeting, think positively, look for any potential bright side, and you will undoubtedly find one."

She is propped up on her elbow, looking down at me still stuck to my pillow but at least no longer under it. I can't help smiling as she smiles, but I have to shake my head in wonder at the same time.

For somebody who doesn't want to be loved, she's going about it very badly.

"You pretty much always do that, don't you?" I say. "Bright side, bright side, relentlessly hopeful, always looking for it."

"And always finding it," she says triumphantly. "It's something I got from my dad. He called it 'Silver Lining Mining,' and he always made me promise I would keep digging until I found it."

I'm about to compliment her and her father when I think about it maybe more than I should.

"But then, he's telling you to go mining, underground, for clouds. That doesn't really work because silver lin—"

Her smile, my main source of light, evaporates.

"Get out," she says.

"What? Wait. No, Joyce, don't."

I desperation-lunge for her arm as she tries to get away. I pull her back down onto the bed, intending to launch the fullest batch of apologies I can think of.

"Ow . . . ow! Stop it, Keir, let go!"

She looks furious and worried as she stares at her arm, my hand on it, and I'm panicked because I didn't mean to hurt her at all.

"I didn't mean to hurt you, Joyce, I swear. I was just playing."

"Then let go," she says.

I do, I let go, of course I do. But now I'm even more concerned about her getting away from me than when she was actually trying to. She sits on her side of the bed, looking at a red mark on her arm that isn't so bad, will probably not even be there in ten minutes, but definitely should not be there now. I know that, I understand that.

"I didn't mean to hurt you, Joyce. I'm really sorry. Really, really sorry."

She nods, more like nodding to her arm, to that red mark, than to me. As if they are agreeing something.

"I said I'm sorry," I say again. "And for what I said about the silver linings and your dad and all. It was just that, well, clouds are up in the sky, not—"

"My father," she says, "is a lovely, gentle man. And a very happy one, I might add. So you might want to try following his advice rather than correcting it." She has turned her full attention on me now in a way that almost makes me wish she'd go back to examining the arm.

"You're right," I say. "I have a habit of saying and doing . . . unhelpful things. I'm trying my best not to be like that anymore, but it's turning out to be harder than I expected. Just like everything else is turning out to be harder than I expected."

"Maybe you should start by doing something about those expectations," she says.

"Well, as of right this minute, I don't have any at all, so I guess that's a start. Clean slate, clean break."

I nod, look down at my hands, which are folded now pleadingly in my lap.

"You haven't had much experience with girls, have you, Keir?"

"I guess it shows, then?"

"Everything shows eventually, if you start getting close to somebody."

"Really?" I ask. "You really think that?"

"You look surprised, for an idea that's not all that revolutionary. That's a little bit cute. But you also look a little bit nervous, which is less cute."

"No," I say quickly, as if I can blow those thoughts out of the atmosphere the way a smoker tries to pretend he wasn't just smoking. "I'm just thinking people can change, right? They grow, they learn, they evolve. They don't wear signs of every place they've been, the people they've been with, things that they've grown out of, the thoughts they don't have anymore."

"You mean, just like resetting the clock at some point? You can't do that."

"Sure you can," I say.

"Not really," she says in that attractive way she has of saying everything with firm quiet confidence. It's not altogether attractive to me just now.

I do not want to debate, but I do not want to agree.

"Time will tell, as they say," I say, joining up with who-ever *they* are.

"It will," she says. "Without a doubt, it will."

"Let's just hope it doesn't tell too much, right?" I say, chuckling and pointing her way like I'm some cheesy comic from the god-awful golden age of television.

The line dies the death it deserves.

"Hmmm," she says, loaded. "How come you didn't have girlfriends?"

I shrug. "Because I never felt like I wanted to try to have a girlfriend."

"Mmmm," she says thoughtfully. "Maybe you should have."

We both sit there for several minutes, silently on either side of her bed. After the talking, this comes as a real bless-ing. I am acutely aware of such things now, gaps in my human file. Like the fact that I have never experienced a situation anything like this long silence with somebody. With a girl. On a bed.

She gets up abruptly, and out of reflex I do the same. I'm anxious about this until I see her looking at me in a softer way, and then giggling a little as I join her in making the bed.

"Are you finding me funny again?" I ask. "Because that would be outstanding."

"Yes and no," she says.

"Great. I'll take that and quit while I'm ahead."

"Listen, will you? Yes, I am finding you funny, but it's

something from before, not something now. When we were first together. I figured then you weren't exactly a lady-killer or anything. I thought to myself, that is definitely not the underwear of a guy who thinks getting any action is a realistic possibility."

I should be mortified. The fact that I'm not may be the strongest indicator yet that my reactions to social situations don't line up the way they're supposed to. Instead this makes my spirit rise.

"That's me, Joyce. I have to say on that one, you got me exactly."

"Yeah," she says, and points. "And you're still wearing them."

But it is a solid lock, guaranteed, I never will again.

I can evolve.

"Remember," Joyce says as she pushes me, forcefully, toward the door.

The time has gotten away from us and I have classes. Academics are my full-time occupation as of now, and dropping *that* ball would look especially bad when the time came to plead with the bursar for mercy.

"Remember to be positive, confident, and optimistic, Keir, and it will go better, you'll see."

"Look for the silver lining," I say as she opens the door for me. And I say it with sincerity and nothing else.

She looks at me, unimpressed. I shouldn't have gone back to that topic, that bad time back there.

"Also remember, a guy with no major and no direction shouldn't try to tell the geology student about mining. Just like he shouldn't question anybody's father on what a good and happy man should say."

The girl waves, and then the door snaps shut.

two hearts telling tales

wouldn't even be getting out of bed if he didn't make me.

"Come on, now," Fabian says. "You have to be on time, and on your game. You have to be sharp." He's snapping his fingers annoyingly but remarkably fast in front of my face.

"Why do I have to be all those things? And why do I have to be them to that rhythm you're snapping at me?"

"You know, Keir, sometimes just trying, making like you care, showing some respect, can go a long way with people."

"I've been trying, I do care, I have respect," I say, but I'm not even doing a good job of selling it to myself. I tip back over and lie on the bed on my side as soon as Fabian leaves me. It feels like some effort to roll my lifeless self over on the bed to look out at the broad bright sky that seems like it has been right there and exactly this perfect every day since I got to Carnegie. I can hardly believe that sky and I are both in the same place, that we are both real.

I start to cry. Again.

It's unlikely that I got more than an hour and a half of sleep in total last night. I would roll and wrestle myself for ages and then finally nod, only to fall into dreams that were waiting for me, and then it would get even less restful than thrashing around awake was. Awake, I could not stop my tumbling mind from rolling through all the things here, in this life, so good, so right, so according-to-plan but that were getting away from me at a sickening pace. It was not supposed to be like this. It was supposed to be so many other things, other ways.

When we danced, her hands did most of the dancing, flittering up and down her back, sides, hips, pursuing my hands like squirrels chasing each other up and down a tree. Somehow, it seemed every place I put them was an inappropriate place, so I had to keep moving them, and then the way I was moving them became the problem, so you can appreciate that Gigi Boudakian was being a little difficult to deal with.

At the table it was more of the same. She was holding my wrist with one hand while holding her idle fork with the other. Then she was elbowing me. Then she was whipping out her cell phone and dialing . . .

"What, what, what?" I said pleadingly, folding my hands prayerlike and earning a reprieve.

"You are drunk, Keir," she said.

"No," I said seriously.

"Yes," she said.

"Not really," I said.

"Yes, really," she said.

"A little."

"A lot."

Hmm.

"Well, everybody is drunk."

"Not everybody."

"Everybody."

"Not me."

"Well, whose fault is that?"

"Listen, Keir . . . ," she said, and there wasn't a tremendous amount of suspense about where this was headed, since she had her phone out and buttons beeping as she spoke.

"I'm sorry," I said into her free ear.

She looked up at me with a hard, penetrating, not unkind or unfair look.

She was so decent. She was lovely and sharp and she was smart and classic. I suddenly felt like I had been wiping my hand on my sleeve, shouting obscenities, fighting, pissing in the punch bowl. She was great. She was lovely and decent, and so, so deserving of all the best things, and would surely wind up with them later on, in college, in love, in the carpet business or on Broadway, in life, if she could get through the degradation of this.

"Please, please don't leave," I said. "Please. Please."

She looked at me harder still.

"Please."

Damn, she could look at you a long, cold minute.

"Get it together," she said firmly.

I felt like the luckiest guy there. I got it together, while Gigi Boudakian and I never did. Though I never stopped thinking about it.

It was a good plan, for good reasons. I would find love here, and purpose and direction and respect, and I was on my way, I was.

Then sleep was no escape at all but instead an even more desperate fight, trying to keep all the other beasts at bay, keep the bad things, the wrong things back there where they had to stay and were supposed to stay. So many miles, so many turns, so many stinking rotten buses were supposed to have settled this. So many separations, endings, shifts. Deaths.

From all that, I should at least have earned my freedom. From what I had to leave behind.

So I spent my night awake, mourning, grieving my pathetic failure to reset the clock. And asleep, in terror of all the dead stuff promising never to leave me alone. It wasn't supposed to be like this. Not anymore, not again. It was a long time now since I felt this, the awful two hearts at war inside me, threatening to break me in half, split me from the chest on out. I'm only supposed to have one now, here. I have done everything necessary to make that happen. Everything has been for that, and everything has been for nothing.

I can feel them pounding so hard, so loudly, I cover my chest with my hands, desperate to keep it to myself. They are two strong angry hearts with two different tales to tell, and one of them has got to win. I thrashed all night with them, powerless to do a thing.

Except, I cried a lot, I know I did. Probably loud enough to keep my innocent roommate awake nearly as much as I was. But he didn't let on then, and here facing the window, I'm trying my best not to let him know I'm at it again now. It would be too much, unfair to him and humiliating to me. I couldn't even explain to him why I'm like this. I'm better than this, I'm stronger than this. When did I lose all that, and how and why?

"You want me to come with you?" he asks from his perch at the foot of his bed. I can tell his location, because I know the dynamics of this room and its residents by this time. Probably better than I know anything else.

This alone, this one small sentence has me emotional again. The mere sound of this odd, unfathomable human, offering me his modest solidarity, is enough to make me feel like bawling again. But I can't, I don't. I say, "No, thanks," instead.

Because Fabian does things according to some unique internal programming I will never understand, he responds in a way that doesn't make any sense to me.

"I can come with you to the meeting," he says, as if the subject has not come up already.

"Thanks," I say. "Good of you. It'll just make me look even sadder and weaker than they already think I am. But, yeah, thanks."

"You're welcome," he says.

Neither one of us moves, or makes a sound, for several minutes. Again, a thing that never happened before, my being in a room with another person and no sound for so long, is happening for the second time this week.

"What are you afraid of, Keir?"

"I don't know."

"What's the worst that could happen?"

"I don't know. I'm trying not to think about worst things."

I've been thinking about nothing else.

"Do you think . . . No, I'm not asking you any more questions, I'm just going to say, maybe it's not completely real, whatever's happening in your head."

He's only trying to be kind, trying to help. But he does not know, could not know, and I can't simply allow this wrong perception of me to hang there unchallenged.

"You don't understand, Fabian, all right? You can't, nobody can, only I can. That is the reality."

He is not lost for words on the subject, and his reply comes quickly and smoothly. "'Is *all* that we see or seem, just a dream within a dream?'"

That is so precisely, murderously the wrong thing for me to hear after the night I had that a chill runs through me. I grasp and clutch and pull the sheet all bunchy over the parts of my back and hip it can reach without my having to work to untangle it. I'm certain now that he heard me struggling through the night. Screamy dreaming the revival of the nasty, old reality. Waking panting over the dying new, pathetic, stupid reality. And over. And over again.

"What the hell was that?" I say.

"Edgar Allan Poe."

"Well, don't do it again."

The silence that happens now is an eerie silence I don't like, one that I can stop and must stop.

I roll over, stand up strong, and give him a look to assure him that I am ready to go to this meeting and ready to take care of my own business.

He stares a few extra ticks. Studying my posture, my face, my eyes in a way he's not supposed to, before hopping up off his own bed.

"Right, that's it, I'm coming with you."

It's our first spat, as I go about the process of getting ready, finding clothes that will help me stand in that room as an equal with whoever is there, an adult whose opinion and point of view need to be taken seriously no matter what outcome results from all this.

I will present myself like a man, dignified, the way I have always known a man should carry himself.

I never iron, I don't make an honest effort at folding, I'm inconsistent in how I decide whether a shirt is clean or dirty after a single wearing. I'm trying my best to assemble outfits one at a time from articles out of my dresser and closet. One at a time I dress in these outfits and present myself to the mirror. Each time when I see what's there, I wince and stoop over a little farther as I skulk out of the mocking mirror's range. It mocks, and it can't even smell the worst of it.

Fabian pretends to ignore me, but even the mirror is onto him. By the time I try to drag myself in front of it a fourth time, Fabian refuses to allow it. He steps between me and the reflection that will defeat me before I even get out the door.

"There is no more time for this ridiculousness," he says, holding a pressed, vibrant sky-blue button-down shirt on a hanger.

"It is pretty nice," I say.

"Put that on," he says. "The black pants will just about do."

I'm putting on the shirt, smelling it, not perfumey detergent or anything, just the scent of clean, just exactly that. It's hard to think of a better scent than clean. He's now slipped over to his closet and returned.

"What's that doing here?" I ask.

"And you'll take a vest, to finish it off nicely," he says.

"What did I do to you?"

"This will make you look smart, sharp, confident."

"Well, that sounds like a powerful vest. But you're thinner than I am. It'll be too small."

"Nah, we just adjust these two straps in back and you're set."

I stare at the thing dangling in front of me like a big spider dropping from the ceiling. It is so far from anything I ever would have worn before.

Which is as good a reason as any to wear it now.

"For luck," I say as he slips it over my shoulders like a professional tailor.

"For luck," he says, adjusting those buckles before I attempt to button up the front.

"I thought I said you couldn't come to the meeting," I say as we walk up the long hill to the admin building and the athletic director's office on the third floor.

"You did," he says. "I'm just on my way to the Yurt, so I thought I'd walk along with you."

"The Yurt is way back there." I point out with my thumb.

"I know. But I need the exercise, you need the moral support, and the vest needs an escort."

"I'm the vest's escort."

"Yeah, well I'm vestcorting both of you. Because frankly, you're a walking disaster right now, as my grandmother would say."

"So, you don't trust me to walk up the hill, without your vest coming to some kind of harm."

"Relax, I don't think it's your fault."

I don't know if it's his intention or not, but Fabian manages to keep me engaged with that kind of nonsense the whole way. Until I'm standing in front of the building, ready to pull the door open, almost forgetting why I'm here.

"What *is* the Yurt, anyway?" I ask as I open the door.

"The Yurt is all things to all people." He shoots past me to get inside.

"No, I don't think it is, and what are you doing?"

"Walking up the stairs. You should join me."

"Fabian, come on now. You shouldn't be here."

"I'm just seeing you to the door. Because right now I wouldn't trust you to find your ass with your own two hands, as my grandmother would say."

I start following him. "That's what she would say, would she?"

"More or less. I cleaned it up a bit because you're fragile."

"Hey, I don't know what you think you might have heard last night . . . but you see *me* as fragile?"

"As a china teacup."

We reach the first landing. "This is terrific. I thought you were supposed to be boosting my confidence."

"That was just motivational crap to get you out of bed. Once you walk out the door into the big uncaring bastard world, you can decide for yourself whether to be predator or prey, young man, it's no skin off my nose."

"Your grandmother?"

"Yep."

"I think I might be starting to understand you," I say, continuing up toward the third floor. "But in that case, you should just scram, save your nose skin, and leave me to it, no?"

"No. If you turn out to be prey, it can be your own shirt that gets shredded and bloody."

We reach the third floor and the sign saying OFFICE OF THE ATHLETIC DIRECTOR. Fabian goes straight in before I can catch him.

"Hello," the secretary says immediately, in a reassuringly friendly manner. She's got soft-looking red-blond hair, painted turquoise fingernails at the tips of fine-boned hands. She could be not much older than us, but with adult-world responsibility. She's the gatekeeper in possibly the most powerful office in the whole college, where I'm just hanging on by my much grubbier fingernails. She has dimples when she smiles, and I would bet somebody loves her a lot.

We're only in the outer office, which is bigger than most inner offices I've ever been in. It's all dark wood, paneling, plaques and trophies and photos of great CC sports moments surrounding us. Most of it relates to the football team, but there's enough broader representation to make it clear that Carnegie College is a very successful NAIA program for boys and girls and badminton players and everybody.

"Hello," Fabian says when I pause too long on the dimples and the athletic display that he couldn't care less about. I don't mean the dimples, which I'm sure he appreciates just fine. "This is Keir Sarafian. He's got an appointment."

"Oh, right," she says. "Hello, Keir."

I startle at the sound of my name, and at the pleasant delivery of it.

"Hello," I say, and wave as if she's passing in a bus or something.

Before she has to do anything, the main office door swings open and the main man comes through it. "Kayley," he says while wagging a very unmenacing finger at her, "I thought we agreed that you would stop mesmerizing my visitors."

"We didn't agree to that, Dad," she says, closing her eyes to him and the scene.

The athletic athletic director strides into the room with his handshake hand already drawn out of its holster. He's six foot two, about 205 pounds, and I would be surprised if his default walk wasn't permanently locked on *stride*. He was a two-sport guy, football and basketball probably. Maybe baseball and basketball, since there's no detectable limp.

"Hello, Keir," he says, and the power of his handshake has me guessing football again. "I'm Mr. Evans, the AD here. But please call me Pete. I'm glad we are finally getting a chance to meet. I know there are a hundred different ways to communicate these days and I love them all, but I simply never feel quite right making decisions and judgments on people when I haven't had the chance to see them face-to-face. You can let your mind go all kinds of silly places before you actually shake a person's hand and get a sense of that person for yourself."

"That's true, sir," I say.

"Okay, I'm not going to force you to call me Pete. But *sir*? We have to be able to improve on that, no?"

I shrug, completely wrong-footed by this guy who is not the guy he was supposed to be. Not yet, anyway.

"Sorry, sir," I say. "That just feels right to me."

"Good home training," he says. "Good for you. You're a credit to your folks."

"Sorry . . . Pete?" Fabian says.

"Yes, my young friend?"

"Do I need to leave?"

"That depends. Are you here for some nefarious purpose?"

"No, not at all. I'm Keir's friend."

"Absolutely, absolutely. Any friend of Keir's is welcome here."

"Cool," Fabian says, very helpfully, "but I'm pretty much it, so no need to bring in a bunch more chairs or anything." He laughs. Kayley gives her head a slight pity tilt in my direction.

"At any rate," Mr. Evans says, "I think it's a good idea, actually, that Keir has a witness for himself in the room while we chat. Kayley will be in there, but she could be considered biased. She can't stand me. Right, Kayley?"

"Right, Pete," she says, dimpling on through the hatred.

"Okay, folks, come on in, get comfortable. I don't intend to keep you long."

As we file into the inner office, I lean close to Fabian's ear. "Hear that? *Witnesses.* That isn't good. When are opposing witnesses required for anything that isn't horrible? I was right. Here it comes."

"Way to go, Keir," he sighs. "Just keep that up, and the power of positive thinking will see you through."

Right, as if *silver lining mining* is going to alter events that were decided before we showed up.

Kayley is the last one in, and as she's closing the door, she says, "Great vest, by the way."

I don't get a word out before Fabian jumps in. "I was going to wear one too. He *made* me take it off because he thought we would look like twins. We don't even look alike. But yes, yes, it is a fantastic vest and ideal on him."

"Right, lady and gentlemen," Mr. Evans says from his high-back leather chair behind his sprawling oak desk. He swivels like a navy ship's radar dish as he addresses the assembly. And he's the first person I ever met who is more intimidating seated than standing up. "You know why we're here. We have a bit of an awkward situation none of us could have anticipated. . . ."

"The one thing he was right about," I say, running dangerously fast, headlong down the stairway. "It was good that I had a witness with me. Jesus, what a shit, huh?"

Fabian led on the way up to the third floor of the admin building, but I am definitely leading the way down. He's fallen off the pace, and when I hit the bottom floor and burst out into the fresh air, he is nowhere near me. I breathe deep and heavy as if I have barely gotten safely to the surface after a deep-sea dive.

"What did you say?" Fabian asks, exiting the building with a lot more breath to spare. It makes him sound more calmly rational, but that's an illusion.

I'm looking down, focusing on the buttons of the vest, which are fighting me as I try frantically to free myself. "You saw it. I'm so glad you were there. The whole thing was fixed. The day those two soccer freaks came to the team as walk-ons who could kick the ball a mile without costing any scholarship money at all, I was a goner. What a snake that guy was."

"A snake? Are you referring to the athletic director? Mr. Peter Evans? Pete? The guy who just served us gingerbread men that he made himself?"

"That's the guy."

The buttons are frustrating me into a frenzy now, refusing to budge, making me feel so trapped and unable to breathe properly.

"Hey, hey, hey, stop that," Fabian says, rushing up and smacking my hands down. I stand still like a good boy while he does some button-whisperer thing that makes them open up for him at the slightest touch.

I feel my chest become a little less constricted as he takes the vest off me.

"It wasn't like that, Keir," he says. "And *he* most definitely wasn't like that. You were treated with respect and consideration, hosted in the office of a very busy guy, who, as far as I can tell, didn't have to bother explaining anything to you at all."

I pivot and start my angry stomp back down the hill.

"See," I say, "once again, you just don't understand this stuff. That man just *stole* my scholarship. Four years. Stole my ticket, my education, my chance. Stole my life, basically, is what he did, because I gambled everything on this plan, everything. This was the life that had to work, because I cashed in the other one to get it. How can you not understand that?"

"I can, Keir, I can absolutely understand."

"How could you ever possibly understand?" I bark loudly, the fat syllables rolling down the hill in front of me.

For a few moments the argument dies down, which is probably good. But as I keep up my fury stride, I sense that he's not just quiet, he's not there.

I stop and turn to see him thirty yards behind me, his arms straight down by his sides, the vest he loaned me dangling from one hand.

"What?" I yell.

He stands.

"What, Fabian?"

He stands. Foot traffic passes him going up and coming down, left and right.

"Are you coming?" I call. Nothing. "Fine, stand. See ya."

I head on my way again, rage and gravity propelling me at a good clip. I pump the brakes some. I slow right down. I stop, and I growl, and I reverse direction.

He's all smug and satisfied as I come trudging all the way uphill in surrender.

"You make me feel terrible, Keir, watching you, listening to you. Miserable stuff."

"*You?*" I say. "I marched all the way back up here to listen to you tell me how terrible it is for *you*?"

"No," he says. "I don't want to tell you that, forget that. But I have to wonder, is this how it went, how it's gone, in the past for you?"

"There is no past for this. I was never cut from any team before. Never."

"But it didn't happen this time, either. You were not cut. You got thrown off, as a result of your actions. That's a critical difference. *The* critical difference. Did you not hear that?"

"Coach was going to cut me anyway. Already made up his mind."

"He says he wasn't. He says he was planning to give you more time to prove yourself. Mr. Evans said that was what he wanted as well. Nobody wanted you to fail, Keir."

"No, but they wanted me to do what I told them I didn't want to do. They tricked me, lured me into coming here to play defensive back when they knew I wanted to be a kicker. Then when the soccer jerks fell out of the sky and dropped a bomb on my whole plan, my whole *second* plan . . . the writing was on the wall for me."

"Well, they say otherwise, but it doesn't matter, because you'll never know, because you made the decision for them."

"Yeah, then if they really wanted to give me more time to prove myself, then why don't they just go ahead and do it?

Take me back on the team. I'm right here. All they'd need to do is ask, say, 'Sorry, Keir, it was just a misunderstanding and we'll get past it.'"

It's his turn to breathe heavily for some reason.

"Because it was not a misunderstanding. And because you practically *forced* them. Teams, of any kind, consider assaulting teammates to be among the most serious of treasonable offenses. Nobody would ever give you a chance to do that twice. If it were me, I wouldn't take you back either."

And there we have it.

"Right, okay," I say, raising my hands in surrender. "You too, I guess. Anyway, you get your private room back like you were expecting before I blew it for you.

"And don't expect me to come crawling back up the hill again," I say, marching back down the hill again. "Because I won't."

"Ah, cripes, Keir," he says, and I'm happy to hear his goofy loafers slapping the ground as he runs after me. Victory is sweet. Not to mention increasingly rare.

"Did you ever even read the commitment you signed with the school?" he says in the same pest voice he was using before I defeated him.

"I'm sure I did."

"Right, then you know that they were never guaranteeing you four years. Those agreements are reviewed at the end of each year to make sure you keep up academically, athletically, and as a citizen who isn't playing football for the respectable college by day and breaking into houses, terrorizing the townspeople by night."

I whip over in his direction as he says this, looking for what he's getting at.

Turns out he's just getting at what he was already getting at. "But none of it matters if you get fired. They don't owe you anything."

I look away from him again, but I don't have any back-lip this time, and I don't have the fight left for it.

"I came so far for this, Fabian," I say.

"I know, man, that's rotten. But look on the bright side: they're paying for this semester, which I think is generous and which, might I say, you would not have gotten without my forcing my way into the meeting to save you from yourself."

I nod, three times, four, then five, then eventually I don't bother raising my head back up.

"You were quite a thing to see in action," he says, and I lift my head because I'm so demented I think for an instant that this is a good story. But I see his sorry befuddled grin, and my head drops once more. "I think if you were left to your own devices, by the time you crawled out of the room, you would have owed *them* a pile of money."

"I appreciate everything you did, and everything you tried to do for me. Despite how it might seem. I am grateful."

"Well, now you have a semester of breathing room to get yourself right. Concentrate on getting a solid foundation laid down academically and socially, while working out your finances for next semester and the three great years coming after that."

"Yeah," I say, meaning nothing. Because I've got nothing. No money, and no clue how this system even works. This sad state of affairs exists, of course, because somebody always took care of all the details for me. And I was always happy to let him.

It felt like a great arrangement at the time. Now look at me. Or better yet, don't.

We reach the bottom of the hill, where a road splinters off to the right toward the chapel and the Yurt beyond it. Straight ahead leads to the halls of residence.

Fabian starts veering right while I'm prepared to let gravity and momentum take me home, a junk car being rolled the last hundred yards after running out of gas.

Until I'm veering. I am being tugged rightward by the tail of the shirt, which I pulled out as soon as I didn't have to play dress-up. This could be a magnetic force, or something more biological, a homing instinct, but Fabian's shirt seems committed to going where Fabian goes.

Or it could merely be that Fabian is tugging me.

"Come to the Yurt. You might enjoy it," he says.

"Aren't you going there to do work of some kind?"

"Work? At a Writing Center? No, no, no, a place like this isn't where people come to write. It's where they come to refine their skills in the equally important craft of assing around publicly, the way real writers do. And if the crowd is made up largely of other assing writers, all the better."

He's still towing me, even though there's no longer any need. I'm happy to check out the place finally. Happy just to be invited along.

"I'm not an assing writer, however."

"Hey, you never know. You could have the makings of a massive assing writer. Personally, I've seen a lot of the right stuff in you already."

I'm not quite keeping up with him verbally, though I often don't. There's a fairly strong sensation of ridicule coming across nonetheless.

The Yurt looks like a flying saucer built by lumberjacks. It's round, with vertical dark wood slats forming an exterior skin, and a band of sly squinting windows running all the way around. It looks like it's wearing a gray felt hat. It is the last college structure on this side of campus, planted midway between the tired-looking old stone chapel and the point where the woods become truly dense. If you kept on going that way, the next stop would be Joyce's beloved glacial erratic stone.

There are flyers and posters tacked up and completely covering the outside surface for about three feet on either side of the door. The door itself is rounded on the top and appears to be arching a big eyebrow above the level of the roofline all around it. There is little activity in the leaf-strewn space around the Yurt, and just some soft words over spare jazz music coming from within it.

It is a strange and strangely isolated little place. Right away I feel at home here, in a way I have been hoping to feel at home since I left my home.

Then I'm caught up short just as Fabian pulls the door open and ushers me in. It's there again, in big yellow painted letters orbiting the room.

O wad some Power the giftie gie us
To see oursels as ithers see us!

"What's that doing here?" I demand, as if Fabian had some explaining to do.

"Why wouldn't it be here? It's poetry. This is the Writing Center. Poetry is writing. . . ."

"Yeah, but that one. That exact one. It's like it's following me. I never saw it before in my life, and now I've already seen it twice since I've been here."

He nods at me, smiling. "The ghost of the plowman poet stalks Keir Sarafian!"

"Shush," says the only other person in the Yurt, a guy with straight long nearly-white blond hair, hunched over a mixing desk and a microphone.

"The campus Internet radio station also uses the space. Campus radio takes things a lot more seriously than the Writing Center, I can tell you."

"I didn't even know we had a campus radio station."

"I think that's one reason that they're so serious. Nobody

really pays them any attention, because for them it's all about the gear and gizmos more than what they do with it. Just proves my point that technology is a fad, and it's only the words that endure."

"Yes, like these enduring words. They're starting to give me the creeps, like they're stalking and talking to me personally."

"Well, maybe," he says, doing a slow-motion pirouette like he's seeing the words for the first time. "I mean, the title *is* 'To a Louse.'"

"What does it mean, Fabian?"

"It's the singular of 'lice.'"

"The rest of it, if you don't mind?"

"Well, basically it means that a person would be much less of a shit if he knew what he really looked like."

I'm doing the same slow spin move, reading the words again, then again, trying to *feel* them better, to see if poetry itself could honestly have the kind of power that can make a guy see things differently.

"So then it's the school motto or something? Has the place got a tradition of attracting assholes, is that it?"

"Yes!" the guy at the radio controls barks, before adding a *shush* that also sounds like a bark.

"I'm outta here anyway," I say, heading right back the way I came. What was seeming homey a few minutes earlier now feels claustrophobic, airless, and unwelcoming.

"Where are you going?" Fabian says, walking right behind me.

"Going to live in the forest," I say, thinking that that would be the ideal situation if I could manage it.

"Want company?"

"No," I say. "I definitely do not want company. The trees and my thoughts will be plenty."

"Okay," he says, dropping back, then heading to the Yurt for whatever it is he gets out of the big stupid coconut of a place.

I am just about to enter the woods proper when I stop and call out to him.

"I was wrong about the thoughts and trees. I don't want to be alone with them. And I think they feel the same way."

We tromp through the woodland, being largely quiet aside from the crunch beneath our feet. It has the effect of talking something out just the same. Better than the same, because sometimes the words themselves can turn out to be your biggest nemeses when you are trying to sort your way through stuff that wants to resist sorting.

"Who was she?" Fabian's voice comes light and stunning, a forest thing with wings and knowing.

"Who?" I ask because that is as much as I dare to ask.

"The girl you loved so much that you couldn't have any girlfriends. Was that who Gigi was? Is that why you dream her, like when you called out her name?"

I walk faster, much faster.

"I told you," I yell out, "that was just a sound I made. Gigi was not a name, it was a sound."

266

The sound of her name. For the love of God, that is the thing, some power, that makes my heart break open again at the sound of it, break right into the two hearts all over again. I am petrified at the combined torture of both of them slamming my insides mercilessly, trying to kill me. For no reason other than that I loved a girl so much, insanely much. And that I still love her absolutely, irredeemably. Guiltily. It's this, causing life to become a pounding, throbbing nightmare until I need to flee from it.

Which I couldn't even do. I know this now, am terrified by it, and am running this very minute because of that fear, as if I can somehow elude this thing by shifting and dodging and sprinting through the woods more maniacally than anyone would have thought possible.

"I'm sorry," Fabian says as I stare down at him. "I promise I meant nothing by it but to try to understand your troubles a little better."

It took him ten minutes to catch up to me, and between the healthy dash through the cool piney air and the bit of isolation to clear my thoughts, things are already significantly better than when we last saw each other.

"I don't have any troubles. But thanks."

He nods amiably, folds his arms in a relaxed manner.

"I'm very glad to hear that, Keir. What with the difficult meeting this morning, the turmoil that I know you suffered through all last night, and the generally accelerating erratic behavior leading to here and now, and finding you squatting like a well-dressed gargoyle on top of a great big boulder, I might have drawn other conclusions. So thanks."

"It's a glacial erratic," I say.

"What, your disorder?"

"No, the rock. It's a glacial erratic, which I think means I am behaving precisely the way I am supposed to. As long as I'm residing up here."

"Okay, that's it, then. You have finally found the place where you belong."

"I have," I say.

He finally appears like he's reached what could be called fed up. He unfolds his arms, holds them straight up in the air, turns, and walks briskly away.

It makes me anxious, to see him go. It's not the end of the world, to have Fabian Delmonico march away from me in a conclusive way, but it manages to have an end-of-the-world feeling to it anyway.

"Can't you be happy for me?" I call at the point where I lose sight of him for the trees.

"I can't, Keir. I'm not going to lie to you to make you feel better. Especially since it won't make you feel better, just like nothing seems like it's going to make you feel better. I can't pretend I have you figured out. I can't even pretend to know you, really. I don't actually know anything about who you were even the day before you showed up at the residence halls."

It's getting very cold very quickly up on my rock, my glacial erratic where I belong.

"Maybe there was nothing before that day, Fabian. Just, maybe that."

"Okay," he calls. "You popped into existence right there. But you had some football scholarship money when you did. Now you don't. How do you figure to apply for any kind of tuition aid or loans or anything if there's no you with an educational transcript, a previous address, a family . . . ?"

"I'm an orphan," I snap.

"You are like hell an orphan. And on behalf of all us *real* orphans everywhere, you can go fuck yourself. I'm going to leave now, in the hope that you are like a tree that falls in the forest and if there's nobody there to hear it, he doesn't make a sound like an asshole. Now, I don't know whatever you did back there, or whatever happened to you. But the only rock-solid certain thing I do know is that you *have* to call your father. And if you don't, then I'm going to do it.

"Good-bye and enjoy your rock."

and a hard place

was just talking to a rock, and naturally your name came up."

"Oh, rocks will talk. Go back and tell them hello for me."

"You look great, Joyce. It's always a better day when I get to see your face. I'm a better me, when I get to see your face."

"That's a lot of pressure to put on one face."

"Is that why the face has been avoiding me?"

"What? Come on, I saw you on date night with Fabian."

I don't even have time to be horrified over the date-night crack.

"Yeah, and the more I think about that night and the more you stay away from me now, the more that night looks like some combination of pity and good-bye."

"Oh, now, I did not tell you good-bye. And I certainly don't pity you."

That's fine, since as of this minute I can do it myself.

"I didn't mean it to sound like that, Keir. Please, look at me."

Even when that face is all she is showing me through her narrowly opened door, I feel lucky.

"Would you like to come on out for a while? Just for a bit, for a walk? It's a perfect night out."

"Keir, it's freezing outside."

"Yeah, you're right. It is, I guess. I never minded the cold, though. Doesn't bother me like it does most people."

"Keir, you're shivering so hard I'm surprised all your joints don't just let go and leave your bones flopping around on the ground."

"I am?" I look at some of my bones and joints to check. "Wow, look at that. See, I was right, I'm not bothered by the cold, and my shivering proves it."

"That's quite a case you make there. Hon, I think you have a rare gift for taking the basic realities of a situation and arranging them into a whole different reality that you can believe and like better. If you are still uncertain about what degree to pursue, I recommend you give serious consideration to law, or theology."

"Okay," I say, as if it is the most obvious thing in the world that a deal is being struck between parties. "I will give your suggestion very serious consideration, and now I hope you will do me the same courtesy and come for a walk."

"No. Sorry, but no. It's cold, I have work to do, and

frankly, I just don't want to. I need to tell you, you seem kind of off. Are you feeling all right?"

I stand there, smiling at her bright star of a face all pinched into that narrow door space. I feel the shape of my smile, aware of doing just like before, trying to match the dimensions of the perfection of her smile. Even if she's not showing me that. Even while I feel myself going crooked and lopsided with the attempt, the failure, the humiliation of trying.

I feel the cold now. I damn do feel the cold now.

"I've had a difficult time of it today," I say, summing up with some dignity at least.

"You should go home to bed. That's the best thing. Before you make yourself sick. Go get tucked in, have a nice sleep for yourself, and then see what tomorrow brings for you. I bet it will be better things."

"Sleeping's not so great lately either. But maybe, if you would just go for a short walk with me, we'll hang our legs over, like remember? Through the bars and dangling off the bridge over the duck pond? That was one of the best times I ever had, and I'm absolutely convinced that if we can just reverse, reverse ourselves back to the pond and that time and then take it slower motion back to forward gear again, everything would get right as righteous this time. The plan could get back on track, and all the results, about us, about football, and tuition, and everything, will go like they're supposed to go. And, Joyce, believe me, the plan and the results are like wildest dream stuff the way I picture it, if things just go like they're supposed to go."

She is giving me a questioning, penetrating glare that is hurting my feelings, scaring me some, and making me angry all at once. It causes me to look away, pretending to notice a bird or a ghost or a blazing meteor that simply must be observed this second.

"That's what happens if I go for a walk with you? All that Shangri-la business will come of that one walk?"

"If everything goes the way it should," I say, encouraged by the progress.

"Go home, Keir. For your own sake, please just take yourself home."

"I don't have a home. I'm an orphan."

"That's very sad, hon, and I'm sorry for you. You still need to go."

"I was wondering, though, Joyce, if you had any more of that wine. Like before. Remember that? What a nice time. I didn't even think I really liked wine. That was delicious, though. We laughed, too. You said you found me funny, which I loved. I've kept that in mind ever since, and I'm making more of an effort to be funny."

"And it shows," she says, closing, then latching, her door before the dust can settle on sarcasm or support or even if she'd left the conversation open.

My face becomes the only warm surface of my body. I stand for just about as long as it takes a refrigerated brain to consider that it might be time to turn back before any more humiliation can take hold.

I am backing away when the latch snaps back in the other direction and Joyce reappears.

"Sorry I took so long," she says. She holds a bottle of red wine high in one hand, while her other hand brandishes a pair of black knit gloves. "I had to find these. Here's the deal. You can have the bottle, but not until you put the gloves on first. They're the cheapo one-dollar-one-size kind, but they'll do you for now."

I pull them on so quickly, half my fingers just about tear through the flimsy stitching at the ends. I raise my hands, wiggle the fingers as proof. Then I reach eagerly, both arms outstretched, for my reward, for the only thing I really want.

"The only thing I can give you is the wine," she says sadly, looking disapprovingly at my grasping. I drop one arm to my side, keeping the other one out to accept the bottle. "And only if you promise you will take it and go straight back to your room with it. Have some wine with Fabian, or have it alone if you must, but sip, and unwind, and let go, and sleep. Promise me that."

"I would promise you anything."

"Yeah, see, that there is a problem. Bad thing, Keir, not good thing. Bad."

"But I mean it. I would promise you anything, and I would not be lying."

274

She doesn't wait for what I might have expected, for the very specific promise about the wine and straight home. She jabs it into my gloved hand as if she doesn't care at all what I do once she closes her door.

"I know," she says. "I know you would mean it, and I know you wouldn't say something to me if you didn't believe it. But I don't think it ever even crosses your mind that just because something's not a lie doesn't mean it's not wrong."

"I don't understand. But thanks for the wine and gloves."

"You're welcome. I hope you have a nice, straight walk back, and a peaceful night."

She closes the door and latches it.

"What is *wrong* with you, you idiot?"

He slaps my face just before and then again just after inquiring about what my flaws might be. I open my eyes to see Fabian's face, upside down, over mine.

"I guess I don't know," I say, "so it's gotta be quicker if you just tell me."

He grabs me from under my arms and starts dragging me, until my feet get caught in the metal rails of the fence on the bridge over the duck pond.

"Hold on," I say, wriggling out of his grip and the railing's at once.

I stand up, look at him looking at me, then figure I'd better look at me. I have on my shoes, pants, and Fabian's blue shirt from the meeting with the AD, and a pair of stretch gloves. But I'm fine until I look at him once more and see him all bundled up like it's winter. He rips off his ski hat as if he's angry at his own head, then jams it down on mine even more aggressively. He gives my arm a wicked yank, pulling me in the direction of our dorm.

"You know it's a miracle the campus cops didn't find you. You'd really be in the shit then. Are you trying to kill yourself or something? Sleeping on the ground, in this cold, the damp cold, that's just what will happen. You'll catch something serious that you could die from. Oh, and you'd take your father with you, which is also very nice."

"Don't talk about my father," I say.

"I will," he says. "I will talk about him, talk to him, talk for him, and I'll call him Ray, and I will not have you telling me to do anything otherwise. I called Ray when I knew you wouldn't, ya big coward."

"You *called* him?"

"I told you I would."

"Yeah, but just because a person says something like that doesn't mean they're actually going to—"

"It does when this person says it."

"God, Fabian, what did you tell him?"

"I told him the truth, of course."

"Yes, but what *is* that?"

"*That* is that you lost your scholarship. That you suffered gross psychological failure, attacked another player, and got yourself banished from the world's most psychotic organized activity for antisocial behavior. That there is no financing in place for you as of the last day of this semester. That you don't have the remotest idea how to respond to this situation in any meaningful way. I told him that you were lost. I told him that you need your dad."

I only realize how profoundly the numbness had taken over my body as the motion of walking replaces it with a bone-coldness that already feels permanent.

"Why did you do that?" I say, breaking into a jog as I see the residence halls come into view.

"Because it's the truth," he says, keeping up. "And I don't know anywhere else to turn with you except Ray. And because even though you may very well not deserve his help, he deserves the chance to offer it."

We hop it into the reception area of the halls and don't stop running as we hit the stairs.

"You know what he's gonna do now, don't you? He's prob-ably gonna come racing all the way out here himself. To fix me and fix everything else and take care of me . . ."

"Yeah, and who the hell would want that?" he says, unlocking the door and letting us in.

"Not me," I say. "Don't you understand? I set him free from all this shit. I set him free from me."

"He doesn't want to be free."

"Shut *up*, Fabian," I snap. "I mean it. Stop talking like you know him, because you don't."

"Well, I know him a lot better than I did four hours—

and six phone calls—ago. And I definitely know what lonely sounds like."

He frustrates me to the point of madness, but right now the cold is doing the same.

"Seriously, Fabian," I say. "I don't know whether to punch you in the head or take a hot shower."

"Do what you want. I don't care if you punch me or not, but my advice is you need the shower a lot more." I'm already headed that way when he adds, "And try to somehow wash the booze out of your voice before you talk to him."

The water is coming up off my skin in thick, foggy steam. If I could get it to a temperature that would melt me and take me down the drain for good, that would seem to be a pleasurable exit to me. But that is neither reality nor right, as I hear my phone ring, and I hear it answered and I feel the good man's presence closer than at any time since I left him alone in that lovely warm confusion that was our home.

When I step out of the shower, I have just about stopped shivering. I dress in underwear, then sweats, then my bathrobe. Fabian is lying on his bed when I walk over to deliver one ski hat, one thank you, and one apology.

"Don't worry about it," he says. "I already forgot the whole thing. Until you brought the hat over. Then that called it all back again. Ray'll be phoning any minute. When he realized he had finally gotten through to the same room where the young prince was dwelling at that very moment, he was kind of overcome, so I wouldn't expect him to hold off much longer. And hey, at least you know he isn't already on his way here."

I don't have any chance to speak before my phone lets out that jingling awfulness that Fabian somehow trained it to do. I become instantly as nervous as the first day of first grade, which he walked me to. He was every bit as scared of that big step up as I was. I knew this to be true because he said as much, right there stepping with me through those big school gates.

He could not help himself, big dopey bear that he was. He couldn't bottle up his worries for me even if his worries only served to make me worry that I hadn't been worrying enough up till then. What kind of horrors did he already know were waiting for me inside once he had to surrender me to them?

I didn't quite get it right away, but that was my first experience with the possibility that people could do dumb and messed-up things to you just because of loving you beyond their brain's capacity to deal with it.

It was not a help to me on that day. It was an incalculable help to me on the thousand different days I recalled it.

"Hiya, Dad," I say, trying to be measured, to be a man.

"Hiya, Son," he says, not trying to be anything, just *being* it. "You sound a little drunk," he says with great pained weariness.

"Nah," I say. "But you definitely do."

"Yeah," he says. "I suppose so."

At the best of times, at the very highly functioning, maximum simpatico peak times in our relationship, Ray and I had a phone manner that sucked beyond belief. There was just such a gulf between what we somehow managed to convey when we shared the same space, and the knotty embarrassment of when our verbal skills alone had to carry the day.

And that was at our peak of understanding. This right here feels like somebody is gradually shutting off the valve that supplies oxygen to us.

"It felt, to me, like you had died, Keir."

And so now it's to be my turn. He's earned it, though. He's earned it and then some.

"I am as sorry as I have ever been, Ray. I should have contacted you. I should have at least tried to explain some things before this. But now, I can explain."

"No," he says, and follows it with a big sweep of a sigh. "You can't. I think I figured so much of it out myself by now, and I'd be afraid if you tried it would get all worse, and I cannot possibly have worse." He does that sigh again, something I never heard before, like the air is being forced out of him by some pressure hose stuck in his back.

"Stop sighing like that," I insist the way I have no business insisting.

"I'm not sighing, I'm breathing. Anyway, I'm not going to keep you long. I just originally wanted to hear your voice, that was all. Just to hear you and know, in your voice, that you're doing well."

I hold back. Just because there is a pause in the conversation does not mean it's my turn to speak.

"And I'm not hearing it, Keir."

"Oh, that's just because you've been talking to my roommate, Grandma here. He's the anxious type, blows everything all out of proportion."

Fabian points a finger at me, indicating a threat of some sort, though I cannot possibly imagine what it could be. I raise a less ambiguous fist in response.

"Yeah, well, that grandma of yours is a wonderful kid, and I hope you know that. He's a top guy, a true friend to you, and a great piece of luck to get for a roommate. If you're too stupid to appreciate all that, then maybe you should just thank him for the fact that he's the only reason I'm not in my car and driving out there to see for myself what kind of state you're in."

I don't even save it for after the phone call.

"Fabian, thank you. I'm serious and I really mean it. Thank you."

He smiles broadly and continues to pretend he's doing something on his laptop other than monitoring this conversation.

"How did that sound?" I ask Ray.

"It's helped me a little, knowing you two had each other to lean on."

"It's helped me, too, to know you two had each other to lean on."

281

He possibly chuckles, probably sighs, and I struggle to ignore this one but just about manage it. "You shouldn't drink, Keir."

"Dad, jeez. I'm fine."

"I thought you didn't want to drink anymore, now that you were starting all fresh at college and everything."

"Well, I think I recall you saying something very similar."

"No, you don't. Because I never said anything like that. In fact, it was my intention all along to *increase* my drinking right around that same time. Guess that makes me the only one who can make a pledge and keep to it."

I knew this. I knew somewhere in me, the place where all the sound sensibility hides from the light, that this was only ever going to hurt. Maybe family can be too tight. Maybe a father can be too great. Maybe there's an equation out there that determines that the power bond you enjoy when you live right inside each other has to be paid for with the agony of the bloody slicing away when it's time.

When we were, all four of us, the intensely great thing we were, it was still going to be tough when my time came to leave. But then when Mary left, then Fran left, and Ray and I had each other, it was bound to fuse into something indestructible.

And then when the girls didn't come back for the regular visits as promised, and when they just had to start picking and pulling at the thing we all shared, they started reversing something that should have been irreversible. That only went and made my becoming melded to Ray, and him to me, that much more absolute.

Which made the severing of us, back into separate beings for good, a long and brutal operation. And unlike when the girls left him, I left him *alone*.

Guilt floods me now, circulating burning and thick throughout my body as if I've been tapped into and injected with hot mercury.

"Can I come home, Dad?" I say in a panting, desperate whisper. The whisper itself is just absurd, since the only two people with any interest can obviously hear me anyway, and every last other inhabitant of planet Earth couldn't give a shit what I say, whether I go home or go to hell.

Unless it's to keep the secret from myself.

"I want to come home. I made a mess of everything. I lost everything that I thought added up to me. Home, and you, and now even football is taken away, which leaves me with, what? Nothing. Nothing I can recognize other than unhappiness and guilt, which are with me *all* the time."

The truth is that I thought I could outsmart the universe and not be responsible for anything. Instead it all started blowing up inside my skull practically from the day I walked out of the house. "I'm sorry, Dad. I let you down, but I don't know what I'm doing, don't know what I am or what I want to be or how I would even go about it if I even knew that much."

At first I can't be certain that it isn't me doing it, but then it's clear that what my father calls breathing and I call sighing is surely neither. It has gained strength and is coming out of him in full whooshy waves one after another until he coughs muffled into a handkerchief or some such and it's gone again.

"Ray, that sounds awful," I say.

"That's what a chest cold sounds like on somebody like me."

"There is nobody like you, Dad. And I want to come home. Can I come home?"

"You did it to yourself," he says without obvious judgment. But without the old absolution, either.

"What?"

"Football, Keir. It wasn't taken away from you. You threw it away."

"Ray, wait. There is a *lot* more to this story than that. Quite a lot more. For a number of reasons, people here turned sour on me, and it was clear they regretted signing me so late in the—"

"You didn't show up in your best shape."

"I worked, Dad. You know that. I had some setbacks, though, and you know that as well. But I was making it back to—"

"But you're never supposed to let yourself down like that. Let them beat you any other way they can manage it. But you don't defeat yourself."

"Would you please stop saying that stuff? That's way too simple for my situation. It does not apply to me. It is not *true*."

It feels as if we're waiting, or at least like he is, for a bell to stop ringing before he speaks.

"*Adversity is the first path to truth.*"

If he started speaking all his words backward, or composing fifty-word palindromes, he would not catch me more off guard than this.

"Ray, what was that? It wasn't you, is all I know. Life is already unrecognizable enough without you morphing into some kind of—"

"Lord Byron," he says serenely.

"Lord *Byron*?" I say, turning just in time to catch Fabian tucking away the tail end of a fist pump. "You did this," I say, possibly expecting him to drop to his knees in remorse.

That doesn't happen.

"Well played, Ray!" he calls right past me to my father.

"Yes indeed," Ray says back cheerily, and proudly.

"What's he saying?" Fabian asks.

"He's saying you should knock it off with teaching poetry to other people's fathers, because no guy's father should be *knowing* poems, never mind quoting them."

Instead of flipping a quip like I'd expect, Fabian nods, smiles weakly. "Tell Ray thanks. I appreciate the advice, since I wouldn't have any idea what a guy's dad is supposed to do."

Goddamn it. Is there any patch of ground anywhere in this part of life that doesn't have a live mine planted beneath it? It didn't used to be like this. It didn't ever used to be like this as far as I could see.

"Sorry," I say across the room.

Fabian waves a hand of absolution and starts burrowing himself down under the covers.

And Ray doesn't talk now. He doesn't sigh or wheeze or perform any function at all that would permit me to hear him. "Dad?"

"I love you, Keir, and it couldn't be any other way if my life depended on it. I'm proud of you. Do you have any idea what the sound is like, when a big fat dumb old baby of a man bawls his heart and lungs out? And he does it in an empty, echoey old house with fragile plaster walls that were already echoing far too much stuff at him even before he started his wailing? Good, I'm going to let you carry on with that silence, hoping and figuring that it means no, you do not know that sound." He's pausing more frequently now, and returning each time with a slightly weaker, wearier, sadder voice. "If you need to hear it, I'll make a recording next time. But those events don't come around as often these days—kind of like your sisters." He allows himself a laugh that has so little joy and so many multiple pains, he cuts it off in the middle. "I kept feeling that you had gone off and died on me, kept letting my brain go all brainless believing Fabian was covering it up, just like the college, the police, whoever. Nobody around here to tell me different, right, so why not? I'm free now to make whatever reality I want just because I say so. Even if I don't realize that it's not me controlling everything in there sometimes. That kind of grief, it turns out, is every bit as destroying to a person as the real kind."

This time I don't need a very large opening to get myself in there. "I am even sorrier now than I was ten minutes ago. I was wrong, and I was selfish and heartless, and I want to come home. I have no business being here, and no good explanation why I did it in the first place."

"I'm much happier now, Son. Just to have heard your voice. I'm getting too tired to talk much more, so just listen. Now, I want you to stop apologizing. You have nothing at all to feel guilty about. I know why you did things the way you did. Took me a while, but I know my boy even after all that's been said and done. And I think it took guts taking that big step without asking me or anybody else to hold your hand. And so, no."

"No?"

"No. I'm not going to allow you to come home. Do what you meant to do. It'll look a little different from what you were expecting, but the notion is the same. You won't quit. You will keep going forward. You will find your way soon enough, and then you'll go on and be who you are supposed to be. You can't do that here."

"What about the money? I don't even know how to apply—

"The college has been in touch with me. You'd be surprised how efficient they can be with financial matters. Anyway, we came to an arrangement on settling your fees for next semester, and that's done and they're settled, so it's time for you to get likewise."

"That's a lot of money, Ray."

"I guess you better turn out to be worth the investment. But the money is spent, the rest of the year all yours, bought and paid for. I don't want you thinking about that end of it, not at all, for the whole of your freshman year. And that's that."

"Dad. Hold on, you can't just chop off the subject without involving me at least enough so I know how I'm managing without my football scholarship, if somebody asks me."

"Nobody's going to ask you that," Fabian says from under the covers.

"Please, just butt out," I snap at him. Then quickly to Ray, "I didn't say that to you, you know that. You know I never would, Dad, right? Dad? Right? Ray?"

I have a short panic attack that manages to pack the wallop of several full-blown ones into ten or twelve seconds.

Then I realize that at the point my father said, "That's that," that *was* that. And if I chose to continue chattering like an idiot, then that would be entirely up to me. Because there wouldn't be anybody else to stop me.

Two semesters, right here in the palm of my hand. Get settled, get sorted. Find out. Learn.

Be the guy you're supposed to be.

How many fresh starts, new first days, can a person expect to be granted? Gotta figure there can't be many more coming along for me.

House money. I'm playing with house money, so I got no chance of losing this time no matter what.

But for the fact that the house money came from the homeowner who isn't rolling in dough by any stretch. There is a loss possible, a great gulping sinkhole of a possibility.

My one and only job is to be the guy I'm supposed to be. But first I have to go out and find him, and he could be hiding anywhere.

. . .

The classes I chose for myself at the beginning of term were not designed to inspire anything particularly, and in that one respect they have been entirely successful. I go to them most of the time, hand in all my assignments, get along well enough to learn a few things and remain essentially anonymous. I'm earning required credits, and that's an essential part of not losing the house's money.

But the other side of things, the intangibles, the things that open up a guy's life at college to the possibilities that could be more than curiosities, those are to be found all over the place at Carnegie.

I get up early, because I remember that I love getting up early. I go to the gym often enough that I have reached the nod-hey-yo-g'mornin' relationship stage with around a half dozen other mourning doves, and I look forward to that fleeting connection so much that I confess to going to the gym this morning for no other reason than a shot of nod-hey-yo-g'mornin'. And once I get it, I'm fortified. The crunchy cold November air under gunmetal gray sky will not wait, and I will not ask it to.

You find out quickly that the campus of a college this size is a tiny throw rug on a massive landscape. I have run every route, climbed every scalable surface, blazed every unbeaten trail the Carnegie College environment has to offer. Done it all a dozen or more times.

I don't see a time I could ever tire of it. But I know how things go, how a place can shrink, how you can get so familiar that beauty and history and love aren't even powerful enough to hold you anymore. No doubt it has happened to thousands and thousands of onetime freshmen who fell in love with these same woods, foothills, mountains, statues that annoyed them right out of town a few short years later.

I dread there ever being such a time, no matter what logic and upperclassmen might say. What has to happen to make somebody not want to sit on the arched bridge and dangle his legs above the duck pond?

And I will recognize one more new first day, not necessarily a good one, when I walk down the sloping path curving past the chapel and I no longer feel the pop of charmed, surprised amusement at the Yurt poking its helmet head up through the earth.

I'm thinking early on this day it's just one more quiet campus touchstone I'm passing on my morning rounds, until I see the glow of some kind of amber light, and hear the murmur of a honey-chocolate voice coaxing listeners gently into the new day.

"Hey," I say when I'm sure the long-hair guy isn't still on a live microphone.

"Oh, hey," he says, rising right up out of his chair to come and meet me in the bull's-eye center of the round room. "I'm George Seldes. I'm the manager of CC Radio. Didn't we meet already?"

"Sort of. I'm Keir Sarafian. I came in one afternoon with Fabian Delmonico."

"Aahhhh," he says, pointing at me with both hands poised like revolvers.

"That's why we didn't quite meet," I say. "The atmosphere with you guys seemed a little . . . challenging."

"Well, yeah, you got it exactly. But as for Fabian and me personally, some days I don't know if I'd bother getting out of bed if I didn't expect him to be out here someplace waiting to do battle. I don't know how well you know the dude, but man, Fabian makes the world go round. You want some really strong coffee?"

"Oh, um, sure."

George leads me over to his post, in charge of the radio station broadcasts, whatever they may be. He monitors the music that is playing, and how long it has to run. Long enough, it seems.

"I noticed you admiring my Yurt," he says.

"Admiring," I say, "yeah, absolutely. But didn't Fabian say this was the Writing Center?"

"I have no doubt that he did. But look around you. Is there anything in this fine upturned bowl of a place that says 'Writing Center' to you?"

I do as told and look all around. There is an unbroken bench built into the wall and running the full perimeter of the place. There is a chunky rustic table and four chairs set up in the center. Aside from that there are puffy throw pillows scattered around, and the radio operation, which stands out as a shock of modern functionality compared to everything else.

"See?" George says, shrugging. It is quite a feat, managing a triumphant shrug, but George nails it.

"Except," I say, and point straight up, to the quote by the poet Robert Burns that won't go away.

"Right, but we are waiting for the right moment to paint it over with 'The medium is the message,' by Marshall McLuhan."

"If I get a vote, I go with that one," I say. "Why is that other one all over the place around here? It's spooking me."

"It's Carnegie-Burns. Andrew Carnegie—the name might ring a bell—was a big admirer of the poet Burns. So all the thousands of Carnegie libraries all around the world that were funded by the Carnegie Foundation try to suck up to the boss by splattering ol' Rabbie all over. So you can imagine a whole college in the Carnegie mold. . . ."

"There'd be no escaping it."

"Exactly. You a little squirmy about that 'to see ourselves as others see us' riff? No shame in it if you feel that way. You'll have plenty of company."

"You?"

"What? Don't be daffy. I know how deadly cool I look to everybody. My only quarrel with that poem is it makes me jealous of all the lucky folks who get to look at me from such a better angle than I can."

This kind of outrageousness must be routine to George, because he doesn't even bother looking for a reaction out of me before turning his attention to the broadcast control desk again.

But he must sense the heat of my blown-away stare. He turns to me with sly-guy eyes.

"I was joking entirely. Read the poem, Keir. Really do. Give it your full attention, all eight demented Scots stanzas of it. It's the perfect antidote anytime you feel the impulse to assume you're better than you really are."

The locked-eyes deal he has trapped me in feels unbreakable. So I try words instead.

"I thought you were on the opposite side from the poetry folks."

"I was just starting to like you, Keir. It would be both tragic and ironic if I had to have you killed to protect the secret shame of my literacy."

I open my mouth to respond, though I have no idea what could possibly be a fitting reply to that. I'll never know, either.

He gives me a shush finger just like that before turning his microphone on. The ON AIR light glows, and I feel a little unscheduled underground coolness of my own at having stumbled into the inner sanctum of this rarefied world of broadcasting. Even if it might not be casting all that broadly at this early minute.

It's a privilege, the very kind I'm supposed to be here for. The kind that will not pass by unnoted or unappreciated.

"That, loyal listeners, was the great John Coltrane, from his seminal album, *Giant Steps*. Now, I'll let you in on a special secret that only my crack o' dawn faithful get to hear. And that is that I do not know what on earth Mr. Coltrane is getting at with that record. Not a clue. But if you don't play some 'Trane every once in a while on a jazz show, then you get dismissed as a know-nothing faker. So, there ya go. If you happen to catch my evening show later in the week, I will be playing that very same stuff and you can just listen to me wax so poetical about that same unfathomable squawk of a record, you'd never know I was talking to you directly from my permanently puckered rear end. See the privileges you get by being part of our smarty-pants early morning population? Now, for a special treat, another of our tribe, Mr. Keir Sarafian, is gonna tell you everything you never knew about our next featured ensemble, Ella Fitzgerald, McCoy Tyner, and Joe Pass. Keir, over to you. . . ."

"What?" I say, as unprepared as it is possible to be for one's radio debut.

"You were just saying," George says, clearly enjoying himself, "remember, about the one thing about this trio that always bothered you?"

I stare over at him in desperation, hoping for a helping hand. But there are no hands available, since they are both clamped tight over his laughing mouth. He keeps gesturing with his eyes toward the guest microphone in front of me.

"Um," I say, "I never heard of the other two guys, I'm sorry. But I know my dad, Ray, has always loved Ella Fitzgerald. So that counts as something I know, right? Hey, Ray," I say, out into the zero point zero zero percentage chance I could be talking to him.

"Well, that was sweet," George says, composing himself enough to come back on and pick me up the way a proper radio station manager should.

I'm starting to feel relaxed a little already, after getting my first spoken words out to the listener-strangers. Getting it done, then getting relieved by the other guy, is a combination of up-and-down swoop of excitement I would not have predicted. It was even kind of fun before I got relieved and I was still dangling precariously.

"Although if I'm not mistaken," George adds, over the beginning notes of some piano and guitar bits fighting for the singer's attention, "Mr. Sarafian forgot to tell us the part he was supposed to tell us about what really bothers him about this recording. Mr. Sarafian, you don't have to be shy or diplomatic on this show, certainly not at this hour. . . ."

Happening just the same as the show, live as we speak, I'm getting overwhelmed by the realization of what seems possible here. A guy could, if he got this right, hold the attention of who knows how many people. He could shape any discussion on any subject according to whatever happened to move him that day, that hour. And he could get away with . . . was even encouraged to get away with . . . talking know-it-all nonsense even about things he knew nothing-at-all about. Meanwhile remaining an unknown person attached to a known persona if he wanted to.

There could be something to this.

"Oh yes, you're right. Sorry, George. The only part that

really bothers me about listening to this record is that I was promised good strong coffee to go with it. And, George, management seems to have lied to me about the coffee."

"Ha! And he's only a freshman, folks," he says, then cuts off my microphone.

"Thanks," I say as soon as I'm convinced we're off air and I'm not being lured into some great radio-biz prank.

"Did you enjoy that?" he says, leaning in close like he's really hopeful about the response.

"Surprisingly much," I say. The thought of having the dawn hours largely to myself and others like me who just want to breathe it in is a powerful motivator for getting out at ungodly hours. The chance to listen for the sound of frost evaporating, and to feel a kind of irrational ownership of the world that isn't possible at any other part of the day, is the whole point.

So, getting up at the same time but with a different purpose—very different, since broadcasting is the opposite of silently absorbing—should be something startling and unappealing to me. George Seldes, who willingly does this all the time, should be a person I politely fail to understand.

Someday I will learn to recognize "should" for the sly deceiver that it is.

"You should think about doing a show," George says as he passes me a coffee that I'm pretty sure was already sitting there when he put on the fresh pot. It is not the good or strong coffee he promised, but he had a lot of time to forget since he promised it.

I used to treat the rookies like this in high school. Maybe he forgot on purpose, and if he did, I will drink my rookie coffee with dignity.

"I should, probably, think about it at least, huh?" I say, doing a crap job of not being completely flattered by the suggestion alone.

George puts on a compilation of what he calls "Scandinavian Torch Classics" that he promises will subdue the last two of his seven loyal listeners while we talk a bit.

"It's a completely manufactured rivalry," he says, "with Fabian and myself as figureheads. He represents the ridiculously antiquated school of thought that holds *the Word* as the one timeless unit of meaning in our world throughout all time. While I get the gravy job of hardly needing to point out that the modes of communication long ago did the job of rendering the ostensible *content* of that communication incidental at best. It's actually a lot of fun, especially since the patterns of history have already declared my side the winner. It's important for morale and enrollment all the same that we keep up the sparring as if there is still anything in the balance. Otherwise, what would all the poor English majors do with themselves?"

"No!" the voice shocks me right up out of my chair.

"No, what?" George says. "You're too late."

"You can't have him. Not this one. He has potential. There might be words in this one."

"How do you happen to know this guy?" George says to me casually as he fetches a cup of coffee for Fabian.

"He sleeps about four feet away from me."

"Oh, this is your *roommate*?" George says as he hands Fabian his coffee.

"Yes, he is," Fabian says. "So there you have it."

"So there I do," George says. "What a score! Even the Gutenbergers will stop listening to you once they realize your own roommate defected to the side of reason and progress."

I keep veering from feeling flattered on the one hand to feeling uncomfortable on the other. And both hands relate to the same, uncommon situation of having two opposing teams competing for me to go with one or the other.

"Fabian," I say, "I think I suddenly discovered that I really like radio."

He nods, sagely, calmly. Far too sage-calmly.

"And did you also suddenly discover that you no longer really like . . . fresh fruit salad?"

"Jesus," I say, shooting right up from my molded plastic chair and my undrinkable coffee. "You guys are relentless. It's like mental schoolboys in the playground seriously debating who would win a fight between, like, Batman and global warming. You're honestly trying to force me to choose between radio and fruit salad?"

The two of them look so relaxed, even satisfied over all this. They lean close, bumping shoulders as they size me up, while they sip their *steaming* and probably identical coffees.

What a chump.

"I did remember to point out to you that this was a

completely manufactured rivalry, didn't I?" George checks just to be sure.

"You did," I say, dropping back into my chair and hanging my head in chumpiness.

"You can do radio and still work with the journalism or literature or creative writing doofs all you want," Fabian says with a reassuring pat on my knee.

"Hey, you can do radio and still work *anything* that floats your boat into a weekly program," George says, patting my other knee.

I feel like a wishbone.

"Okay," I say, hoping to get at least a firmer grasp of what the Yurt honestly is. "But I thought this was the Writing Center."

"It is," Fabian assures me.

"Where's your typewriter, then? I would think if there was a writing center that you'd have that machine as the center of everything."

"Well, that *E* key is sticking again, and I want to treat it just so before—"

"It's banned," George says.

"Huh?"

"It's not here because Fabian's diabolical contraption was such a loud clacky nuisance that it provoked an uprising. Even the writers joined in."

"Ha," I say, "so it wasn't just me."

George shakes his head emphatically no, and eventually even Fabian joins in.

I notice, as the end of the night-crawler hours give way to the early bird hours, we are now passing the baton to the mainstream morning shift of gourmet coffees, smoothies, loud pre-class chatter.

"So," I say, finally strung far enough along, "is this the Writing Center or isn't it?"

"Yes," Fabian says.

"Yes," George concurs. "But it is also the Chess Society, Mindfulness Meeting Space, CC Chapel Micro-Choir rehearsal hall, Photo Phellows Photography Club (close supervision division), Interfaith Outreach, First Friday Folk Freaks—"

"Ah, I think I get it," I say. "It's every group's space if they request it."

"Most of them don't even bother requesting," Fabian says. "They just show up."

"And they don't even have to be groups," George adds, "since any old stray is likely to come in at any time."

"The Yurt is the epicenter of the entire community," I say.

"Yes," George says. "And the radio station is the epicenter of the Yurt. Through it all, we broadcast. And when all the special interests go home for their beauty sleep, we broadcast right through that, too."

I give my faithful roommate a taunting, restrained shove.

"All things to all people, that was how you first described this place to me. Even when you're just trying to be a smart-ass, you can't seem to help coming up with all the exact right words to fit everything everywhere right in its place."

He looks, for Fabian, strangely uncomfortable with the compliment. I figure it must be me and choosing the wrong way to say the right thing, so I let it go for now. I'll tell him again, and better, when it's just the two of us. I always speak better when it's just the two of us. I don't know why that is, and I don't know that I want to know.

But I know this, and I know I want to know it.

I have found the place. The Yurt is the place where I will find things I'm here to find. Where I'll begin to know who I'm supposed to be. And where I'll figure out how.

Most remarkable of all is that I was sent here, directed by my dad to find this thing.

And Ray wouldn't know a yurt if it fell out of the sky and landed right on top of him. It would probably fit him too, that great big beautiful bear head.

orphans

You know what I love about radio?" I say loudly over Fabian's bashing away at the typewriter.

"No, I do not know," he says while remaining in his hunchback, forehead-to-the-page writer-man posture. "I'm expecting to know very soon, though. But first, have you called Ray?"

"No. I will."

"You have to call him, ya shit."

"Okay, I plan to, but listen. It's the one-wayness of the arrangement with radio. I love having the freedom to talk about whatever I want, in exactly the way I want to, without anybody's beady judgmental eyes throwing me off and making my words fall all over each other and land all wrong. I control the conversation, and that gives me the confidence to plow on until I get everything just right."

"You do remember that it is Internet radio, yes? That there are a whole bunch of different ways people can get their messages to you, instantly. In fact, chances are that with the number of misfits, maniacs, and malcontents out there squatting like carrion feeders over their keyboards, there could come a tipping point where the number of people reaching you with their thoughts could well exceed the number of actual listeners you're reaching with yours."

Well.

"Well, Fabian my friend, I guess that leaves me with just two thoughts. One: Asshole! And two: How can you keep on typing while having a conversation at the same time?"

He stops typing and turns around to face me. "I can't," he says. "I'm curious to see what kind of gibberish I've got on that page, right after I finish with this conversation in the next twenty seconds."

"No, I need you for longer than that."

"Twenty-two seconds."

"No. More."

"Agreed. No more."

He whirls around and is most definitely typing gibberish, because he's attacking the keys with great smashings that come from way over his head like a mad Mozart at a piano.

"You're a very funny guy," I say.

"I know," he says.

"That's one of the reasons I want to interview you."

This manages to get him right up out of the chair. He

ventures all the way into my cramped but cozy corner office. My desk, which sits against the window wall about three feet from the foot of my bed.

"What are you up to?" he says, bringing some extra comedy to the situation by putting his hands on his hips and staring down at me fiercely. Third grade felt very much like this to me.

"Are you a writer?" I ask.

"Not at the moment I'm not. I happen to believe that writing and talking are mutually exclusive pursuits, and furthermore, that the population who self-identify as writers in reality break into two groups: writer-writers, and talker-writers. And I don't think there is very much overlap at all."

"See, I knew you would make a great interview."

"That is kind of you. But now, as I would very much like to be able to think of myself as a writer-writer someday, I'm going to stop talking and resume writing."

Fabian walks, upright and with very little excess of motion, back to his desk in just the way I would imagine a real writer would walk. It's not sufficient to escape from me, however.

"Come on, Fabian, it won't take too long. And it'll be a laugh, too. You know how you love having opinions and stuff."

"Keir, you don't even have your own program slot yet."

"I'm working up to it. George is letting me sit in with him for longer and longer stretches, especially during the late-late, early-early hours I'm coming to love. He says when I'm ready, I can make it whatever format I want. Music, interviews, remote stuff I collect around campus with the portable gear we're allowed to check out of the media center."

"That's all great," he says. "So just go and do all that stuff, then."

"Maybe," I say. "Sometime. But I want to focus, see this through, do it right, and make it special. Something with a great framework to build on, that has an honest point to it. So that it could keep gaining depth and meaning the more I add to it, you know?"

He nods a whole bunch of times in his way I recognize as saying, *Hold on a minute, wait right there, I'm thinking something. . . .*

So, waiting's no problem.

"You're exactly right," he says. "Anybody can just jump on the mic and talk crap and waste everybody's time. It's the very foundation of most commercial radio. But taking your time with this chance is a good move. Does George have any suggestions for what he thinks you might do?"

"Yeah. He says with my background I should do a bunch of sports-related pieces. Not enough sports on the air, apparently. Said it would be cool to maybe start by talking to the football team, players and coaches and all, since they are having another stellar year."

"Cool. Is that what George said, cool?"

"Cool," I confirm.

"Yeah, ah, no, not cool."

"Ah, no, probably not."

"So, your backup plan to a series on the football team is . . . me?"

"Yeah. How's that for social climbing?"

"Very impressive. So, are you going to tell me what your hook is? Your through-line? Your connective tissue?"

"Thought you'd never ask. The best part is, I stole the idea from you."

"Excuse me?"

"'Stole' was the wrong word, because I didn't take anything away from you, other than inspiration. I'm going to build up an archive called 'Interviews with Insufficiently Famous Americans.' What do you think of *that*?"

He's decided to get back to me later on that one, or else he's answering me in mime, because he bolts like a greyhound out of his chair, to his closet, jumping up to the shelf to check that I have indeed not stolen anything from him.

As he walks slowly back in my direction, his eyes look like they are crossing slightly. His arms are at his sides, but spread uncharacteristically wide of his body.

"What, are we about to have a gunfight?" I ask.

"Not if you answer the following question correctly. Keir, did you touch my book?"

"What? No, I promise I never laid a finger on it. I saw the spine when I went in to borrow a vest, and it instantly sent my mind spinning with ideas just from the title alone."

He's still poised to draw. "You swear?"

"I swear. You told me the book was special, and that was all you ever needed to tell me."

"All right then," he says, his body visibly relaxing. "But about the other thing, I know I said help yourself anytime . . ."

"I'm borrowing your vests a lot, aren't I?"

"Well, since I have now had to go into your closet *twice* to find one I wanted to wear, maybe we'll just suspend the vest-lend program for a while to give them a chance to settle again."

"Fine. Cool. Sorry for abusing the program."

"That's all right, it's done now."

He stands there with his thinking, pondering face on for a few seconds, then goes back to the closet to retrieve the book. He smiles at it, cradling it gently in one hand and barely touching it with the fingertips of the other. He looks like a guy who's just been reunited with his beloved pet cat. That he had lost when he was a little kid.

He sits on the bed with the book, and though I have never felt this before, I clearly feel welcome, invited to sit next to him and be properly introduced to the book.

He slides it carefully out of its slipcase. *People One Knows: Interviews with Insufficiently Famous Americans*, by John Updike. He shows me just one page, and opens it only the minimum required for me to see.

"Signed by the author," he says proudly. "And numbered, number two hundred ninety-seven out of three hundred.

There were another hundred done in a deluxe edition, but
that was all they ever produced."

"Whoa," I say, reflexively moving my hand just slightly in
the direction of copping a quick feel of the cover.

He stands, re-cases the treasure, and takes it with him to
his desk again. I had run full gallop into brute running backs
who did not protect the football as well as that.

I remain on his bed because, why not? Something in this
situation is loosening him up, and I don't want to do anything to break the spell that gets this insufficiently famous
American talking from his deep.

"That's one special fancy book for an orphan," I say,
thinking maybe humor was the thing to move us along. And
it probably was the thing, but this was a sorry idea of humor.
"I'm sorry," I say when I see his fractured features aimed my
way. "It was stupid to say, but I meant nothing. Bad joke, just
really bad, forget I said it."

He nods, but says no at the same time. "No, I want to tell
you about it. But I'm going to tell it quickly so I can be done
with it. It was my gran's book, her one real, shameless item of
showing off that she would allow herself now and then. Rare
special item, piece of class, piece of elegance, in a poky plain
little life and a poky plain little house that possessed nothing
else of the kind. Bought for her by my papa on one very rare
and special day during the two sweetheart months between
his retirement from sixty years in leather tanneries and his
retirement from everything else. When I was really young, I

believed his hands looked like suede because he never took off his fine calfskin gloves. He was the wise guy who fed me that story in the first place, so of course I had no trouble swallowing it whole. If that man told me his hands looked and smelled like buckskin because his own daddy was a stag, I would have believed that just as easily.

"So there was your romance angle stirred in with the intellectual and the valuable. The trifecta for Gran and more power to the book."

He is nodding at the story, looking off into some distance. He is nodding at a specific something, but I'm not asking because I'm already learning lessons about this, about asking people for their *stuff*, and how much harder it is than it looks. About how their stuff, unconnected to your own stuff, still somehow sets things alight that maybe won't burn well.

"That was a great story," I say. "I knew you would be a dream interview subject, but you've already surpassed anything I was thinking. Great stuff."

"Oh, it gets greater, but I can see you're anxious to get going somewhere. . . ."

I only now become aware of standing up and edging toward the door.

"No, no, no," I say, rushing right back to my spot on his bed. "I do have to get down to the Yurt to meet a tech guy who's gonna teach me stuff, but I have time."

"This time I will edit myself down to the essentials. The point where the story gets greater is when I tell you that I stole the book from Gran. Huh? Huh? I told you, right?" he says while pointing and winking in a showy *got-cha* kind of way.

"Yyyuuup," I say.

"There's more to it, of course there is. Papa died, we cried, like it was our one and favorite pastime. And then, after ages, after months, Gran finally stopped weeping. She had flushed it all out. From right then on, every day she was worse than before. Every day she was less than before. She was going, and she was going willingly.

"I took care of her, was the only thing to do. It was no more than she did for me when I needed it. I couldn't even remember what age they took me in, was how long ago it was. And she took care of me, washed my face and my shit-ass underwear and stretched meals that were skimpy for two old skinnies like them and somehow found more for me and loved me like their own, or even better, I think, than if I was their own. That's how loved I felt.

"And I felt it even stronger, after a short staggery spell, felt stronger for myself and crazy insane gratitude for them, when in my duties as caretaker of life at the poky little house, pieces of details started accumulating into a sus-picion, then into a possibility that these two lovely people were never who I thought they were.

"Sorry, I left out a piece. I thought all along that these old folks were just my very old parents. Yeah. Like life became one giant game of Clue or something. My actual mother, their daughter, fucked off right after I was born. Presumably going after the father-like substance who fucked off just prior to the blessed event.

"Gran told me herself, which makes me happy even today, even after I already knew. She was sinking fast and didn't recognize me more of the time than she did. But she broke the surface, like a beautiful old silvery fish jumping its way up the river. She saw me, she told me, and she thanked me, before disappearing just that quick again into the river.

"By the next day it was really as far as we could go together. The ambulance came and the paramedics, who were so fantastically great, told me where she would be for the next week or two of tests and stabilizing whatnot and where she was almost certainly going for her long-term care whether or not the term was long or not.

"They would take the house. I knew because I had studied. And they would take the contents, which still wouldn't come near to paying the bill, and they would kick me out. So I took the content I wanted, took the long-buried records of my long-dead sleazebag biological warfare parents to a hostel, and started the process of getting the orphan to the college in the hills."

I can't speak. I can't tip over sideways on the bed either, because it's his and I would have no right even if it was mine. That was one hell of an interview I conducted there. If I were one of my listeners, I'd be thinking this job is the easiest gig in show business, just sitting there in a chair across from one true soul who is willing to cut himself wide open and howl as long as anybody cares to listen.

The supposed interviewer himself, on the other hand, is thinking he is not nearly tough enough for this.

"That the kind of stuff you have in mind, for your radio project?" Fabian asks helpfully.

"I can't imagine anybody has that kind of stuff in mind before you tell it to them."

"Alas, I'll have to remain insufficiently famous for a while longer, since that was off the record."

Now I do move toward the door and my blessed tech appointment. "You can come into the station once I'm up and running. We'll do it live. Or we could record it any place and play it back later. Could even record it here, maybe."

"Yeah," he says, "maybe."

I almost escape before he catches me, calls me to poke my head back in.

"Did you suppose you could run a bunch of inter-views, get people to pour out the bloody stuff for your show while you remained hidden behind them, safe and secret, unharmed and unexposed? It won't be possible, you know. I mean, it's a great idea, but you need to know that."

"Thanks," I say, and see my permission to flee in the way he turns his body and hovers over the book on the desk. But I don't flee. "Fabian," I say, and he looks up. "Thanks. And thanks. And, y'know, thanks."

"You're welcome. Now off you go to get sufficiently famous."

It makes me smile for several seconds after I get out the door. But then it doesn't. It almost sounds like a curse to me now. And by the time I get to the Yurt and the screaming yellow letters circling and seeing us from every direction, I still cannot get out from under the crush of that awful feeling.

reachable

There is a meditation class, four guys, eighteen or so girls, scattered about on mats while a visiting lecturer stands on the solid wooden oval table built right into the center point in the Yurt's floor. George has been trying to make some kind of radio out of this man's soothing and barely audible instructions on how to achieve inner peace, spiritual enlightenment, and excellent posture.

The idea, the broadcast part, is so bad that George gave up on playing it straight and is now doing very quiet sports reporting in a voice that mimics golf commentators but content that hews much closer to a frat-boy film. I nearly fell asleep with the sedation of the first half of the program, but now I'm feeling uncomfortable, disgusted with myself even though I've not done anything to trigger anything as vile as what I'm feeling. Every time George makes reference to his new obsession, yoga pants, the tar pit that I swear is drawing me down pulls another six inches toward searing suffocating oblivion. My heart is heaving to the point of actually, certainly bursting even before the shock of the door crashing open and causing screams to swing rings around the room.

"You have to carry this thing with you, goddamn it!" Fabian says as he rushes at me, brandishing my phone. His voice is high volume, high pitch, and when he gets close enough, I can see him fighting tears and losing. He pounds me hard on the collarbone with the phone, then again on the jaw and finally in the middle of my chest. I take it then, and he starts yanking my arm, hauling me straight across the room full of petrified innocent students, who won't be likely to find peace again for some time.

"Call your sister!" he shouts, letting me go but leading the way back to our place.

"My sister? Call my *sister*?"

"Fran. Fran called. Your sister Fran called, and she sounds like a nice person and I talked to her for only a couple of minutes, but you have to call her right *now*, Keir."

I follow obediently as Fabian continues to berate me for not carrying the stupid phone, but aside from thinking Fran's calling was odd, and aside from the meditation class sick-feeling like I was ramping up on a post-traumatic seizure from some war I was never in, my main thought right now is if Fabian is all right, because this is a crazy he's never even hinted at—

"Is it Ray?" I say when I come out of the density of my personal fog. "Fabian!" I yell, though he's just a few feet ahead of me and we're both sprinting toward the dorms. "What is it? What's wrong with Ray?"

"Does it make me insensitive if I say that I might find this easier to get through if you weren't crying so much?" I'm speaking to Fabian, who is sitting on *my* bed, hugging his knees and indulging in *my* sky view while he prematurely mourns *my* father. I am occupying myself with stuffing dirty and wrinkled and inappropriate items into my travel bag. Fran has arranged a flight for me. I have to hurry if I'm going to make the only plane that'll give me a chance to say good-bye.

"No," he says. "Of course that doesn't make you insensitive. It's the complete lack of any emotional response at all that makes you insensitive."

"I'm sorry about that, Fabian. Still, I have to get moving." I zip the bag, pick it up by the fraying cloth handles, and already I cannot picture one single item that wound up in there.

I turn toward the door, leaving him staring up out the window at the big-sky view that can surely mend anybody's broken self if he looks at it for long enough.

"I should be going too," he blurts out, and pulls me back.

I go to where he is at the window. "I wish that was possible," I say. "If my sister didn't come up with the money as quick as that, I wouldn't be able to make it on time myself."

He nods fanatically. He's actually gotten himself up into the windowsill, taken that same knee-hugging pose, and with the added turbo-nod he looks like a big version of one of those wind-up monkeys that bash the cymbals together really fast.

"Ray was my friend, Keir. I know how stupid it sounds—"

"Not to me it doesn't. I know exactly the how and the why of how you feel, and you're completely right to feel it."

"Like, one of the best friends I ever had. Maybe the nicest guy I ever talked to. The realest, that's for sure. Jesus, I never even laid eyes on the man and I'm falling to pieces over not saying good-bye to him."

"I will absolutely tell him good-bye from you," I say, checking my watch. "That is, if I get the chance to say it for anybody."

"Right, go, get out of here."

"If it's any consolation, not that you won't be missed, but there will be a big crowd of people there to send Ray Sarafian off. Every person who ever met my dad became a close friend forever. It will be nice to see that, at least."

"It should be a consolation, might eventually be a consolation, but right now it's nothing. Go, Keir. Just go."

I go.

At the airport I have to wait twenty minutes for the gate to open. I don't feel like I can sit down, so I just walk. I walk the complete circuit of the sleepy quiet airport three times and find that leaves another ten minutes still to go. I don't feel like eating anything, drinking anything, reading, or listening to any goddamn thing at all. There is a card shop.

What is a person supposed to do? What does he do with himself? What are all these horrible sticky slow minutes *for*, anyway? What are they doing? What am I doing? What should I be doing?

What should I have done?

What shouldn't I have done?

Card shops exist for the purpose of telling us how we're supposed to behave, that much I know. It's with a sickly kind of hope that I walk into the card shop fifty yards from my departure gate. I stride through the door expecting instantaneous divine clarity to come to me. I even sense, powerfully, that the envelope will be kelly green.

"Hello, sir," says the strawberry-blond girl, who looks young and cheerful enough that she must not have been stuck in here for too many hours, months, or grievings yet. I'm glad I get to see her now, with her freckles still stars, and not after.

"Hello," I say, standing cluelessly just inside the door.

"Can I help you find something?" she says, and it sounds like a person who really, really does want to know if she can help another person.

"Thank you," I say, "but I'm just browsing."

"Oh," she says, mentally regrouping after a customer said something the training day definitely did not prepare her for.

"Don't hear that very often in here. With, y'know, most of the kind of things we sell being aligned to specific dates, birthdays, anniversaries . . ."

She is being sweet and extraordinary, and I make sure to repay her consideration by being at the far corner of the shop and looking elsewhere when she gets to the grimmer end of the inventory in her mind.

Sorry for Your Loss has always bothered me. There is simply a frigid, soulless, stiff detachment in those words, in that arrangement that seems to practically make a joke out of how *not* sorry they are to *not* be you, you poor sad bastard.

Final boarding call. Final boarding call. How did I miss any incremental boarding calls? Is this a joke?

Right in front of me, as it has been for too many minutes, is the "Sympathy" row of cards, right next to the "Sorry" row. I don't even read, but instead pluck every green card I can find out of each category, race to the counter, and run off before the nice girl still intact with her niceness calls after me about my change.

"Thank you," I call as I sprint toward the gate that is now seven hundred and fifty yards away, so I turn on whatever jets I have left and I get there just in time. Just in time to see the woman and the man in their forest-green regional airline uniform jackets slam the door closed to any more passengers.

"How could this be? How could this ever, possibly be happening?"

"I am very sorry, sir," the lady with the lemon shade of

blond hair says with her head tilted to the two o'clock sympathy position.

"But it's right there," I say. "People are still walking along that tunnel thing, I can hear them. I'm not arguing, there is no question that this was my fault, my responsibility. But it can't be a problem for one single person, anywhere in the world, for you to let me onto that plane right now."

"Sir, there is another—"

"No," I snap, making my task all the harder, "there is no other one. That one"—I point—"is the only one there's ever gonna be."

"We really are sorry, sir," the slim and serious gent says.

"Okay then," I say. "In that case, everything's good. As long as you're sorry. I must have missed that part before. What kind of sorry was that, anyway? Sorry for your loss, I imagine? It's got to be sorry-for-your-loss sorry. Which is cool, all set now. You have a good day."

It is not their fault, and I know that as I berate them over the whole mess. The more I bark at them, the more I know that I have nobody to blame for what I did, and the more I know that, the louder I bark at them. I stand, holding my duffel bag in one hand and the bunch of sorry sad sympathetic cards in the other. I stand in front of these two perfectly innocent polyester rule books who are possibly just holograms who don't even comprehend why people keep getting onto these planes, plane after plane until that moment when they have to stop letting them on. So they can't be expected to comprehend why this one solitary, careless, cowardly shit of a man should be so upset with having not gotten onto the plane, even though he had every chance to get on it earlier and he clearly simply fucking just didn't. It is logic-defying, and utterly, utterly inexcusable.

"Well, I won't have any use for these now, so happy anniversary, you two," I say, and heave the stack of cards straight up into the air. They flutter and flap their way to the floor as I walk to the nearest row of padded waiting area seats and lay myself down. This is where I should have been from the minute I entered the terminal building.

I am staring at the floor, allowing my arm to dangle, and my fingers make contact with the pleasant cool of the tile floor. It is an especially quiet time at this quiet airport, but I hear murmurings and the distant business of maintenance and a midsize passenger plane starting up its engines.

I am startled crazy by a hand squeezing my arm, and I almost take a swing. When I hesitate, the woman gets suddenly muscular. She pulls me up out of my lie-down, hands me my bag and the collection of misery cards she picked up off the floor. The man waits until I am right there before popping the door open and waving me quickly inside like some life-or-death commando operation is happening right this minute.

Too stunned, too slow, I turn around to thank them just as the door bangs, shut and locked.

• • •

Finally I am flying home. During the time it takes to get me back over my endless sneaky switchbacking escape route away from home, I write. It takes all of seven sad, sorry, sorry, sad cards before I manage to say it. Finally.

The front of the card is mostly plain, pale flowers in a bunch, looking like they are surging toward the reader. The shiny green lettering says only, *Words cannot express . . .* Under that I wrote as neatly as I could, *But they have to try.*

In the event that she might actually open the card to read beyond that, I tried.

> *I know you don't want to hear from me. But the option to receive certain words should be available to you in any case. You deserved that long before this.*
>
> *Life has been far more difficult to manage than I ever dreamed it could be. So I tried to snuff it out altogether and invent a new one. It came for me, though. And by the time it did, I had destroyed whatever good was still lingering right up till the day I ran.*
>
> *I'm learning now, what I never did before it was too late. I know that there are truths and there are lies and there are different ways of interpreting them. Especially if your mind can't live with one horrible interpretation that changes every last molecule of your life, including your whole future and even your whole past.*
>
> *It's a blessing if you've read this far, and I won't test*

your patience further. But I have to tell you that I see now. The way I could not see before.

Two people telling opposite stories is pure wickedness to try to get right. I felt all along that in our hearts it was possible we could both not be lying. But in our hearts or in the dark or in the full bright light, what we can't both be is, we can't both be right.

I've already seen more of myself than I want to see, but I plan to keep on looking. I still can't see me ever doing anything to hurt you.

But I have seen enough to feel like I can believe you and whatever you say, more than I can believe myself.

I'm sorry for what I did to you. I will be forever sorry, forever knowing it.

Whatever you want, whatever you say, I will do that. I will come back, now, a year from now, a hundred years from now. I will surrender, confess, plead guilty, keep it out of public sight as much as possible. Then you can be done with it, and I can get what I'm due.

Good-bye. You are a fine person and I hope life manages to tell you that, in some way, every day, forever.

as we see each other

They don't notice me, which is the best break I could ask for. As I peer through the small square window into my dad's room, it looks just unreal enough that I can hold a brief hope that that's what it is. Everything there is blue lighted, like an aquarium. My two sister fish are fully absorbed in studying the machinery, and the sheets and their wringing hands, to see me. As for the father fish, he has seen all the sights of his life now, and all I can do is hope the good ones are playing on a constant loop in his mind.

I am not going to move until somebody comes and forces me to. I'm trembling, every bit of me, and when I struggle to get a grip on it, it just shakes me harder to teach me a lesson.

Mary is the one to look up first, and she comes dashing right up to look at my face from just the other side of the glass. I genuinely have no idea what to expect from her, and frankly, her noncommittal expression holding fast in the glass is scaring me further out of my wits.

But I don't think she's doing it at all deliberately. Her face has no more idea what to do with itself than the rest of us do. Finally she tries a small smile that shatters into weeping before it ever has a chance.

Within seconds I am on the inside, and Mary and I are in a hug-to-the-death. Then I find enough arm to fit Fran in, and here we are. For now, for a fleeting moment, day, two days, too short and for all the wrong reasons, we are us again, and we are great like I knew we were.

I am submerging myself in this for as long as it will hold, this hug, this revisit, this historical reenactment of when love came easy to this family and nobody ever forgot to show it.

But I have already kept the old man waiting too long.

When I step up to the bed, I get a shock far beyond all I had tried to prepare for. The respirator pumps him up and down and hisses at him, through him, toward his children, whose combined hearts would never match up to even that exploded and decommissioned thing he's got left now.

His was a massive and open and happy heart, and it was every bit about two daughters and one son who became the Grand Project that remained when his first best beloved went and died and the first Great Plan followed her down. We were his life's work, the source of his limitless warmth as well as the beneficiaries.

For most of those years we didn't comprehend how much

he counted on us. For those early years after Mom, when we needed him most of all, we just took it all as a given. Took him as a given. Took everything that was given. Then when we started preparing for next lives, next grand projects of our own, it became more and more obvious. We found out his big secret, how much he needed us. And we punished him for it.

He is shrunken by so much compared to when I left him alone in the house that last day. This is not just one massive heart attack that did this job.

"Was he starving himself?" I ask. When nobody says anything, I turn around to face them.

Their faces tell the tale. They didn't know what he was up to those days and weeks and months. No more than I did.

"It's tomorrow," Fran says in a whisper. "They're giving him till tomorrow morning to see if maybe, if there's some improvement . . ."

"And if not, they are switching off the ventilator mid-morning," Mary says. "To give us all time to get back."

"Not an issue for me," I say, slouching myself down into the vinyl upholstered chair near Ray's beautiful big bear head, the one part of him undiminished.

"I'll be here," I say, slipping right into the man-of-the-family coat that is still quite roomy on me.

And there will be improvement.

When there are no more distractions, the lights are dimmed to almost nothing and I can fight no longer. I crawl up into his bed, work into as close an approximation as possible of the hundreds of times his big burly arm had pulled me in, warmed me up, calmed me down, and drove the demons out.

"*I* still need you, Ray," I say to him. I always hated this, in stories, movies, people talking out loud to somebody who's already kind of busy with the dying. It bothered me enough to want to tackle the talkers and eject them from the poor tired soul's room.

But now I'm here. I'm here and it's us and as I am discovering practically every day now, everything is different when you get there yourself. And telling him these things, out loud, was what he was cheated on so badly already. So, not now.

"I need you something fierce. I need you to sit down and eat with me. I need you to play another game of infinity Risk. I need you more than I needed you when I was seven, and I'm terrified ten times as much. I'm ashamed of things I've done in the past, and when I think of how you never, ever, ever quit on me, I become so filled up with hate and disgust that I think I could go and do it. I think the big thing that's the issue, that makes killing yourself so reprehensible most of the time, is the leaving behind that vicious mess for your loved ones. That is what you cannot do.

"But this is it, Dad. After you, there is no such anybody for me to hurt. And don't think the girls count, because they don't. I expect not to see them again, once this week is done.

"I'll shut up now, Ray. I should anyway, shouldn't I? But not before I tell you that the last truly awful thing I did during your lifetime, I did to you. I pretended I didn't need you. And then I pretended it was for your good even more than mine. I lied on top of lies and lied about the lying until I got scared that I was losing the last real thing I had, the last lifeline back to myself as I knew me.

"Then I decided that was exactly what I wanted. What I thought I wanted. I don't know what to do. I don't belong anywhere, except right there, right inside that big fat heart. It was so big that we had to all pull together just to pull it apart.

"I'll shut up now. See."

I lie there, feeling the almost nothingness of my wonderful dear dad's final breaths that don't even belong to him as much as to a machine. But my head stays right where it is now, not to miss one single beat of it.

"I'm gonna hold you, Ray, right through. I'm gonna see you off to sleep, see that you go untroubled, just like you always did for me. Because I did learn. I did, and I hope you can feel me now and know.

"And I have no idea how this kind of thing works, how it actually transpires at the very moment it does. But if there is any possibility, and your time comes to close you down, if there is any way you can pull me along as you slip through, I wouldn't mind that at all.

"Good night, Great Man."

He declined to take me with him.

But my father did the next best thing when he let me

hold on to him as his life was letting go. It was a quick thing when it decided to happen, and by the time his medical team reached the room, I had ushered him safely beyond their reach. I don't think I made lifelong friends of the staff by lying there clinging like an overgrown bat to Ray's corpse. But they allowed me that, and a few more minutes with him alone. We hung on until I could start to feel the cold transaction of my dad's remains transforming into a chilly, stiff facsimile that had nothing of the man within it at all.

This is when I'm ready. And I leave knowing that the two of us got at least this thing right. The final thing.

wrong and wrong again

Now we know what Ray did to fill up all that extra time once we left him to get on with his life, like the girls had already been doing and I was starting on myself.

He planned for his death.

The funeral is all organized and paid for, as is the law-yer handling the orderly wrapping up of details that would not have a chance to get messy. Messier. The house is being sold immediately and the proceeds divided three ways. Bank accounts, insurance benefits, any remaining scraps of the man's worldly possessions that have real-world cash value are all likewise to receive the logical, clinical, unsentimental resolution.

In other words, the most un–Ray Sarafian way to go about it.

We all agree this is sensible, it is for the best, and the way it's all laid out, we couldn't fight over anything if we wanted to.

But we don't want to fight, Mary, Fran, and I. We just want to get going.

There is no great heaving mass of bereaved humanity at the quick and clean graveside service. Maybe a dozen mourners who might be vaguely recognizable to me from sometime when I was still little and my dad was still big and everybody adored him.

They did. They did. He was adored because he was adorable in the most literal and most authentic sense of the word. I am not making memories do what I want them to. I know this beyond mere *knowing*, because this ache is far deeper and weightier than any words could possibly reach. To disturb, distort, destroy, as words are ever ready to do.

The minister's words do none of those things as he murmurs along, but they don't do anything else, either. I'm grateful for the assembled decent dozen, even if the more I look at them the more I think they are some of those lonely sad souls who come to funerals for the juice they get out of not being dead themselves or out of simply being thoughtful, if morbid, fellow travelers.

It occurs to me that eventually it might not be possible to be thoughtful without also being morbid.

I stand on the opposite side of the grave from my sisters.

And just behind them is their roommate, Grace. The sight of her, for the first time since a very different tragic night, shakes me up terribly. I fear for a shaky second that I could fall right into the hole before Dad can even get in and finally rest. I steady myself quickly, though the flash of Grace's face is almost as upsetting as the event that has thrown us back into each other's view.

The moment that matters is here anyway, and every one of us—strangers, loved ones, and some combinations of the two—edges up close as Ray is lowered into the ground, into the hole they reopened for him fifteen years after they did it the first time. Slowly down he goes, where she waits to receive him and lie side by side, snug in the dirt. The perfect reward for a guy who lived and died desiring nothing more complicated than a long lie-around with a beloved. And despairing when it couldn't be as simple as that.

The girls are driving directly from the cemetery back to Norfolk. I'm spending a last night in the house before taking the identical meandering bus route that took me away from here the last time. The same journey, except for an utterly different journeyman.

Mary and Grace are already at the car. Mary and I said our good-byes and regrets honestly, minus the malice but with only traces of what may have once been a finer thing than this. Even the moderate flare-up of shared emotion from the other night has already died down to embers of no glow and very little warmth.

"Are you sure you don't want to just fly and forget about the stupid, stinking buses?" Fran says as we hug. It is the familiar hug, and we linger in it. It's a different hug too, and we let go of each other knowing that.

"No, thanks for doing that, though, and getting me here that quickly. I don't know what I would have done, if I hadn't been able to—"

She stops me. "We would never have let that happen. Hell or high water."

"I think I've had enough of each to do me for a lifetime."

"Good," she says. "I hope so, Keir, for your sake. I want your new place to be a better place. I want to know you are thriving in the real world, the one that's mostly not going to tell you exactly what you want to hear. And when it tells you what you don't want to hear, that's when you need to listen hardest to it, and not to that other voice, the sweet talker that knows you better than you know yourself and that means you nothing but harm."

She stops herself, crosses her arms, and cocks her head to one side.

"That's a lot of listening you're doing there, Sarafian," she says.

"I'm getting in as much practice as I can. And who better to chew my ears than you?"

She heaves an inconclusive sigh, adding, "You're talking a good game, anyway. But then, that part was never your problem, was it?"

"I guess not," I say, and quickly draw the envelope out of my pocket and stick it in her hand.

"You've missed my birthday by six weeks, Keir."

"I have to ask a favor," I plead.

Mary punches the car horn twice. Fran waves to acknowledge her but stays looking at me, and the card, and finally at me.

"Grace sees her still, doesn't she?"

She steps back like I've suddenly turned radioactive. "Oh . . . oh, Keir, what are you asking me to do here? Things are only just starting to lose that constant, miserable edginess that you started. I can't be a messenger for you. I can't do that, and you can't ask me to. Do you forget? Do you still forget, that easily and willfully, that I do not accept your version of certain events? And that I have had to come a long way just to be able to relate, on any level, to you since that horrible time?"

"Things do change sometimes," I say cautiously.

"Some things don't," she says, and shoves the card back at me. "And my position on this has not changed one bit."

"Read it," I say, and notice the instant startle in her eyes, across all the muscles of her face. "I left it unsealed because I wanted you to know what was in there so you could decide what to do. Actually, whatever you decide to do, I very much want you to read it anyway."

Mary beeps again, four times this time, and spurs an already frazzled Fran into fumbling the envelope into

335

releasing the card. Her hands shake as she reads it, and mine shake while I wait.

A straight and simple outcome here was never going to happen. But the parade of all the spirits of all the human emotions playing rapidly across Fran's articulate features is close to horrifying for me to witness.

Finally she just fits the card, with some difficulty, back into the envelope.

Then she seals it.

She grabs me fearsomely in a final hug around my neck that is intended to inflict pain on me in equal parts with better intentions as well. But in the end, yet again, it's the words that will linger.

"Do you know what a tragedy you have been for everybody?" she says, and pushes off me to run to the idling car, which barely waits for the door to slam before peeling away.

I make my solitary way back, covering the streets and blocks of my hometown, between my parents' final resting place together and their original one they built and maintained for us all to be happy in. I make the walk at a crawl, taking note of every familiar sidewalk crack, every shop, every ballfield.

I reach the house that's Forever Ray but tomorrow is for sale and tonight is for myself.

I have actually had this planned, since the moment I realized I would have this night, this once-only opportunity to pay a tiny fraction of all due respects.

It's a farewell tour, and it doesn't take long to scan it all in once more for the details, and then bank it for a lifetime.

"So long, kids," I say as I poke my head into the girls' old room. In this vision, the weights are not yet there, but the girls still are. Fran screeches like a police whistle, "You have to knock!" and Mary hurls herself so hard at the door that my head gets battered on either side, smashed between the sharp edges of the door and the frame.

I go into my parents' short-term heaven room and Ray's long-term widower's roost. I walk up and touch the bed, the left side facing the window onto the silver maple tree. It was my mother's side of the bed and then it became my retreat from every fear known, and I knew them all. It was not likely a coincidence that the fears and the visits came timely enough that I could still fit myself into my mother's impression pressed like a mold into the mattress. I felt it, I know I did. And the first few times some of her body warmth was still there too.

The place where Ray never talked me out of being afraid. His strategy was that we would talk about the fear right in front of its face until it eventually got bored or ashamed enough to leave us alone.

I stroll into the kitchen like I have a thousand times before. But it's a first to find it scrubbed and sanitized of the faintest hint of any meal cooked here in the recent past. I get a distinct whiff, however, of the sage, peppercorns, and Worcestershire sauce of a meat loaf that marked the final day of my eighth-grade year.

I pass through the living room, where so much of every-thing happened that I'll be editing that film in my head for years before the narrative reveals itself clearly. But the piano that lost its music when we lost the lady who loved it needs no narrative. Her picture perched on top could still bring Ray to tears. The dining table stops me cold.

The game, our game. Risk, which we played for probably five complete years of my life, is laid out on the table, ready to launch.

Christ. As if he could have been waiting for me. Waiting and ready for me to come through the door and play with him like always.

The tour is over. It is all over, completely, well and truly, over.

I lie on my bed, the blue bed I can still remember helping Ray put together for me. I thought this bed was so tremendous, I couldn't sleep the first two nights just knowing he actually went out and bought the right one and it was under me every time I opened my eyes.

I try for several hours, but I'm returned to that day. I'm returned to not being able to sleep in the blue bed. Mostly because the blue bed is inside the house, and I cannot sleep in this house anymore.

When the relentlessness of the knocking at the door finally pulls me to my senses, I realize exactly where I am. I have no recollection of coming to this spot, but I am in my tiny wooden hideaway chair in the cellar, wedged next to the archaic bulky furnace the new owner is going to need to replace immediately. Serves him right, whoever he is. Usurper.

The knocking continues as I mount the creaky steps, go through the door to the kitchen, and say "All right, all right," right up till I open the door.

"What the hell?" I say.

"I told you I should be here," Fabian says. "You should know I say what I mean."

"This is astounding," I say, waving him inside. "How?"

He pulls a crumpled couple of pages from his pocket and holds them up like a kid just in the front door with his proudest schoolwork.

"I just got out your old itinerary, the one Ray forwarded us before your arrival at the school. And I just organized one in reverse. College bereavement policy allowed me five days for the loss of my uncle Ray, plus two travel days. I'll still miss a few classes, but that'll give them a chance to catch up at least."

I shake my head in admiration and shock. Then I look down at mail that came in through the slot sometime earlier. It's a card. It has my name handwritten on the envelope but no postage or address.

"Keir?" Fabian says.

"Yeah, sorry, man."

"Are you doing okay? You look a little unwell."

"What? Oh, not at all. Listen, give me just a minute, will ya? Feel free to poke around all you like."

"Great," he says, starting his own self-guided tour. "I love poking around."

I take the card into my room, the last time it will still be my room. I started loving Gigi Boudakian as a little boy living in this room. I sit on the blue bed and open the envelope as a very anxious man.

The outside of the card is printed, *With Sympathy, through these difficult days.* The inside is all Gigi, all lovely script and brevity.

I was truly saddened to hear about your father. He tried to be a good man. He was kind.

It was good that you wrote. Even if only for yourself, this was an important move forward. But no, I do not want to pursue anything. I don't want to see you in jail (anymore). But I don't want to see you anywhere else either. You offered to surrender yourself quickly and quietly so I could be "done with it." You still have a very long way to go to understand what you did. I will never be "done with it." It is mine, every day, until I die. Just like it is yours, until that day comes for you.

The only thing you can do is go. And stay gone. I should not have to look at your face ever again, and you should not deny me that one small gesture to spare me any more anguish over your actions. If you have any true remorse, then don't ever come back here.

You said before that you loved me, and I hated that. I told you to stop it. Stop saying it and stop thinking it. But if you were not lying, if you did ever feel love for me, I want you now to remember that. Finally admitting your guilt to me was a start. But it's a start to something that doesn't have a finish. You cannot undo what you did that night. The effects are irreversible.

What you can do is remember me. Remember loving me, and remember destroying me.

If there is any human soul to you at all, you will be sickened whenever you think of that. And if so, then you will never be able to do this to anybody else.

"Ah, um, Keir? Hey, how you hanging in there, okay? I already saw all the other rooms, but I can go back out if you need more time by yourself."

I shake my head no, then place the card inside my duffel bag, which is all ready at my feet.

"I just have to do one last thing, Fabian. I don't want to go until I leave a message for Joyce."

"I guess it won't wait till you're on the bus."

I shake my head, point at my feet, and say, "Right here."

• • •

"Joyce, I'll make this brief because otherwise I'll get stupid.

"I came home and buried Ray. My dad and best friend. I closed down our house.

"I also saw a lot of myself. Not the best stuff. Some of it you saw before me, I think.

"I believe the world probably shows us true fineness only a few times ever.

"I believe one of those was you.

"In three days, two hours, and twenty-five minutes or so, I will be perched on a big glacial erratic.

"Hoping to see true fineness there."

"I guess that's all she wrote, as they say," Fabian says.

"That, my friend, is very much all she wrote. You sort of missed everything," I say to him. "I'm sorry about that. You came all this way."

"No problem at all. I knew I was going to be too late. I made up my mind to come all this way anyway. Just to see. To make the connection. And to bring you home."

"To bring me . . ."

"Figured company just now might be no bad thing."

"You're ready, to turn around and get right back on that bus, and the five more after that?"

"Ready if you are," he says.

I grab my bag, and my friend, and together we leave this house permanently behind.

"Are you still ready if I say I need to tell you a terrible story on the way? About something I did that was inexcusable?"

"I am ready for that," he says. "I've been ready for that for some time now."

"It's time now," I say, locking the front door behind me, sticking the keys back in through the mail slot. Leaving no way back to this place.